Only with Me

KELLY ELLIOTT

one

Nicholaus (Nic)

"SO, WHAT DO YOU DO when you're not . . . SWAT teaming?"

I glanced up at the young woman standing at our table. Her bright-red lips puckered out in an attempt to look sexy while she leaned over and put her tits on display. All I really wanted to do was tell her she had lipstick on her front tooth. Focusing back on my sandwich, I ignored her. It was a dick-move, but damn it all to hell, I just wanted to eat.

Phil, another SWAT team member, answered her. "We train, ma'am."

The waitress laughed. "Ma'am? Holy shit, how old do I look?"

None of us answered. Hell, we knew better than to touch that shit with a ten-foot pole. If I was to guess though, I'd say she couldn't have been more than twenty.

"What kind of training?" she asked.

Cole kicked me under the table. She wasn't going to go away until I talked to her. With a sigh, I put my sliced brisket sandwich down and wiped my hands on my napkin.

I cleared my throat, flashed her my signature smile, and replied, "Ma'am, if we told you, we'd have to kill you."

Her smile faltered a little before it grew wider. She got what she wanted, me talking to her. "How about drinks later, handsome?"

Damn. That was fast.

Usually it took the new waitresses at least a week before they were throwing themselves at one of us.

With a fake chuckle, I replied, "I don't think my wife would like that very much."

With a pout, she shrugged. "Well, you can't blame a girl for trying."

Spinning on her heels, she headed to another table.

"I hate new waitresses," Phil mumbled.

"I hate that they always want Nic. What the fuck is wrong with the rest of us?" Cole asked. "I'd have taken her up on the drinks."

"Yeah, if you want your ass thrown in jail. She looks sixteen," Phil stated with a deep rumbled laugh.

"It's the Greek in him. It's like a magnet for women. I have yet to see one it hasn't worked on," our sergeant, Oliver, said.

"I almost laugh every time you say *my wife*," Cole said.

Rolling my eyes, I went back to eating. Was it too much to ask for us to eat in peace? We'd been coming to this restaurant for over six years now. Once the newness of seeing all of us walk in wore off, the waitresses usually treated us like every other customer. But when there was a new one and she saw us walk through that door in tight T-shirts, muscles on display, and the word SWAT splayed across said shirt, something happened. It was like their hormones were turned up into overdrive.

"Yeah well, it keeps the ones I'm not interested in at bay."

Phil laughed. "And you're not worried the ones you've fucked aren't going to say you're a lying bastard?"

It was true. At times I did worry about my little lie. Over the years I had screwed one or two . . . or maybe six . . . of the waitress at Roy's Place. None of them bothered to even ask if I was married. Each was a fast fuck. In the alley behind the restaurant, in my truck, outside the bar before we even made it in, the backseat of their car, Roy's office, and my favorite, fucking Scarlett in the bathroom while the rest of the guys sat out there and ate. Bastards still had no clue about that one.

I smiled. Something to be said about public sex.

With a shrug, I responded. "They got what they wanted. Besides, they never stay long enough to care."

Cole looked over to the long counter. "Scarlett's still here."

Glancing over my shoulder, I watched as Scarlett, Roy's daughter, poured a cup of coffee for a customer. Her dark hair pulled up in a ponytail and one of her signature Dierks Bently T-shirts on. She winked and said something to the old man before turning around and grabbing a few plates.

I turned back to Cole. "Scarlett's different. She's part owner, you asshole."

"And the occasional hook-up."

Shrugging, I replied, "What's wrong with that?"

Holding up his hands he laughed. "Nothing at all, my friend. Nothing at all. We've all had the go-to fuck buddy at one point."

I wasn't sure why, but Cole's comment bothered me more than it should have. *Was that all I was ever going to have in my life? A fuck buddy?*

My phone buzzed on my side. Pulling it out, I frowned as I read the text.

Mom: Don't forget dinner tonight.

I quickly typed out my response.

Me: Can't make it tonight. Training session.

Mom: Don't lie to me Nicholaus. I will find out.

Laughing, I turned to Oliver. "If my mother sends you a text, we're training tonight."

He nodded, like what I had said was nothing new. It wasn't. Ever since Thad and Thano had settled down, my mother was even more eager to set me up with a good Greek girl. I was almost positive the last girl she tried to set me up with was a distant cousin.

"Hiding again, huh?" Oliver asked.

"Yep," I replied as I typed another text.

Me: I've gotta run, Mama. Love you.

Mom: Love you. If you finish up, stop by. Maria's daughter is in town.

I lifted my brows. Hmm. That might be fun. Cassie was beautiful with her long, dark hair and brown eyes that begged for more. The last time she was in town we had one night of hot sex. The girl knew how to work her tongue, that's for sure.

Oliver's pager went off. Without a word, everyone jumped up and headed out as he called and got the information.

"We've got a high-risk narcotics warrant. Let's head back."

My heart pumped harder. I fucking loved my job. It was dangerous and required fast thinking, planning, and balls of steel to be on SWAT. My career choice had also kept me single. I'd yet to meet a woman who could handle the fact that I was a cop. Let alone, a SWAT member. Not that I was looking. Far from it. I liked my single lifestyle. No one to answer to and plenty of women to go around. At least that was the mantra I repeated to myself all the time.

Once we made it back to the station, we went over the plans down to every last detail. Every single thing was planned. Where our entry points were, where the pull teams would go, and what the backup plan would be.

Five hours later we were ripping the iron gate off and breaking the door in on a house that was suspected of selling heroine out of it.

"Police! On the floor!" I shouted as we rushed in. Three guys immediately dropped to the floor and one dumb fuck took off running for the back of the house to try to get out.

Idiot.

I'd have him in less than thirty seconds.

Thud.

"Don't even think about it. Give me your hands."

Fighting me every step of the way, the suspect shouted out, "I didn't do nothing!"

I restrained his hands and pulled him off the ground. Heading into the main living room with the dirtbag I had caught, Liam walked around the corner. "The rest of the house is clear."

I called in, "Three in custody. All clear for narcotics to come in."

My heart was still racing as we headed back to our vehicle. Another successful bust. This would never get old. The thrill of my job was all I needed.

The drive back to the station was filled with Oliver going over the operation. What went right, what could have gone wrong, and what we could have done better.

"Beer?" Cole asked as we stripped out of our gear and threw it into the back of our police cars.

"Sounds good."

"Drivas!" Oliver called out. "Your mother texted. Told her you were on a warrant issue."

With a roll of my eyes, I sighed and slammed my trunk. Turning to Cole, I said, "I'm going to need something stronger than a beer."

His face lit up. That meant we were heading out on the town and would most likely both end up getting lucky tonight.

"Hell yes! I was hoping you'd say that."

With a smile, I shouted, "Later guys!"

Oliver, Phil, and Liam each lifted a hand. They were all heading home to their wives or girlfriends. Not me though. The last thing I needed was a woman tying me down. I was perfectly happy being alone.

At least that was what I kept telling myself.

two

Gabriella (Gabi)

I STARED OUT THE WINDOW as I wound the yarn in a ball.

"It's a new pattern I'm trying for my granddaughter."

"Oh, I love it, Beth!"

Glancing to my right, I watched as Lou and Beth oohed and aahed over a new blanket pattern Beth had bought.

Beth looked up and showed me the pattern. Smiling, I nodded. "It's precious! She's going to love it." The look of pure happiness on Beth's face made my heart fill with happiness as I let out a soft sigh and went back to my busywork. I loved coming to knitting club. It always relaxed me and made me think of my grandmother. She was the one who had taught me to knit, and being with these women reminded me of a happier time.

My eyes scanned the mountains out the window. One of these days I'd build up the courage to hike up one of them. My somewhat fear of heights kept me from venturing out to them. Until then, I would sit in a room with four other women who were significantly older than me, and knit.

Lou gasped as Beth showed her the yarn she was using for her future grandbaby. She insisted it was a girl, even though her daughter and son-in-law decided not to find out what the gender was.

"That pink is perfect!" Lou gushed.

Beth held it up for the rest of us to see.

"Beautiful!" Karen said.

"Love that pink!" Nancy added.

With a smile, I said, "Lovely."

Everyone turned to Charity. My best friend, roommate, and business partner. She was sulking in the corner like she did every week when we came to knitting club.

Clearing my throat, I said, "Char?"

She snapped her head and lifted her thumb up. "Great."

Beth seemed disappointed by Charity's response. I wasn't sure why, it was pretty darn clear Charity was not here of her own free will. She lost a bet. I won. That meant knitting club for both of us.

Beeping from across the room caused Charity to jump out of her seat and cry out, "Times up!"

Lou and Nancy let out a yelp and covered their hearts.

"You scared the fright out of me, Charity," Nancy said.

Charity grinned. "I scared the piss out of you, Nancy. Just say it."

With red cheeks, Nancy waved her hand to dismiss Charity as she giggled and said, "You're such a bad girl. It's a good thing I'm not your mother, young lady."

Charity glared at me then fake laughed while turning back to Nancy. "Oh, you know I'm kidding. Enjoy your day, ladies."

She was out the door and to her red BMW faster than I could say knit one, purl two.

Slipping into the front seat, I waited for her to start her weekly bitch session.

Right on cue she went for it. Dropping her head back against the seat, she closed her eyes and groaned. With a quick snap of her head up, she turned and glared at me. "I cannot believe I let you drag me to this thing called hell."

My lips pressed together tightly to keep from laughing.

"Honestly, Gabi. The damn club is called Knitters are Purls. That should have been your first clue!"

This time I did laugh. "Oh, come on it's not that bad. You're not even trying."

Her mouth dropped. "You want me to socialize with women who are old enough to be my mother. Did you know Karen tried to set me up with her son! She told him I was a virgin! Why in the hell would she think I was a virgin?"

I covered my mouth in an attempt not to laugh harder. Shrugging, I said, "Maybe cause you're in a knitting club?"

"Exactly my point! Ugh! I hate you so hard right now."

My phone buzzed in my purse. Reaching in, I read the text from Max. "Dang it, Max has an issue."

Charity pulled out onto the main road and punched the gas. "Max always has an issue. What's it this time?"

"He said Ms. Loft is in and wants to know why I didn't make zeppoles."

"Fuck Ms. Loft."

Gasping, I cried out, "Charity!"

"What? The lady is crazy. She comes in everyday and buys *your* desserts and then pawns them off as her own for her rich boyfriend. I hope she gets caught one of these days."

"That still wasn't nice."

Charity came to a stop and turned to me. "Just say it. You know you want to say it."

I looked into her feisty hazel eyes. "I don't want to say it."

"You do. I know you don't like her."

It was true. I loathed the woman, but I'd never call her names. Only under my breath.

"She's a customer. I love *all* of my customers."

Charity hit the gas, causing my head to hit the headrest.

"Bullshit. One of these days you'll say it. The woman will push you too far and you'll crack."

I shook my head. "Nope. I've worked too hard to be where I am. I will not call our customers names. I leave that to you."

"And like I said, she is a fucking bitch."

I rolled my eyes and groaned. This was my payback for dragging her to knitting club.

Ten minutes later, we were parking in the garage of the building we lived in. My bakery was located on the first floor. Four years ago when I came through Colorado Springs, I never thought I would fall in love with it. But one drive through Old Colorado City and I was hooked. As I walked around the shops, I came to the bakery that was for sale. I instantly knew it was a sign this was where I belonged. After spending two years jumping from town to town, I finally felt safe enough to settle in one place.

At least until my past caught up with me, if it ever did. As long as I stuck to the original plan my brother and father set up, I'd be safe.

"You okay? You seem like you're in another world?" Charity asked, pulling me from my thoughts.

"Yep. I'm heading to the bakery to see what's going on."

She rolled her eyes. "*Right.* Max and his *emergency.* I'm going to pour myself a hard drink to forget the last two hours of my life that I'll never get back."

With a chuckle, I shook my head and bounced down the stairwell. Charity swore Max had a thing for me. I disagreed. Besides, I was almost positive he had a girlfriend.

Unlocking the back door, I stepped into the hallway. One side housed the restrooms, storage room, and cleaning closet. The other side was my office. I'd converted the two existing offices into one when I bought the bakery. It was where I lived for the first six months after I bought the place. It was convenient when I had to get up at three in the morning to start baking.

Stepping into my office, I grabbed my apron, tied it on and took in a deep breath. Glancing around the space, I grinned. *I love this place.* I still couldn't believe I was lucky enough to get the second and third floors when they became available.

The top floor was my apartment. Two bedrooms and two and a half baths. The remodel took forever, but it was worth it. That's when I met Charity. We instantly hit it off and when I learned she loved to bake, we became business partners.

"Hey, what are you doing here on your day off?"

I jumped when Liza spoke. "Shit! You scared me," I said as Liza stood there staring at me with a smile on her face. Liza worked at the bakery part-time while she went to culinary school.

"Thank God you're here!" Max cried out.

"What's wrong?" I asked.

"That woman! I want to hit her in the face so hard she won't remember her name for a month!"

My eyes widened as Liza laughed. "Oh yeah. Ms. Loft. She's still here."

"What?" I gasped.

"I'm telling you, Gabi. You need to ban her. Ban. Her," Max said as he pushed his hand through his short brown hair.

With a moan, I replied, "All right, let's go get this taken care of."

Pulling my long, blonde hair up into a ponytail, I cracked my neck, popped my knuckles and got ready to deal with the worst customer on the planet. If she was in New Jersey, she probably would have been taken out by a friend who knew a friend.

I walked into the main area of the bakery. With a smile, I glanced around at the handful of people who filled the tables. I mainly served dessert, with a few options for salads and cold sandwiches, so it made my heart happy to know my creations were bringing people in. For years I was told I needed to add wine to the menu. It hadn't been announced yet, but the second floor was being turned into an upscale wine bar. A dream of my father's that I was making my own reality.

"Well, it's about time you showed up."

Ms. Loft jumped up and made her way over to me. "Where are the zeppoles?"

I was about to answer her when the bell on the front door chimed, I glanced that way, strangely drawn to see who was coming in. Everything stood still, as if time had ceased for a few brief moments. Opening my mouth to talk, I was stunned into silence. A burst of excitement and curiosity for the man who walked in caused tingles throughout my body.

Holy. Crap'ole.

I'd never in my life seen a guy so drop-dead gorgeous. My eyes roamed his perfectly fit body. Dark hair, sun-kissed skin, and stubble. Damn . . . I loved stubble. Then my gaze landed on his shirt.

Colorado SWAT.

Oh yes. A police officer. How I loved a man in uniform.

My eyes took another gander over his body. Black pants, black boots, and a gun strapped to his side.

Hot. As. Hell.

What would it feel like to be under such a guy like that? The thought alone made my panties wet.

Ugh. Stop it, Gabi. What in the hell is wrong with you?

He walked over to the counter where Liza was attempting to wipe the drool from her mouth. There was something about this guy that kept my attention drawn to him. I'd seen plenty of good-looking men, but this guy. He seemed . . . different. So very different.

That broad chest. Those delicious arms. I bet he could pick a girl up and fu . . .

"Did you hear what I said, Gabi?"

Ms. Loft's voice pulled me from my naughty thoughts. *Good lord. What is the matter with me?*

"Is it hot in here?" I asked as I fanned myself and looked around. "Do we need to turn the AC on in here?"

Ms. Loft's expression hardened. "What? Stop changing the subject."

I really didn't want to be dealing with crazy lady right now. I wanted to walk away, push Liza to the ground and finish helping Officer Dreamy.

Liza laughed and my eyes swung back to the counter. I was instantly jealous that Liza was talking to him.

Bitch.

Putting my fingers to my temple, I groaned. "What in the hell?" I mumbled.

"What was that?"

I lifted my head and glared at Ms. Loft. "I didn't make zeppoles today. I don't guarantee certain things to be made every single day."

"But my Henry wanted zeppoles today! I need zeppoles!"

She raised her voice, causing the patrons in the bakery to look over at her. Including Officer Dreamy.

Great. That's all I need is for crazy to draw the police's attention to me. It's one thing to look and dream about a police officer, but to actually draw his attention to me . . . not so much.

"You're not listening to me! My man wants zeppoles! Gabi, I need you to make me zeppoles. Now!"

And that's when it happened. I snapped. There was really no reason why I picked this moment to have had enough. Maybe it was because I was missing out on Officer Dreamy, or that Charity was right. I had wanted to call Ms. Loft a fucking bitch.

"What did you call me?" Ms. Loft asked as her face turned red.

"Oh no," I whispered.

Max laughed and said, "Yeah, you didn't think that in your head, darling. You said it out loud."

Looking over my shoulder to Max, I mouthed, *shit*. He smiled and said, "It's about time."

"You called me a bitch!" Ms. Loft exclaimed.

"I believe she called you a . . . fucking bitch."

My head snapped over to the customer sitting at a table who had filled in Ms. Loft's oversight. "I'm sorry, but this lady is rude every time she comes in. It was deserved."

I lifted my hands as I gestured for everyone to stop. "Wait. Ms. Loft, I'm sorry, it slipped, but you seriously cannot expect me to make something your husband wants on a whim."

She guffawed. "Boyfriend. Christ, do you even listen when I talk to you? Blonde bimbo."

Oh no she didn't. I'm finished with this lady. "If he wants them so bad, you could always . . . I don't know . . . bake them yourself and stop lying about it."

At first she stood there glaring at me. Then she started laughing, which made me laugh in a nervous way. Peeking over to the counter, Officer Dreamy was watching what was happening. His stare caught mine and my breath hitched. The way his eyes darkened had my insides flipping all about. I couldn't help but wonder if his thoughts about me had gone just as naughty.

Don't be ridiculous, Gabi.

"Listen, cupcake, get your ass back in that kitchen and make me my zeppoles!"

Focusing back on crazy lady, my hands went to my hips as I opened my mouth to tell this bitch off. I'd had enough of her kind of crazy. "Listen here you—"

"Excuse me, is there a problem here?"

Glancing up, he was standing there. Up close he was even more attractive. His muscles more apparent. His voice was smooth as silk and felt like a warm blanket wrapping around my body. I was instantly calmed. And then it happened. Stupid took over.

"Wha . . . ma . . . ba . . . prob . . . um . . ."

I seriously could not form a word to speak after hearing that man talk. He not only looked like a God, he talked like an angel. His hazel eyes sparkled as he tried not to smile. There was a touch of gold specks that seemed to shine a bit brighter.

Crazy lady spun around and went to lay into Officer Dreamy when she noticed he was a cop. She dropped her pointed finger and stared at him.

I know how you feel, lady.

He glared at her before speaking again. "Vivian Loft."

Huh?

He knows her?

"Um, I was just leaving."

My eyes darted back and forth between crazy lady and Officer Dreamy.

"I'm sure you were. And I bet you were telling this nice young lady that you won't be coming back. *Ever.*"

Her eyes turned black. "You're a real asshole, Nic Drivas! Ass! Hole! I hate you and I hope you get shot!"

All that could be heard were gasps across the bakery. I was pretty sure my eyes were about to pop out of my head from sheer shock. Not to mention I'd have to scrape my jaw off the floor. How could she say that?

What. A. Bitch.

He laughed as everyone watched Ms. Loft storm out of the bakery. The second the door shut, the entire bakery erupted in cheers. Turning to me, Officer Dreamy smiled.

Lord. I'm for sure going to have to change my panties.

Closing my eyes, I got a grip on myself. This was what happened when you didn't have sex in forever. I took a deep breath and got my thoughts back in order.

Clean. Thoughts. Only.

My eyes snapped opened as I tried to shake away my wandering thoughts. I smiled as I looked up at the tall, dark, and handsome man standing before me. "I take it you know her?"

Officer Dreamy's smile faltered a bit as he narrowed his eyes at me and stared at my mouth. When his eyes slowly moved up and caught mine, I held my breath and prayed he didn't recognize me. There would really be no reason why he would, unless he lived in New Jersey six years ago.

Then his smile grew bigger and my stomach dropped fast and hard.

Lord help me. The man could probably make a woman orgasm simply by smiling at her.

"I wish I could say I didn't, but unfortunately I do."

Huh. Interesting. Old girlfriend? Old lover? Either way . . . lucky bitch.

"She's an old . . . family friend."

Yep. Old girlfriend.

"That is a roundabout way of not saying she's an old girlfriend."

I thought he was going to fall over laughing. "Now that made my day, agapiméni. Vivian and me? No. Not a chance in hell. She's honestly an old family friend who wanted more with me than I wanted with her."

Agapee what? I had no idea what he called me, but it made my insides melt and I was pretty sure if he told me to drop to the ground and get ready for him, I'd do it willingly.

Nodding, I lifted my brows. "Ah. I gotcha. Anyway, thank you for stepping in. Dessert is on me. Pick anything you want."

I didn't think his smile could get any better, but I was wrong.

Cue the dimples.

Yeah, I'm pretty sure I just moaned out loud.

three

Nic

*W*HAT. IN. THE. FUCK.

I just called this woman sweetheart. I never called women pet names and I certainly never said it in Greek. She showed no reaction which confused the hell out of me.

My heart was racing, and I had to fight to pull my eyes away from hers. Her smile about knocked me off my feet, not to mention the angelic way she spoke.

What is this weird feeling in my chest? Jesus. Snap out of it, Drivas.

It finally dawned on me she asked me a question when she tilted her head and scrounged her nose in the most adorable way. Fuck. All I could think about was having her under me.

"What was that?" I asked.

She laughed, and it hit me square in the chest. The warmth that spread through my body was something I'd never experienced before. It left me feeling both confused and turned on as fuck.

"Dessert is on me."

Fuck yes. I'd lick dessert off of this girl's body any day. I could only imagine the beautiful body hidden under all those clothes.

Nodding, I motioned for her to lead the way back over to the display.

"How long have you been open?" I asked while I examined the treats before me. Everything looked amazing.

"Four years."

My head snapped up. "What? You've been here for four years? Always as a bakery?"

She giggled. "Yep."

I ran my hand over my stubble as I thought about how I'd never seen this little bakery before. "How have I missed this?"

Shrugging, she replied, "Do you live nearby?"

"Not really. I just got back from looking at a little house over on Twenty-third and Kiowa St."

Her eyes widened in surprise. "The blue one?"

"Yeah, some asshole keeps outbidding me. I went to look at it again to see if I wanted to put in one more offer."

Her cheeks blushed and I couldn't help but notice how her blues eyes lit up. Chewing on her lip, she mumbled, "Um."

The corners of my mouth rose into a smile. "You're the asshole, aren't you?"

Pressing her lips together tightly to keep from laughing, she nodded. "I am."

"Damn, I'm sorry I didn't mean to call you that."

She waved me off. "It's okay, how would you have known, right? Besides, I pulled my offer earlier today."

My eyes traveled her body again. Well, what little of it I could see now that she was behind the counter.

"What? Why did you pull your offer?"

Another customer walked into the bakery, but the other girl who was helping me earlier walked up to them.

"I'm opening a wine bar upstairs on the second floor. With the amount of work going into that, there was no way I could put time into another project."

"A wine bar, huh? I like wine."

What the hell? I like wine? Where in the hell is my game?

Her brow lifted. "Well then, you'll have to stop by on opening night."

"I'd like that."

We stared at each other for a few seconds before she broke away and looked down to the desserts. "So, do you have a favorite Italian dessert?"

Glancing again over the desserts, I saw the panna cotta. I loved panna cotta. The creamy custard-like dessert was one of my favorites.

"I'll give your panna cotta a shot."

She smirked. "You'll never look at panna cotta the same again. It was my great-grandmother's recipe."

"Don't you think before I taste your panna cotta I should get your name?"

Seriously?

If I could, I'd punch my own face right now.

What is this girl doing to me? Everything I say makes me sound like an idiot.

There went that radiant smile again. Her blonde ponytail swung around as she turned her head to cover the blush in her cheeks. Peeking back at me, she answered. "Gabi Mandola. And yours is Nic Drivas."

I smirked. She had remembered.

Her teeth sunk into her lip and my dick instantly strained against my pants. I couldn't help but imagine those lips wrapped around my dick. The thought of grabbing that ponytail while sinking my cock deep inside her from behind had my heart racing and all the blood rushing to the only thing that was thinking right now.

All right. Down boy.

"Is that Greek?"

My heart felt like it dropped in my chest. "Yes. I'm impressed."

She chuckled. "Don't be. When I was little and visiting family in Italy, we went to visit one of my father's best friends. Their last name was Drivas."

"Huh. That's interesting. Could be a relative of mine."

"You never know," she said with a smile and a wink.

Yep. I needed to get this girl under me. On top of me. Anywhere the fuck on me.

Holding up my plate, I said, "Thank you for the panna cotta."

"Sure. I hope you enjoy it."

I made my way over to a little table. The lady sitting one table over smiled then ran her tongue along her dark-red lips. With a polite smile,

I made sure to sit with my back facing her. Plus, that gave me a better view of Gabi.

Glancing down at the panna cotta, I smiled when I saw the raspberry sauce on it. I popped the single berry into my mouth and let the flavor burst inside while I slid my spoon into the custard and took a bite.

Holy. Fucking. Shit.

I wanted to moan. Hell, I wanted to pick up the plate and devour the heavenly dessert in front of me. I'd never in my life tasted something so amazing.

Closing my eyes, I let the taste linger. It was amazing.

"If your mother saw you with that look on your face, you'd be dead right now."

My eyes snapped open. "Cole?"

He sat down and placed his plate of tiramisu on the table. "You finally discovered my favorite bakery in Colorado Springs."

Anger raced through my body. "You asshole. Why have you never told me about this place? We eat at Telly's all the time."

He shrugged while he took a bite. "I only found it about six months back. And maybe because I've been trying to get the owner to go out with me for the last month. If you walked in, she'd be all over your Greek ass."

I laughed and took another bite. "Well, if it makes you feel any better, she didn't go all crazy over me. Well, she did stumble on her words when I first walked up and talked."

Cole rolled his eyes. "And there you go. She's probably been dreaming of you ever since. Tell me the other hot chick who works here hasn't seen you yet."

"The young girl?" I asked in shock. The first girl who originally helped me couldn't have been more than nineteen.

Cole laughed. "No, not Liza. Her name is Charity and fucking hell she is gorgeous."

Glancing back over, I watched Gabi moving behind the counter. "I can't imagine this other girl being as beautiful as Gabi."

"Yeah well, they're both knock-outs."

I turned my attention back to Cole. "I still can't believe you kept this from me. You know Italian food is my favorite."

"That's blasphemy in the eyes of your mother, you know that, right?"

Laughing, I stared down at my dessert. There was one more bite of panna cotta left. *Maybe I should get a to go box and bring it home. Savor it later while I thought about Gabi naked and waiting in my bed for me.*

"How are the desserts, gentlemen?"

I glanced up and my stomach dropped at the sight before me. Cole and I both answered at the same time.

"Great!"

"Good as always!" Cole added.

I glared at him while he ignored me and kept smiling up at Gabi.

"So, you seem to know everyone today, Nic?" Gabi said with a chuckle.

"Nic?" Cole asked as he shot me a dirty look. "We're on a first-name basis already, huh?"

There was no way I couldn't hide my smirk. That's what the bastard got for keeping this place a secret from me.

"We work together," I replied. "Cole here is on SWAT with me."

I watched as Gabi turned and smiled at Cole. It wasn't the same smile she gave me earlier. It was a polite smile. One I figured she gave to all her customers. For some reason that made me feel good. *Really* good.

"I didn't know you were a police officer. Well, thanks for telling Nic about the place, Cole."

"Sure, of course. I tell everyone about . . . ouch!"

I kicked him under the table. "He didn't tell me. He's been keeping it a secret."

Gabi lifted a brow. "Why?"

"Would me telling you I've been sharing your bakery with my friends make a difference in you going out with me?"

"Nope. Not at all."

Her response was quick and made me smile even more.

"There ya go. I kept Nic away simply for selfish reasons." Cole jumped up. "As always, it was great, Gabi. I've got to run. Later, Drivas." Cole took Gabi's hand and kissed the back of it. "Enjoy your day."

Taking a step back while withdrawing her hand, Gabi replied, "You too, Cole."

I was going to kick his ass the next time we were alone.

"So, did you not like the panna cotta? You left some on your plate."

The thought of eating the last bite almost made me sad. "Don't be crazy! I loved it. I was holding off on the last bite. Trying to savor it. Cole was ruining the mood."

She laughed, and it rumbled through my body again. "I'm glad you enjoyed it."

Scooping up the last bite, I put it in my mouth and moaned. Gabi's mouth opened slightly, and I swore her eyes turned dark with desire. I might have been jumping the gun, but I didn't care. There was something about that woman I needed to learn more about. She had an air of mystery surrounding her. I'd never been so drawn to anyone before in my entire life.

Reaching down, she took my plate. "Best you've ever had?"

"If I say yes, will you let me take you to dinner sometime?"

Her eyes lit up and my chest squeezed in a delicious way. "No. But, how about if you let me cook *you* dinner? That's if you like Italian food?"

Holy fuck. Even better.

"Like it? I love it."

Her smile grew wider as I handed her my card. "Send me a text so I can get your number and we'll plan it."

She nodded as I stood. Staring at her perfect lips, I added, "Now, Gabi. Send me a text now so I know you're not blowing me off for Cole now that you know he's SWAT."

The giggle that came from her mouth had my dick growing painfully hard again. Grabbing her phone from her back pocket, she typed in the number on the card and ten seconds later my phone beeped.

Desire raced through my veins like I'd never experienced before. The possessive way I had told her to text me shocked me but hadn't seemed to phase her at all. I bet she'd respond to a bossy lover in bed. I was dying to find out.

A loose strand of her blonde hair dangled in front of her eye. Reaching my hand up, I ran it through my fingers before tucking it behind her ear. Her breath caught as I traced my finger along her jawline.

"When can I see you again?" The need to feel this woman against me grew by the second.

Her tongue darted out and ran over her lips quickly while she nibbled on it a few seconds. She was deciding on what to say next. "Are you free tonight? I have tomorrow off, so I can stay up late."

My brows lifted and her cheeks immediately blushed. "That's not what I meant!" she said while pushing my shoulder back. The zip of energy from her touch made my knees weak.

"I only meant I wouldn't have to be going to bed at seven!"

"Tell me what time and I'll be here." *Please don't let me get called in tonight. Please.*

Glancing at her phone, she peered back up at me. "Seven too early?"

The urge to lean down and kiss those perfectly plump lips was hard to ignore.

"Seven's perfect."

A sweet, shy smile played across her face. "Just ring the bell at the side of the bakery at the door. I'll buzz you up."

With a grin, I leaned down and kissed her cheek lightly as I whispered, "See you then."

The pounding of my heart in my ears was all I could hear as I retreated out of the bakery. Each breath was labored as I walked away.

Gabi Mandola had just turned my life upside down. My head was spinning as I headed down the street to where I parked my truck. I rubbed my hand over my chest, trying to get rid of the feeling that had settled in there the moment she smiled at me and those blue eyes met my gaze.

My brother Thano's words swirled around in my head.

"The moment you meet her, Nic, you'll know. Your breath will catch, your chest tightens like a vice clamped down on it, but it's a feeling so good you want it to last forever. Your world will feel like it's been turned inside out. She'll affect you like no woman has ever done before and you can't help but count down the minutes until you see her again."

I didn't do relationships. I fucked. And boy did I want to sink myself deep into Gabi and forget everything else in this shitty world. There was something very different about this woman and I couldn't wait to figure out what it was.

The vibration of my phone in my pocket pulled me from my dirty thoughts. Cole's name scrolled across it and I instantly laughed at the beginning of his message.

> *Cole: Please tell me you didn't get a date with her!*

> *Me: Dinner tonight at her place.*

> *Cole: I hate you. Greek bastard.*

> *Me: That's what you get for hiding that bakery from me asshole.*

> *Cole: I hope your dick breaks out in some weird rash.*

> *Me: You still have hope with the other hot chick that works there.*

> *Cole: That's true. I still hope your dick breaks out in a rash.*

Laughing, I didn't respond as I got in my truck and started it up. Before pulling out, I glanced at the clock.

Six hours until I could see those beautiful eyes again.

four

Gabi

*T*HE SMELL OF BASIL FILLED the kitchen as I got out my great-grandmother's recipe for chicken parmigiana. I found myself singing "Tied Up" along with Olivia Newton-John and Charity. The song was blaring from her room. Her obsession with Olivia had caused me concern when we first moved in as roommates. After countless hours of hearing her songs, going to two concerts in Vegas, and repeated viewings of her movies, I was a bit of a fan myself. *Nothing* like Charity though.

"Why are you cooking dinner? I told you I had a date."

Glancing over my shoulder to Charity, I replied, "I know. I'm making dinner for someone else."

I turned before I could see her reaction. Charity was pretty much the only friend I had in Colorado Springs. Well, besides the ladies from knitting club and Max and Liza.

She was next to me in a flash. "Really? Who?"

"Just someone I met earlier down in the bakery. It's sort of a thank you dinner. He helped get rid of Ms. Loft once and for all."

Charity took a step back, held up her hands and said, "Wait. Hold on. Back things up a bit here. First off, Ms. Loft is gone? What happened?"

"She freaked out on me and I might have accidentally called her a name when I thought I was thinking it."

Laughter roared from Charity. "It's about damn time."

"Funny, Max said the same thing. No thanks to you though. I wouldn't have thought it had you not have said it earlier in the car."

"You can thank me later. Now tell me about this date."

With a quick chuckle, I shook my head. "It's not a date. It's a thank you dinner."

She leaned against the counter, folded her arms and stared at me.

When she quirked her eyebrow up, I knew I needed to be truthful not only with her, but with myself.

"Okay fine. It's a date!"

Charity grabbed my hands and began jumping. "Oh my gosh, this is the best news! Finally your vibrator will get a break!"

I stopped jumping with her and pulled my hands back. "Hey!"

Staring at me like I was the one who was insane, she tilted her head. "Since I've known you, Gabi, you've only gone out with one guy and I'm pretty sure you were not getting any nookie from him."

My mouth opened, but I couldn't argue with her. Jack was a nice guy, but we never hit it off. We went out a few times and that was it. He never even tried to kiss me.

"It's just dinner. And really, Char. Nookie? What are we, ten?"

She bumped my shoulder. "Oh! I see it in your eyes. You want the nookie! Who is he?"

The heat on my cheeks was hard to hide. "His name is Nic Drivas. He's a police officer." Peeking over to her, I added, "A SWAT officer."

Her eyes widened. "Shut up. Was he in uniform?"

Sinking my teeth into my lip, I couldn't help but think of Nic in that tight black T-shirt. It had been a long time since a man had made my body come to life like he had. "Oh, yes he was in his uniform. Well, kind of I guess. Everything was black, including the two-sizes-too-small shirt he had on."

"Holy shit. You totally want nookie! If he is SWAT, he's got a rocking body."

I nodded. "That's putting it lightly. He was all muscle."

"What did he look like? Oh, my gosh! My roommate is finally replacing her BOB with a real life dick!"

I pushed her away. "Stop it! I'm not looking to have sex. It's just dinner."

"Liar. It's written all over you face. Now, answer me. What did he look like?"

Putting the knife I had been chopping the basil with down, I faced her. I couldn't help but smile when I thought about Nic.

"He's tall and built. *Really* built."

She nodded. "Right. I got that."

"He's got dark hair, almost black. Some stubble on his face with the most beautiful hazel eyes and olive skin I've ever seen."

Wiggling her eyebrows, she asked, "Italian?"

I shook my head. "Nope. Greek."

She stumbled back. "What? Like full-on Greek?"

Shrugging, I answered, "I'm not sure. He sure looked like it."

Charity grabbed my shoulders. "You know what they say about Greek lovers, don't you?"

I frowned. "Who is they?"

"That doesn't matter. You know what they say?"

Laughing, I tried to break free of her hold. "No, enlighten me, Char."

"Well, there is one thing they say, but I'll save that for later. Gabi, they are sex gods! Sex. Gods. Alpha's in and out of bed. Slightly possessive of their women, which works for me and is hot as hell. And they can't keep their hands off their women. Always feeling them up."

I stared at her with a dumbfounded expression. "Where do you come up with this stuff?"

"Do I need to Google it for you?"

"No, that's quite all right. I think I'll wait and get to know him before I label him in one of your groups."

She let go of me. "Oh, it's not one of my groups. I'm telling you now. I know. I've had Greek cock before."

"Oh, my gosh, Charity!" I exclaimed. "Really?"

Lifting her eyes up to the sky, she seemed to be taken back to a moment in time that I knew I didn't want to hear about. "It was the best sex

I've ever had in my life. I lost my virginity to that boy."

I went back to chopping up the basil. Charity had no problem sharing every detail about her life with me. I, on the other hand, shared very little. The less lies I had to remember the better. I told her my parents died when I was in high school and the rest of my family lived in Italy. Charity never really asked me anything about my childhood. Every now and then I would share something that I didn't think would hurt to share, but for the most part my life was not an open book like hers.

"What was his name?" I asked.

She looked up and smiled. "It's kind of funny. His name was Nicholaus too."

I dropped the knife and turned to her. My heart started pounding.

"Don't look at me like that, Gabi. I went to high school in New York. Your Greek dick is not the same as mine."

A sigh of relief washed over me before I snarled my lip at her.

Charity laughed. "I'm pretty sure that's a common Greek name."

"Yeah. I'm sure it is."

Her eyes roamed over me as she took a step back. "Um, you're not wearing that, are you?"

I looked down at my clothes. I had on sweats and a cropped black T-shirt.

"No. I'm going to change."

"What are you wearing?"

"Um, well. It might be a little . . . smutty."

She laughed. "Is it the black dress we bought a few weeks back?"

"You mean the black dress that you *forced* me to buy? Yes."

"Holy shit. Who are you and what did you do with my best friend? Inviting a guy to dinner, cooking for him, and dressing like a whore."

I wasn't surprised Charity was shocked by my actions. I was as well. But it was time for me to move on with my life. My cheeks heated as I let out a giggle. "I don't know! It's like my libido is in charge. Besides, it's been a while since I've dated."

She nodded. "She's tired of plastic. She wants real dick. Greek dick."

I rolled my eyes. "Why are we friends?"

"Because I speak the truth. Look at me and tell me you don't want some Greek dick."

Laughing, I grabbed the fresh pasta I had made earlier. "Don't you have a date to get ready for?"

"Yep, as a matter of fact I do. And this girl is hoping to get her own dick tonight."

Ugh. "Seriously? Keep your dick thoughts to yourself."

"When is he due? I'd fix your hair, but Scott's expecting me at seven."

The buzzer for the front door went off. Charity and I both looked at each other.

"Please tell me your date is picking you up."

She shook her head and smiled wide. "Nope."

"Oh crap."

five

Gabi

I STARTED WRINGING MY HANDS together nervously.

"What time did you tell him to be here?"

"Seven! It can't be him, it's just after six."

The buzzer went off again.

We both rushed over to the intercom, pushing and shoving each other out of the way to try to get to it first.

"Did you tell him six or seven?"

Pushing her as hard as I could, Charity jumped to avoid the chase lounge and fell. "I said seven! I'm positive."

I pressed the button and took a deep breath and cried out, "H-hello?"

"Gabi? Is everything okay?"

I jumped back and covered my mouth. Whirling around, I looked at Charity who was now sitting in the chair, wearing an *I told you so* expression. "Are you going to answer him, Gabi?"

"Right!" I quickly hit the button again. "Um, yes. This is Gabi. Everything is fine. I um, I stubbed my toe. Nic?"

"Yeah, it's Nic. I hope you don't mind me getting here early. I couldn't wait to see you again."

My hand dropped to my side as Charity walked over to me and whispered, "Oh hell. He wants nookie too! Greek dick, meet Italian pussy."

"Shut up!" I said while I pushed her away from me.

Lifting her hand, she called out, "I'll be in my room with Liv!"

Turning back to the intercom, I pressed it again. "Sorry, my roommate was talking to me. Come on up, I'll buzz you in."

I stood there like an idiot as I stared at the door. There was no time to change my clothes or touch-up my makeup.

Shit! Shit! Shit!

The knock on the door caused me to jump. Taking in a deep breath, I walked over and opened it. Clearly I was not prepared for the sight before me because I gasped. If you looked up Greek god in the dictionary, there would be a picture of Nic Drivas next to it.

My eyes leisurely roamed his body. He wore jeans, cowboy boots, and a tight long sleeve black shirt. He was holding a bottle of wine in one hand and flowers in the other. I didn't even care I was ogling him.

Oh yes. I want to have nookie with this man.

"S'up?"

Oh gosh. Did I really just say that?

Nic's gaze moved over my body slowly. The air between us instantly charged, and I was suddenly wondering if I had shaved my legs.

Please let me have shaved my legs. There was no time to shower now.

"Damn, you look hot."

I glanced down. *Huh?*

Jerking my head back up, I replied, "I'm wearing sweats and a T-shirt."

He was staring at the only skin I had exposed. My stomach.

"You make sweats and a T-shirt look hot as hell, Gabi."

I let out a giggle. "Um, well I'll change in a bit, these are my cooking clothes."

Nic lifted a brow and asked, "May I come in?"

"Yes! Gosh sorry about that."

A slow smile grew over his face. His stubble had grown even more from earlier today, making his dimples harder to see.

My eyes glanced down to the wine.

"I hope you like shiraz."

"I love it! Do you mind if I open it now or do you want to wait until dinner?"

"I'm game for having a glass now. What's for dinner?"

Smiling, I replied, "Chicken parmigiana."

Nic closed his eyes and groaned. "Damn, that's one of my favorites."

Swallowing hard, I tried not to think about how I wanted to push him onto the sofa and crawl all over him.

Ugh. Stop it, Gabi.

"Want to help?" I asked as I walked into the kitchen.

Nic followed me and replied, "I'd love to help."

Glancing over my shoulder, I asked, "How good are you in a kitchen?"

He chuckled and reached for one of my aprons that was hung up. I couldn't help my smile when I saw the apron he had put on as I read it.

Caution . . . hot stuff coming through.

"You'd be amazed at the things I can do with these hands."

Digging my nails into my palms, I fought to keep the groan from leaving my lips.

Oh, I can only imagine what you could do with those big, strong hands.

Swallowing hard, I tried to ignore the throbbing between my legs.

"Basil. I love basil."

Smiling, I said, "Good. It's from my own herb garden."

"Nice."

"Do you want to pound the meat?"

The moment I said it I knew I had made a faux pas. Nic's eyes widened in shock and his smile looked a tad on the evil side.

"Wow. You're moving faster than I thought. I'd love to pound your meat, Gabi."

He moved closer to me and I held my breath. The way he stalked up on me had my stomach in a fluttering mess.

My heartbeat was so loud in my ears I could hardly think.

When I hit the island, he turned and picked up the package of chicken breasts behind me. "Do you have a meat mallet I can use for these?"

I looked at the chicken and smiled.

Bastard.

Reaching into the drawer, I pulled it out and handed it to him. "Pound away."

His eyes turned dark and his voice dropped to a whisper. "Is that an invitation, Gabi?"

"To pound her meat? Yes. That was."

We both spun around to see Charity standing there with a shit-eating grin on her face.

"Don't you have a date you need to be getting ready for?" I asked as I shot her a dirty look.

Nic laughed and stuck his hand out toward her. "Nic Drivas. It's a pleasure to meet you."

"Charity Maxwell. Nice to meet you too, Nic."

When he turned around and started on the chicken, Charity looked at me. Eyes wide open with her mouth slightly ajar. She shook her head and mouthed, *holy shit*.

I motioned for her to go away. She acted like she was grabbing him and began air humping. Shooting her a dirty look, I mouthed, *stop it*.

"So, Nic, Gabi tells me you're a cop."

Handing him a plastic bag for the chicken, he smiled at me. "Thanks. And yes, I am."

Charity reached into the refrigerator and took out a Diet Coke. "What made you want to be a cop?"

I glared at my best friend. She needed to leave. Now. We were in the middle of some seriously hot flirting and she is throwing cold water on it.

"When I was seventeen my best friend got caught up in the wrong crowd."

That was eerily familiar.

"He ended up getting involved in drugs and some pretty bad stuff. One day this punk guy walked up to him, pulled a gun and shot him. I chased the guy down while my other friend called the police. From that moment on, I knew what I wanted to do with my life."

Charity was the first to talk. "I'm so sorry you had to witness such a horrible thing. I can't imagine seeing someone killed right before my eyes."

My hands shook as I was instantly taken back six years in time. Blood was everywhere.

On my hands.

The walls.

The loud bang caused me to scream and jump back.

Warm hands touched my arms, calmly pulling me from the nightmare I had been sucked into.

"Hey, are you okay? Gabi?"

Nic's voice pulled me out. My eyes found his and a warmth spread through my chest. "Yes. I'm fine. I'm so sorry about your friend."

Nic smiled then searched my face. "Are you sure you're okay?"

Forcing a smile, I nodded. Nic still had a hold of my arms and a part of me wanted him to pull me in closer. It threw me for a loop how I felt safe with this man. I glanced down to where he had a hold of me and Nic quickly dropped his hands. I instantly missed his touch.

"Loud bangs always scare her." Charity took a drink and added, "She's a basket case anytime fireworks go off."

Nic looked into my eyes again, almost as if he was searching for his own answers.

I cleared my throat and headed to the refrigerator to get the cheese out. "Again, don't you have a date you need to get ready for?"

Charity laughed. "I do! Nic, it was a pleasure meeting you. Have fun with that meat."

Nic chuckled. "It was nice meeting you as well."

Pointing to me, Charity said, "Have fun, but don't get wild. We both know how long it's been."

My jaw dropped as I stared at her in disbelief.

She disappeared and I wanted to crawl into a hole. Warm breath tickled my ear.

"I like her. She's fun."

Jumping, I turned and came face-to-face with Nic. My eyes drifted to his lips before I swung them back up. "She's a pain in the ass."

Tossing his head back and laughing, Nic went back to work on the chicken while I sliced the mozzarella cheese for the top of the chicken breast.

We quickly fell into an easy conversation about . . . of all things . . . food.

"So you grew up cooking?" I asked while mixed the flour, pepper, salt, and parmesan cheese into the bread crumbs for the breading.

"I did. Mostly all Greek cooking. My mother was big on my brothers and I learning to cook. What about you?"

I tensed up. How much should I share? The last thing I wanted to do was have a cop snooping in my past. But the connection I felt with Nic was different than anything I'd ever felt before with anyone. I quickly decided, I wanted to share more than I normally would.

"I remember being little and watching my grandmother cooking. She didn't speak a word of English, only Italian. I couldn't have been maybe five at the time. I'd pull up a stool and stand there watching her throw this and that into a pot. She never measured a thing when she cooked. I asked her once if she would write down her favorite recipes for me. She asked me why I wanted her to write them down."

Nic was totally enthralled with my story, which made my chest flutter. "What did you say?" he asked.

I laughed and looked away. "I told her I needed to learn how to cook for my husband. She made me promise I'd marry a good Italian boy."

Turning back to Nic, I watched as he raised his brows. "Did you promise her that?"

I shook my head. "No. At the time, I was madly in love with Jerry Knox. My first unofficial boyfriend from kindergarten."

Nic chuckled. "Knox doesn't sound Italian."

"No, he was not Italian. My grandmother simply laughed." I looked down at my hands. "She passed away six months later. When I graduated high school, my father gave me a box filled with recipes. She had done what I asked and written down her favorite recipes. I've treasured that box ever since."

Nic placed his finger on my chin and lifted it. "You were lucky to have known her and even luckier she shared her love of cooking with you."

I fought the tears in my eyes. I never spoke of home, or memories. It was too painful. The way Nic was gazing into my eyes scared me and thrilled me all at once.

"I want to kiss you, Gabi. I've wanted to since the moment you smiled at me."

My breath caught. I realized I desperately wanted the same thing he wanted. The spark I felt in my chest was unlike anything I'd ever experienced before. Suddenly, everything else faded into the background and all that mattered was this man standing before me.

He leaned in closer. We were inches away from each other. My heart picked up its rhythm in my chest. I was sure it would burst out any second.

"May I kiss you?"

My mouth parted, giving him the silent invite he was looking for. He stopped just short of my mouth. Waiting for me to give him permission.

I was frozen and completely unable to speak. The air around us was charged liked I'd never experienced before. I said the only thing I could manage to say. His name off my lips sounded like a whisper on a breeze.

"Nic."

The moment his lips touched mine, I felt the spark. Beautiful, intense, magical. It was the only way I could describe the feeling of Nic kissing me.

Softly and gently he moved. When his tongue asked for permission, I granted it to him without hesitation. The kiss deepened and Nic pulled my body against his.

An explosive fire ripped through my body. All I could do was moan. Nic's hand moved around my waist, pulling me to him so I could feel how much the kiss was affecting him as well.

Then it happened.

Music came blaring from Charity's room.

She. Did. Not.

Nic pulled back and looked at me with his brows pinched together. "What in the hell is she playing?"

I rolled my eyes. "Olivia Newton-John. The song's called "Magic"."

The corners of Nic's mouth rose into a beautiful smile that had my knees shaking.

"I'd say she hit that spot on."

Matching his smile, I giggled. "I'd say."

Nic took a step back as his eyes gazed into mine. His smile slowly faded. The confusion in his eyes was hard to miss. I was pretty positive I had the same look in mine.

six

Nic

*W*HAT IN THE HELL WAS *that?*

Staring into those beautiful blue eyes, I couldn't figure out what was happening. My heart was on the damn floor the moment she moaned into my mouth. Then she opened up to me and I was overcome with a euphoria I'd never experienced before.

"Your world will feel like it's been turned inside out."

Fuck that. There is no way. I needed to break this weird connection we were sharing. I was in uncharted territory and not sure how I felt about it.

I turned back to the food. "Are we frying or baking the chicken?"

Gabi stood there for a second, her forehead creased in confusion. We'd just shared the most incredible kiss of my life and I totally blew it off.

"Um, I bake mine. Healthier and all."

"That sounds perfect."

She moved to open a cabinet where she pulled out a baking sheet. "Just put them on here after you coat them in the breading."

Somehow I needed to get things back on track and easy like a few minutes ago. We were talking as if we'd known each other for years then I fucked it up with kissing her. Damn if I didn't need to feel those lips. Taste her.

"Have you always wanted to own a bakery?"

Her face lit up. There we go. My dick-move forgotten.

"Yes. For as long as I can remember."

"What do your parents do?"

She tensed. That was twice now she reacted that way when I asked about her past.

"Um, they passed away when I was in high school."

I frowned. "You said your dad gave you your grandmother's recipes at your graduation."

A panicked expression moved over her face.

"They passed away in a car accident a few days after I graduated."

"I'm so sorry, Gabi."

She shrugged. "Thank you."

"Did they own a bakery?"

She shook her head. "No, they owned a restaurant in Italy that my uncle owns now."

I lifted my brow. "Really? Wow. Were you born in Italy?"

Gabi chewed on her lip. Talking about her family seemed to be a sore subject. "No," she said with a chuckle. "My parents moved to America after they got married. They had the restaurant before they moved."

I couldn't help but notice she failed to mention where she grew up. Although the cop in me could tell she was hiding something, I let it go.

"I've always wanted to go to Italy."

Again, her face beamed with happiness. "It's beautiful there."

"How many times have you been?"

"Dozens!" she said with a light laugh. "We have a lot of distant family still in Italy. I haven't been in about seven years though. I was actually planning a trip to go in a few months. If everything works out."

I lifted my brows. What did that mean? "Really? Sounds like fun."

Her smile slowly drifted away. "Yeah. I hope so."

"I'm off!" Charity called out as she walked by the kitchen. "You two kids have fun and just as an FYI, I won't be home tonight."

"What?" Gabi gasped. "You're staying the night with him?"

Charity tilted her head and smirked. "Awe, that's kind of cute that you're concerned. Yes. I haven't had sex in weeks and plan on getting a lot of it tonight."

Spinning on her high heel, Charity was out the door before Gabi could respond.

She turned to me. "I swear, she's not a slut. She's been dating this guy for a few weeks now."

I laughed and held up my hands. "None of my business. If things don't work out for her and this guy, you should introduce her to Cole."

Gabi chuckled. "Cole tried once with Charity. She shut him down so hard I actually felt sorry for him. He wouldn't stand a chance with her."

"You don't know Cole."

Her smile grew. "You don't know Charity. Besides, she likes Cole."

"And that's a bad thing?"

"I think it scares her how much she was attracted to him, but you can tell Cole's a player."

"What about Charity?"

Gabi laughed. "No. Scott's the first guy she has dated in a few years. She's not one to sleep around."

"She seems like a pistol. And Olivia Newton-John? Wasn't she in *Grease*?

Gabi shuddered. "Yes. I know every one of her songs by heart after four years of living with Charity. I've seen *Xanadu* I don't know how many times."

My brow lifted in question.

"It's a movie she did. After *Grease*."

"I've never watched *Grease*."

Gabi dropped the spoon and turned to me with a look of horror on her face. "Don't *ever* tell Charity that. You'll be watching it within five minutes of the words leaving your mouth. And no potty breaks."

Damn this girl was adorable. "No potty breaks, huh?"

She shook her head. "It was pure hell. I had drank a lot of water that day too." She shuddered as if the memory had hit her again.

I had the urge to pull her into my arms again, but I fought it.

"How are you at chopping veggies for a salad?" she asked with a wink.

"Bring it on. I'm the master at chopping shit."

Gabi soon had everything you could possibly think of that would go in a salad in front of me.

"I bet next time you won't show up early," she said with a chuckle.

The fact that she was already planning a next time had my chest feeling light.

She must have realized what she said. "I mean, that's if you enjoy my cooking and want to come back."

I chopped the cucumbers and put them into the large salad bowl. "Don't you mean *our* cooking? Since I'm helping and all."

Her nose scrunched up in the cutest way and my heart stopped. Like, honest to God, it felt as if it froze.

She winked. "It's my recipe though."

"Touché. But, I did pound the meat."

Her tongue ran over her lips and the dark blue specs in her eyes lit up like sparklers on the Fourth of July. "I guess we'll have to see how it tastes for me to decide if you're good at that or not."

Fuck this. If she was going to flirt then so was I. "I know another way you can find out."

Her mouth formed the perfect O while her breathing picked up. I'm going to guess Charity was spot on when she said it had been a while for Gabi.

"Sounds promising," she shot back.

The alarm went off on her phone. Without taking her eyes from mine, she spoke. "Would you put the cheese on the chicken and stick them back into the oven? I'll put the pasta in and then run and change."

Lifting my hand, I tucked a strand of hair behind her ear. "You go get changed. I'll take care of the rest and get the salad put together."

"Are you sure? The pasta needs to be put in the water."

There was something about Gabi that was so different from any other woman I'd ever been with. I wasn't sure if it was her smile, the way her eyes lit up when I said something funny . . . or sexual . . . or the way she made my heart feel like it was floating hopelessly in my chest. Whatever it was, I wanted more of it. A whole hell of a lot more.

"I'm positive. Even though I think you look great now."

"I'm not wearing sweats while you look all dashing and handsome."

"You thinking I'm handsome, huh?"

A hint of pink moved across her cheeks. "Give me ten minutes."

I nodded as I watched her walk away. Fucking hell she had a nice ass. I wanted my hands slapping it pink while I took her from behind. The bedroom door shutting brought me back to reality.

Turning, I got to work on taking the chicken out, placing the slices of cheese Gabi had ready on top and then putting them back in the oven. The pasta went into the boiling water and the last of the vegetables were added to the salad. The smell of Gabi's perfume still lingered in the air. Inhaling, I shook my head and chuckled. I never would have imagined I'd enjoy being in a kitchen and cooking with a woman.

One quick survey of Gabi's kitchen, and I walked over to where I thought she'd keep her dishes. I couldn't help the smile that spread over my face when I opened it and saw the plates. Grabbing two dinner plates and two bowls for salad, I set about getting the table ready.

The timer went off for the chicken. Taking it out of the oven, I set it off to the side while I drained the pasta and mixed it with Gabi's homemade marinara sauce. The smell of garlic and Italian spices filled my senses and made my stomach growl.

One quick taste and I was letting out a satisfying moan. The moment I tasted the pasta, it exploded on my tongue. "Holy shit, that's good." I could totally get used to this woman's cooking.

I set off looking for one more thing.

"Gabi? Do you have any candles?" I called out.

"The drawer to the left of the sink. There are some candles and the holders are in the cabinet underneath."

Finding what I was looking for, I added the candles to the table and finished it off with the flowers I brought.

"Sorry that took longer than I said. Wow, I'd say you've done this a time or two."

I spun around and nearly dropped to the damn floor.

"My God," I whispered while my eyes roamed over the beautiful sight before me.

"Too much?" Gabi asked with a shy smile. All I could do was shake my head.

She wore a black dress that hugged her body in all the right ways.

It showed a hint of her breasts, enough to leave me imagining what else was under the dress. And her legs. Holy hell. Those long toned legs were perfect. The red fuck-me shoes finished the whole outfit. Gabi had pulled her hair up and into a sloppy, yet sexy as hell bun.

My chest squeezed, and I found it hard to breathe. If I thought I wanted Gabi before, now I was fighting a goddamn hard-on as well as trying to figure out how to breathe.

"Looks like you've got everything ready. You sit and I'll get the food to the table."

I watched her walk by and all I could think about were those legs wrapped around my body with me buried deep inside her. Nothing but the red shoes on while I pounded into her over and over again.

Jesus. Get a grip, Drivas.

Gabi placed two platters down in the middle of the table, pulling me from my daydream. The pasta and sauce was on one, and the chicken parmigiana was on the other. The large bowl of salad appeared last.

Gabi sat down across from me. "Dig in!" she said with a huge grin.

After taking another bite, I moaned and nodded my head. "This is good. So damn good."

She chuckled. "I'm glad you like it."

"So, how was the rest of your day today?"

Her eyes lit up. "Well, I played around in the kitchen downstairs with a recipe I'm trying to perfect."

I smiled. You could see the excitement in her eyes. "What are you trying to do?"

Her face turned scarlet. "Make macarons."

My brows lifted. "Macarons? Those little colored cakes? They look easy to make."

She laughed. "Yes! Those little colored cakes. They're not as easy as you would think. To get a smooth and shiny shell takes practice and honestly, I suck at it."

Taking another bite, I winked. "I say screw the macarons and give me more of this dish right here."

A smile danced on her lips as she said, "Thank you, Nic."

Before I knew it, dinner was over. Gabi pointed to my wineglass. "Do you not like the wine?" Gabi asked.

"On call tonight, so I'm going easy on it."

She simply nodded then stood. "I should get this cleaned up."

The chair almost knocked backward when I jumped up. "Let me help."

Gabi smiled and we quickly got everything cleaned up and the leftovers put in a to-go container for me.

"I can put some music on and we can finish this wine on the balcony if you'd like."

With a nod, I followed her into the living room. My dick was throbbing as I watched her lean over while picking out something to listen to.

Fucking hell, that ass was perfect. And her tits were begging to be kissed and sucked on.

"Anything in particular you'd like?"

There was no way I could stop myself any longer. Walking over to her, I placed my hands on her hips, causing her to jump.

"There is something I'd like, now that you mention it."

Gabi spun around and looked up at me. She searched my face until our gaze locked. I could get lost in those eyes for hours on end.

"Nic, I'm not the type of girl who falls into bed with a guy I hardly know. I need you to know that."

Lifting my hand, I twirled a piece of her hair with my finger. "I'm not asking to sleep with you, Gabi."

She quirked her brow up.

"Don't get me wrong, I'd love to fuck you, but I'm a patient man."

"Nice," she said with a smirk.

"What I'd really love is for you to fall apart on my fingers. Will you let me make you come, Gabi?"

"Oh my," she whispered as she grabbed onto my upper arms. Leaning in closer, I licked my lips.

"Nic," she gasped as I pulled her closer to me. "I . . . I don't know."

"Tell me you'll let me touch you, Gabi. I want so badly to touch you."

Her mouth parted slightly as I ran my finger along her collarbone and straight down her chest and through her cleavage. Gabi gasped and held onto my arms tighter.

"You're so damn beautiful. Do you know that?"

Her eyes closed as I moved my hand and cupped her breast through her dress. It took every ounce of strength not to rip the damn thing off and bury my face between those perfect tits.

Backing her against the wall, I slowly moved my hand down and under her short black dress. Her body shuddered and I couldn't help but catch my own breath. Her skin felt like silk.

I lifted her dress and felt her body tense.

"Do you want me to stop, prinkipissa?"

As fast as her body tensed, it relaxed. Her eyes caught fire, and I was positive if I went further she'd let me. But I wanted to move slow with her. Honor and give her the respect she deserved. Well, I had my goddamn hand up her dress, maybe I wasn't being so respectful. And in that moment, I didn't give two shits.

My lips moved to her neck where I placed soft kisses and repeated my question.

"Do you want me to stop?"

"W-what . . . what did you . . . call me?" she gasped between breaths.

Smiling, I spoke against her ear. "Prinkipissa. It means princess."

"Oh, you're good."

With a light chuckle, I trailed my hand up further, brushing my fingers against the lace fabric of her panties.

Slow. Go slow.

Inhaling a breath, Gabi pushed her hips out, silently begging for more.

I fought the urge to rip her panties off. With slow movements, I slide my hand barely inside. The hint of hair leading me to the prize I was after.

Beep. Beep. Beep.

My heart dropped as I said, "You've got to be fucking kidding me."

seven

Gabi

MY BREATH WAS LABORED AS I pushed my hips into Nic's touch. I felt like a slut, silently begging this man I had only met hours earlier to touch me. I'd never needed to orgasm as bad as I did right then. His touch drove me insane.

Wildly insane.

Then his pager went off, and it felt as though a gallon of cold water had been poured over us.

"You've got to be fucking kidding me."

Nic rested his forehead against mine as I desperately tried to catch my breath. He pulled his hand out and rested it against the wall, next to my head.

So. Close.

I was so close to having a real orgasm. Okay, I've had real ones with BOB, but one with an actual man present would be nice.

"I'm so sorry, Gabi. Damn it. I'm so sorry I'm leaving you hanging. Do you want me to finish?"

Yes! Yes, I want you to finish!

"No. It's totally okay."

His eyes turned dark. "It's not okay."

I swallowed hard.

He leaned in and kissed me. When he pulled back, his eyes were filled with nothing but lust. "Don't make yourself come."

"Excuse me?"

Stepping back, Nic pulled out his beeper and looked at it, then looked back at me. "I don't want you to touch yourself. The next time you come will be because I'm the one who makes you fall apart into a million pieces."

My eyes widened in shock and I couldn't help but laugh. Nic stared at me with a deadpan expression.

Holy shit. He's serious.

"Wait. Are you serious?"

Pulling me against him, I felt his hard dick pressed to my stomach. I found myself loving the alpha vibe he put off. That was something I'd never experienced before and I wanted more. The idea of waiting for him to finish what he started shot my libido even higher up.

Gulping, I whispered, "I promise I won't."

He smiled and my knees went weak. "That's my girl."

My girl? My lower stomach pulled with desire at his possessive tone.

When he released me, my head was spinning and my heart raced. "I've got to go. Tomorrow I have off. Are you free?"

My stomach dipped at the idea of spending time with Nic.

"I am. I have the day off tomorrow."

He leaned in and gently kissed me on the lips. It was so tender I swear my heart melted. "Thank you for dinner, agapiméni. It was amazing."

There was that other word again.

"Y-you're welcome, Nic."

And just like that he was gone from my space. He made his way into the kitchen, grabbed the leftovers and walked to the door.

My fingers traced along my lips where they still tingled.

When I heard the door open, I faced him and called out, "Be safe."

He stopped, glanced over his shoulder and smiled.

Oh Lord. Did the earth just move?

With a wink, he replied, "Always."

The door shut and I stumbled back against the wall. My hand clutched to my chest as I tried to steady my heart and scattered thoughts. It was hard ignoring the throbbing in my lady bits, but I forced it out. I'd wait for him. As much as I wanted to come, I actually wanted Nic to be the one to fulfill that longing. From the tease I just got, I was positive I'd be in a blissful euphoria.

My hands came to the sides of my face. Shaking my head, I asked, "What in the hell just happened?"

══ ♥ ══

"GABI?"

With a quick glance over my shoulder, I called out. "I'm out on the balcony."

Charity stepped out onto the balcony as I flashed her a grin. "Did you get lucky?"

"Yes. But he sucked in bed."

Laughing, I asked, "Why, what happened?"

She groaned and flopped onto the seat. "It's what didn't happen. He was a wham, bam, thank you ma'am kind of guy. No foreplay, no touching, no sucking of any kind."

"That sucks."

"Ha. Yeah, I'm glad I charged my vibrator. I didn't even get an orgasm out of it."

Wrapping my hands around my mug, I took a sip of tea. "I take it no more dates with Scott?"

Her head dropped back and she let out a long frustrated moan. "Ugh. I tried so hard to like the guy. He has a zero-fun level. Not spontaneous at all. Not a good lover. It's all wrong. Damn it. Why can't I find a guy who likes to have fun and fucks good?"

"Never one to mince words, were you?"

Spinning in the chair, she pulled her legs up and rested her chin on her knees. "Speaking of fucking. Did y'all?"

My lip curled. "Gosh, Charity."

"What? I like to get to the point. You should know that about me by now."

"For your information all we did was kiss."

Her head jerked back. "Say what? That Greek god didn't try to make a move on you?"

"Oh, he did. Then his pager went off."

Her eyes about popped out of her head. "No!"

I nodded. "Yes."

"How close did y'all get?"

Heat moved over my cheeks. "Well, he had his hands under my dress, right inside my panties."

Charity closed her eyes and slowly shook her head "That. Blows."

With a light chuckle, I replied, "Yeah it does."

"Well, looks like we're both having to hit BOB after these dates."

I took another sip of my tea and looked away. From the corner of my eye I saw Charity leaning out to look at me.

"What? Did you have phone sex when he was on a call or something?"

Turning, I hit her on the leg. "Of course not! He made me promise him something."

Her mouth dropped open and her eyes danced with excitement. "Tell me!"

My hand covered my face as I slid down in the chair. "Ugh! I can't!"

"Oh. My. God! What did you promise him?" Then she gasped. "He told you not to get off without him, didn't he?"

"How did you know?" I asked while sitting back up and staring at her.

"I told you, I've been with a Greek guy. They are possessive as fuck, but in a hot way. That would drive me even more insane, and I'm pretty sure ole Nic knows that."

Rolling my eyes, I set my mug down on the small metal table. "Char, I'm going insane. I've never in my life been this turned on and it's growing by the hour. No . . . by the second! My mind keeps wandering back to last night. To his touch and his insanely good kisses. I feel like I'm going to explode. This has never happened to me before. It's like my libido has taken control of my mind and body."

Charity stared at me for a good thirty seconds with a serious look on her face, then lost it laughing.

I swatted at her. "I shouldn't have told you!"

Her hands waved about in an attempt to stop herself from laughing.

"I'm sorry. I'm sorry. It's just I've never seen you this way before. You're horny as hell and that man knows exactly what he is doing."

My brow lifted. "What do you mean?"

"Gabi, he knew you were worked up. He also knows by telling you not to give yourself relief, you're going to fall apart the moment he touches you. It will get him off even more. If either of you can resist full-on sex the next time you're together, I'll sign up for another year of knitting club."

"Really?" I asked with a chuckle.

"Yes, because I'm positive you're gonna have nookie next time you see him."

My arms wrapped around my body. "I feel like such a . . . a . . . slut."

She dropped back in her chair again. "What? Why in the hell would you say that?"

"Because I've just met the guy and all I can think about is having sex with him. What does that say about me?"

With a wiggle of her brows, Charity answered me. "That you're normal. Gabi, it's okay to be turned on by a man. By his touch. Besides, I bet that scruff would feel good between your thighs."

Jumping up, I cried out her name. "Charity! Stop! Ugh, you're such a . . . a . . . slut!"

Tears were now sliding down her face. She didn't even attempt to stop laughing.

My phone buzzed and I let out a yelp.

Charity was up and wiping her face. "Is it him? Is it?"

I pushed her hands away as I fought to get to my phone in my pocket.

Nic's name lit up the screen.

"Oh, my God, it's him!"

"Answer it, Gabi!"

With shaking hands, I slid my finger across my phone. Charity and I stood perfectly still. When she bumped my arm, I remembered to breathe . . . and talk.

"Hello?"

Ugh. I sounded too eager.

"Hey, Gabi. Did I wake you?"

I laughed. "No, I've been up since five. That's sleeping in for me."

"Awe, the whole bakery getting up at the crack of dawn thing."

Smiling, I felt my body warming. Just the sound of Nic's voice did things to me.

"Something like that."

Charity was trying desperately to put her ear to mine to listen in. Pushing her, I walked into the living room.

"So, how do you feel about a hike?"

"In the mountains?"

Nic laughed. "Yeah."

My heart about leapt from my chest with excitement. "I've never been before."

His silence on the other line scared me. "Are you serious? You've never been hiking or up in the mountains?"

"Both."

"Well, this makes me rethink my plans for where I wanted to go. Do you have good shoes you can hike in?"

Smiling, I spun around and looked at Charity. "Yes! Charity actually made me buy some hiking boots a few months ago. We had planned on taking a trip up to Pikes Peak but she keeps backing out on me."

"Well put them on, girl, I've got a day planned for us."

I could hear the smile in his voice. "Should I meet you somewhere?"

"No, I'll pick you up in an hour."

My eyes widened in shock. "An hour?"

"Is that too soon?"

Not wanting Nic to think I was high maintenance, I chuckled but wore a look of horror on my face. "No. That's plenty of time."

Charity clutched her chest then took off running to her room.

"Great, see you then, agapiméni."

Butterflies galore took off in my stomach. I'd never had a man call me sweet names before. So when Nic called me one, and said it in Greek, it pretty much made me weak in the knees. "K. See ya then."

The moment I hit End, Charity was yelling for me to come to her room. "We are at emergency level one! From what I got we have hiking and mountains. Anything else?"

I stared at her with a deer caught in the headlights look on my face.

"Um, no that's all he mentioned."

She tapped her chin. "Okay, I can work with this. Hair, clothes, make-up, and keep it natural."

I nodded. "Sounds good."

The clap of her hands scared me. "We need music." Spinning, she rushed over to her iPod and searched frantically. A huge smile spread over her face. "This one! It's perfect!"

When the song started, I groaned. "Seriously, Char? *That* song? Why *that* song when I'm going hiking?"

Her hands went to her hips. "It's the words, Gabi. It's perfect!"

Olivia Newton-John started belting out the lyrics to her song "Landslide". It was true though. It felt like I was riding a landslide and I had to confess, the last twenty-four hours was the most fun I'd had in years.

eight

Nic

AFTER HITTING END, I STARED out the large set of windows in my bedroom that looked out at the mountains.

Goddamn that voice of hers.

What was it about this girl that had my mind spinning and my chest feeling like I was on a freaking roller coaster?

I wasn't sure what in the hell was going on with me, all I knew was I couldn't wait to see Gabi again. After four hours in a standoff with a drugged up nutcase last night, I drove by her place at almost three in the morning. Tempted to call her, but knowing how crazy that would make me.

I couldn't stop thinking about that kiss. Or the way her body shuddered when I touched her. I loved how responsive she was to my touch. I couldn't wait to pick up where I left off last night.

Fuck. I've never in my life longed to see a girl again after a date. Hell, I didn't even do dates. There was something different about Gabi Mandola.

Something very different.

Pulling my jeans on, I got to planning out the day with Gabi. First stop, Woodland Park. I couldn't wait to show Gabi my favorite hiking trails.

My doorbell rang and I froze.

Shit.

Maybe if I stood here and was really quiet.

It rang again and then my phone went off.

Mama: Your truck is here. Wake up!

Groaning, I sliced my fingers through my hair and headed to the door. Opening it, my mother pushed in.

"First you don't come to the family dinner the other night, then you don't answer your phone yesterday or last night."

"I was working, Mama."

"Hmph. That job of yours, it scares me and keeps you from the family."

Pulling the T-shirt over my head, I replied, "I love my job."

"What you need is to not love that and find you a nice Greek girl to settle down with and love."

My heart seized. Surely if my mother accepted Kilyn into the family, she would Gabi.

Wait. What am I even saying? No. Relationships are not my thing.

But if I dated an Italian girl, how would my mother feel? All hell broke loose when my youngest brother Thano fell in love with Kilyn, an Irish girl.

"I brought you some moussaka. I'll put it in the refrigerator for later."

"How's Pa?"

With a grunt, my mother answered. "Grumpy. He wants to go on a trip. See the world he says."

"That sounds like a great idea. Why don't you?"

She turned and glared at me. "I have a feeling there is something about to happen. Something big."

I swallowed the lump in my throat. "R-really? Like what?"

With her eyes narrowed at me, I took a step back. "I think Kilyn is pregnant. That girl is so damn stubborn. It's the Irish in her. But I see the glow on her face."

I breathed a sigh of relief and laughed at myself. It wasn't like my mother was a psychic. There was no way she'd know about Gabi.

"What. Is. This?"

Jerking my head up, I saw her holding the Tupperware container that Gabi made for me.

"Food."

Her head slowly turned to the side. "I know it's food. It's homemade food and not in one of your containers. Who made it for you?"

Holy shit. My mother new the type of food containers I owned? That was almost borderline crazy.

No. It was crazy.

"A friend."

Her lips pursed as she casually nodded her head. "This is Italian food, Nicholaus. You missed family dinner for Italian food made by a . . . *friend*?"

"No, Mama. I missed family dinner because I was working."

She glanced up. "That's right, Oliver said you were delivering some warrant or something dangerous."

Moaning, I blew out a frustrated breath. "You cannot keep calling my sergeant when I miss family night. I'm a grown man. And I can like other food besides Greek."

"Who is she?" Her hands went to her chest as if I had mortally wounded her.

"W-what?"

"The girl who cooks you this . . . this . . . *food!*"

"What makes you think it's a girl, Mama?"

"It isn't?"

I was at a crossroads. Did I lie to my mother? Or tell her the truth.

"Liam's wife made it and had leftovers. That's all."

A look of relief swept over her face.

Shit. I'm going to hell.

I had never lied to my mother.

Okay, that's a lie.

Opening the lid, she smelled it. "Ugh. Too much basil, my goodness. Poor girl needs to go to cooking school. Italians. I swear."

I watched as she opened my garbage and banged the dish on the side. Sending my heavenly delight into the trash.

Stumbling back, I asked, "Why would you throw perfectly good food away?"

Holding up the moussaka, she grinned. "This is good food. That . . . that was nonsense. Make sure you eat this today. Now, your brother Thaddeus and Phoebe are planning a baby shower. The whole family will be there. A week from tomorrow. I have the perfect girl I want you to meet."

"Mama, please don't set me up with anyone."

She held up her hand. "Shh! You are thirty years old, Nicholaus. Your sperm is growing weaker by the day."

My mouth dropped open. What had I done in my life to deserve this?

"Aunt Maria's niece from Greece will be there. Her name is Aphrodite. You know what that name means in Greek?"

Rolling my eyes, I nodded. "Mama, I've met her a dozen times. And yes . . . it means Greek goddess of love."

"Equal to the *roman* goddess Venus."

Why was she bringing that up?

"She is probably a good lover, unless you have tested those waters with her. I know you like your women, Nicholaus."

My hands raked down my face. "Mama, why do you go there?"

"Don't be ashamed of your sexuality. Greek men are very proud of that. Take your father for instance."

I held up my hands. "No! Let's not talk about what a great lover my father is. *Please.*"

With a shrug, she washed out the container that held my leftovers from last night. "I'm just saying, there is a reason I had three sons. Your father's sperm was young and strong."

"Ugh! La la la la la."

There I stood, almost thirty-one years old with my fingers in my ears trying not to hear my mother talk about my father's sperm while singing out a tune.

Hitting my chest, my mother frowned. "Stop that. I worry about you. Now, what time will you be over for dinner tonight? It's your day off, right?"

"Um, I . . . ahh . . . well . . . I . . . um."

"Nicholaus, what are you hiding from me?" She gasped. "A girl? Are you spending the day with a girl?"

I laughed. "No. Cole and I are going hiking."

She frowned for a moment and looked deep into my eyes before her smile returned. "Bring him, I'll make sure there is a good Greek girl there for you both."

"No, Mama, we can't. We're planning on camping out all night."

The lies! The lies were flowing from my mouth. I made a mental note to text Cole. I didn't trust my mother.

Her eyes searched my face, looking for any sign I was going to be with anyone other than Cole.

With a pat on my chest, she said, "You be careful. There are wild animals up there, Nicholaus. You two boys would give them a lot to chew on."

She squeezed my arms as she lifted on her toes and kissed my cheek. "Se agapò."

Kissing her on the forehead, I replied, "I love you too, Mama."

"Bring that food! You can heat it up."

"Yes, ma'am."

One quick look at the clock told me I was going to be late picking up Gabi. "Cole is waiting on me, Mama. I need to get ready to go."

Taking her hands, she grabbed onto my face and stared into my eyes. She smiled and said, "I think you're going to find love soon, o gios mou."

I forced a smile. I had a feeling I'd already found something close to it and my mother was not going to be happy about it.

nine

Nic

"HOW DID YOU DO IT?"

"Well hello to you too, Nic. I'm fine. Kilyn's fine and Kira misses her uncle and would like to see you before she turns ten."

I rolled my eyes. My little brother Thano could be a serious pain in the ass.

"Hello, Thano. I miss Kira too, I'll plan to come over soon and speaking of your wife, Mom thinks Kilyn's pregnant."

Silence.

Laughing, I rubbed the back of my neck. "I'll take your silence as a yes, she is."

"How in the hell does she do that? Kilyn will freak out if Mom says anything to anyone."

"Well, she already said something to me, you can only imagine who else she voiced her thoughts to."

"Son-of-a-bitch."

"The reason I was calling, is to ask you how you dealt with telling mom about Kilyn?"

"Why? Are you dating someone?" He said it with a fake laugh.

I didn't say anything.

"Holy shit. Who is she?"

"We're . . . hanging out, that's all. Her name is Gabi."

"Kilyn! Kilyn!"

"What are you screaming about?" I asked as I grabbed my keys and headed out the door.

Thano laughed then called out, "He's dating someone!"

"Who's dating someone?" Kilyn asked in the background.

"Nic's spending the day with a girl and he's hiding it from mom."

I sighed. There was a lot of noise and all I could hear was Kilyn demanding the phone.

"Nic! Yeah, hi . . . it's Kilyn. For the love of all things that are good in this world, please tell me you're dating someone. *Please!*"

I couldn't help but laugh. Poor Kilyn would finally get a reprieve from my mother if I had a girlfriend. *Especially* if she wasn't Greek.

"It's only a second date. And she's Italian. Very Italian. Like both her parents were from Italy."

Silence.

It sounded like the phone dropped to the ground.

"What did you say to my wife, you bastard? She's crying."

Laughing, I replied, "I told her I was going on a second date with a girl who was Italian."

"Dude, don't fuck around with me. This is not the time. Are you serious right now? I mean, the whole you going on more than one date is freaking awesome, but she's not Greek? Don't do me that way if you're fucking around."

Shit. This should be a warning sign for me.

"For real, it's only a second date though. Do you really think Mom will freak if she finds out?"

"A second date for you is huge. And yes. She's going to freak the hell out. I need to go. Kilyn and I have some celebrating to do!"

The line went dead. Pulling the phone back, I looked at it before tossing it on the passenger seat.

My fingers laced through my hair. "Shit," I whispered. I'd have to keep Gabi a secret for now. That wouldn't be so hard.

Ten minutes later I was parking and heading to Gabi's front door.

The door to the bakery opened and Charity came walking out. I smiled and waved.

"Hey, Charity."

She stepped in front of me and held her hand up. "Listen, Gabi is like a sister to me. She doesn't open up to anyone, not even me half the time. If you hurt her, I will find a way to hurt you. I don't care that you're the po-po."

My head jerked back and I chuckled. "The po-po?"

"I will find a way to hurt you. Capisce?" She stood on the tips of her toes and stared me down.

Clenching my jaw to keep from laughing, I nodded. Charity was all five-foot-two and probably weighed next to nothing. It was kind of cute how she thought she was a threat.

"Got it."

"I'm serious, Nic. Gabi means a lot to me and I need you to know how big this is for her. I've only known her to go on two dates and they were both not something she wanted to do. She likes you, don't play her."

The thought of playing Gabi caused a tightness in my chest. The last thing I'd ever want to do is hurt her.

"Don't get me wrong, I like the whole alpha male thing you've got going on, but heed my warning, mister."

I held up my hands in defense. "Charity, from the little I know of you, trust me, I won't be getting on your bad side."

She smiled. "Good. Now, she doesn't know this, but she has tomorrow off because I'm hoping you're planning a nice evening for her and I don't want her rushing home."

"I hope I am. At least I'm trying to. I'm not really good at the whole dating thing."

She narrowed her eye at me. "I figured as much. Just blow her mind away with some earth shattering sex."

Holy shit.

"Wow. You went from don't hurt her to earth-shattering sex? It's only our second date."

She nodded. The way her smile crept over her face, I couldn't help but smile back. Charity tapped her hand on my chest, "I love her, but

Jesus Christ she needs to loosen up. The kind of loosening up you do after you've had mind blowing sex."

"You realize how much pressure you're now putting on me, right?"

She laughed. "Please, I've been around the block, Nic. I know your type. I seriously doubt you have problems making a girl—" Her eyes traveled down to my dick and I instantly felt violated.

I covered my junk and her eyes lifted back to mine.

"Loosen up," she finished with a wink.

Pinching my brows, I said, "I don't know if you complimented me or insulted me just now."

With a one-shoulder shrug, she turned and headed back into the bakery.

I shook my head to clear my thoughts and also made a mental note to hook up Charity and Cole. Cole would love the feisty attitude of Charity and I had no doubt she would keep him on his toes. They would be perfect for each other.

Pressing the bell, her sweet voice soon filled the air.

"Hello?"

"Hey, it's Nic.

"Come on up!"

I could hear the smile in her voice and that caused my body to warm. All these feelings were new to me and I wasn't really sure how to read it. Is sex on the second date to soon? Maybe I should have asked Thano.

Stopping, I pulled out my phone and hit his number.

"Hey, if you're calling to tell me that was all a joke, I'll hate you forever."

"No. No that's not why I'm calling. I need to ask you something."

"Shoot."

I pulled in a deep breath. "How did you know Kilyn was . . . different . . . from other girls?"

Thano didn't say anything at first before he smiled. "Um, I just knew. I felt things I'd never felt before. Not even with Savannah."

His words from before came back to my mind.

"I couldn't stop thinking about her. Wanted to see her every chance

I could. Would think of excuses to call her on the phone just to hear her voice."

"What about sex? Is the second date too soon?"

"Do you like her? I mean, *really* like her? Not like a *I want to get in her pants and fuck her* like her."

I nodded even though I knew he couldn't see me. "Yeah. I do. I've never had a woman make me feel this way before. I mean, don't get me wrong, I want in her pants. Bad. But, if she told me she wanted to wait, I'd wait as long as she needed. I love being around her. Gabi makes me laugh. I feel relaxed when I'm with her."

"Take your time, Nic. Get to know each other."

"So you're saying no sex today?"

"I'm saying let your heart lead the way. You'll know when the time is right."

There was a few seconds of silence before Thano laughed.

"Damn bro. I never thought we'd be having *this* convo."

"Me either. I'm not saying it's anything more, but I'm also going on a second date and hoping for more."

"Well, don't push her, dude. If she's the one, she's worth the wait."

Knocking on the door, I went to reply when Gabi opened the door.

My God. She was beautiful.

"Gotta go, Thano. Later."

Hitting End, I shoved my phone in my pocket.

"Good morning!" she said with a huge smile on her face.

I said the only thing my brain could muster up. "Hey."

She opened the door wider, motioning for me to come in. "Am I dressed okay? I mean for hiking and all that?"

My eyes raked over her body. She wore black yoga pants, and a T-shirt that had the name of her bakery on it in hot pink. Her hair was pulled up in a ponytail and she wore a wide hot pink headband. Her makeup was light, like the first day I met her.

She looked adorable as fuck. And sexy as hell. I couldn't believe her dressed this way was sexier to me than last night.

"You're perfect."

Her cheeks turned pink. "You're too sweet. I'm only in yoga pants and a T-shirt. Hardly perfect."

I shook my head and took a step closer to her. Her tongue instantly ran over her lips as she prepared for my kiss. All I could think about was tasting her again. She tasted sweeter than honey.

Leaning down, I wrapped my arm around her and rested it on the small of her back. "I've been thinking about kissing you ever since last night."

Her chest rose and fell quickly. The corner of her mouth rose as she whispered, "Then kiss me."

Before I had a chance to, Charity came walking out from her bedroom and up to us. She dropped a bag at Gabi's feet. "Well, don't you two look like you're getting to know each other?"

I jerked my head back and gave her a confused look. "How in the hell did you get up here before me?"

"Wait what?" Gabi asked as she looked between the two of us.

"Back steps. I ran. Fast."

"I'd say," I replied.

"Did you see each other or something?" Gabi asked confused.

With a cocky grin, I answered her. "Charity here was nice enough to offer me some tips about our date today."

"Really?" Gabi asked as her brow rose up in question.

Charity grinned from ear to ear. "I packed you an overnight bag. Don't come home tonight."

"I have to work tomorrow, Char."

"Nope. I'm making you take another day off."

Gabi laughed. "I've already had two days off. I need to . . ."

Lifting her hand, she placed her finger on Gabi's lips and loudly said, "Shh, we've got this. Go have fun. Loosen up."

She shot her eyes at me and nodded, as if reminding me of our conversation downstairs.

"I don't know, Charity. I don't think I need to be taking another day off."

Finger to lips again. "Shh." Charity took Gabi by the arm and walked her away from me. "Gabi. I mean this as a friend. An opportunity like this—"

She pointed to me. I looked around like there was someone else in the room.

"He doesn't come along all the time. You *need* this."

Gabi's head pulled back in question? "Need what?"

With her hands on her hips, Charity titled her head. "Hello, Greek dick meet Italian pussy? Remember?"

Gabi's mouth dropped open, and I was pretty sure I choked on my own spit.

"Charity! What is wrong with you?"

I attempted to clear my throat and stop coughing as Gabi walked over to me. "I'm so sorry. Water?"

"Please."

After handing me a glass of water, Gabi looked at me with sadness in her eyes. "If you want to cancel today, I completely understand."

Stopping, I took her hand in mine and pulled her to me. "I was taken by surprise, Gabi. There is nothing more I'd rather do than spend the day with you."

Her eyes lit up like fire. You could almost feel the desire bouncing between us. She chewed on her lip. Reaching up, I pulled it free and ran my thumb her soft plump lip. "The night part will come when you're ready."

"She's ready."

Gabi's eyes snapped over my shoulder. "Charity, please go away."

Focusing back on me, her cheeks turned red and she looked down. "It's just, I haven't been out with anyone in a long time and . . . well . . ." She swallowed hard. "I feel it too, Nic. So much so it scares me. Can we just take it day to day and let things go how they go?"

"Of course, Gabi, I'd never pressure you to do something you're not ready to do."

She smiled and my damn stomach dropped again. Fuck I wanted this girl, but I needed to be patient. I liked that she wasn't eager to jump into bed with me. Not that I would argue if she wanted to.

Her smile dropped and doubt crept into her eyes. "I'm sure a guy like you isn't used to waiting on a girl."

Lifting my hand, I traced my finger down her jawline. "Agapiméni, some things are worth waiting for."

ten

Gabi

I WAS GOING TO KILL Charity.

Kill. Her.

I couldn't believe she had said that in front of Nic *and* packed an overnight bag for me. Why didn't she just put whore on my forehead?

Of course, after how sweet Nic was, the only thing I could think about was having sex with him. What he would feel like inside me. Was he gentle or a little rough? Did he take his time or was he the type of guy who didn't care if the girl was pleasured or not?

No. Not Nic. I could tell already by the sweet things he said to me he would be the type to take care of me first then him.

My heart raced the more I thought about sex with Nic. I needed to stop now. This is what happens when you go so long without sex.

Of course, it wasn't lost on me that Nic picked up my overnight bag. Truth be told, I was hoping our hike would lead to his house, which would lead to a shower, which would lead to other things.

Stop it, Gabi! Focus!

"We're almost there," Nic called back. "Just around this switchback."

I breathed in a deep breath. The air up here was amazing. It felt so pure. But at the same time, it was kicking my ass. I needed to get back to the gym. As I came up behind Nic, I gasped at the sight before me. The grassy meadow was unlike anything I'd ever seen. "Wow."

"It's called the Garden of Eden."

"It's beautiful."

Nic turned to me. "I can't believe you've lived here for so long and never been on any of the hiking trails."

With a weak smile, I didn't want to tell him I was afraid of being alone. That I craved the peace, but feared someone was following me.

"Charity isn't much of an outdoor kind of girl. Even though she made me buy everything clothes and shoes wise to go hiking."

He took my hand in his as we walked across the meadow. "I love being outside. I've hiked all over these hills. It helps me find the inner peace I crave so much."

"I bet you need that with your job and all."

"Yeah, my job can get pretty intense."

I kicked at a rock while drawing in a breath. "And dangerous."

Nic came to a stop and squeezed my hand as he turned to me. I could get lost for days in those eyes.

"Yes, but that's why we train as much as we do."

Running his finger along my jaw, I saw the excitement cross his face when my body reacted to his touch. "Does that scare you? My job?"

I thought for a moment. It didn't feel like it was too soon to be having this conversation. There was no doubt we were drawn to each other, and I was positive more dates would be in our future. I got the feeling this was new to both of us. The last time I had a serious boyfriend was six years ago and even then, I wasn't drawn to him like I was Nic. What started out as an attraction soon led to something far more dangerous.

"It scares me, but not in a way that would scare me off. Does that make sense?"

The corners of his mouth rose and a hint of his dimples showed through where he had trimmed up his five o'clock shadow. "That makes perfect sense. It also makes me happy."

The way his green eyes lit up had my heartbeat racing. I'd never been so drawn to a man's eyes. Or ever felt this way about a guy before. It was as if I couldn't get enough of his smiles, kisses, and his touch. Lord knows

I wanted more of his touch. I got the feeling Nic felt the same. We were both guarded, but curious as hell. Each time he touched me my body trembled, and I knew he saw it. You could see in his eyes he liked to see what his touch did to me.

"I've had fun today," I said as I leaned against his body. He gently spun me around, wrapping his arms around me. It felt so natural. Like we'd been seeing each other for months. Like we fit together like two puzzle pieces.

He leaned over and whispered against my ear, "I've never brought a girl up here before."

His confession thrilled and stunned me all at once. Looking up at him, I watched while he looked straight out over the meadow to the distant mountains. Like his statement was hard to admit.

"Why not?" I asked.

He held me tighter. "I've never wanted to share it with anyone before."

Turning, I placed my hands on his chest, "Why share it with me?"

When his eyes met mine, I felt the air leave my lungs. I'd never had anyone look at me the way Nic did. Like he was searching deep within my soul.

"I don't know. There's something about you that draws me to you. Then last night, I couldn't stop thinking about you and that sweet wet pussy of yours, aching for me to make you come."

Oh. My. God.

I never in my life thought I would like a guy talking dirty to me. But I sure as hell liked Nic talking to me that way. My panties instantly were wet, and I longed for him to pick up where he left off.

He then added, "I can't help the way you make me feel. The things I long to do to you."

My teeth sunk into my lip as I grabbed his T-shirt and lifted to the tips of my toes. "You do things to me too, especially when you talk naughty like that."

He smiled. "Oh yeah? You like it?"

Nodding, I felt my cheeks heat. "I do, and that surprises me."

Nic ran his fingers down the side of my cheeks. "You look beautiful when your cheeks get flushed. When I talk to you like that, they turn a beautiful pink."

I dropped my gaze.

"Don't be shy, Gabi. A nice girl can have a little bit of naughty in her too."

My head dropped onto his chest and I felt his body rumble with laughter.

When I finally gained the courage I need, I dropped my head back and looked up at him.

"I've only ever been with one man. And even then it was a . . . forced relationship."

Nic frowned. "He didn't . . ."

I shook my head. "No, no, nothing like that. We were friends and our families thought we needed to be more. He never hurt me, but he certainly didn't care how I felt about things. If that makes sense."

There was no doubt that was anger I saw in Nic's eyes. Maybe I needed to think about getting into a relationship a little harder. No. No I've waited long enough and I'd never felt like this with anyone else before.

The deal I made when I went into this was to wait three years before I became romantically involved with someone. It had been six.

There was only one thing I was unsure of though. Did I want a relationship built on a lie? The truth hidden deep within me and the fear it could show its ugly head at any time.

If Nic ever found out the truth . . . the thought made me sick to my stomach. He would hate me.

Bending down, his finger lifted my chin. "Hey, are you okay? You're shaking."

Forcing a smile, I nodded. "Yeah, just a little chilly with the wind up here."

He didn't believe me. When he looked like he wanted to press me for more information, I stepped away and walked a little further into the meadow. My arms wrapped tightly around my body.

I had only known Nic two days, and I was already longing to tell him everything. I was greedy though. The longing for happiness outweighed the need for the truth.

"Gabi, you can talk to me, you know that, right?"

Smiling, I replied, "I know. I'm just taken by how beautiful this is and how I've been missing out on it."

"I've got so many more places to show you if you want."

In that moment I knew what I wanted. It was time to move on and leave the past in the past. I'd go to Italy, do what I needed to do and then never look back. It would destroy both me and my family, but the only way to be truly free was to break the tie.

Nodding, I softly replied, "I'd like that very much."

eleven

Nic

I PUSHED AWAY THE NOTION I had that Gabi was hiding something from me. I didn't have to know every single thing about her past, just like she didn't have to know everything about mine.

"I'm starving!" she gasped as we made it back down to where we first started.

"There's a great place to eat in Woodland Park."

The drive into town was comfortable and easy. Like always. There was never a moment of awkwardness between the two of us. The only time Gabi wandered away from the conversation was if it had to do with her past. Anything that had happened the last four years was open game, before that, forget it.

"This is it. Joanie's. Best damn place in town."

Gabi chuckled. "What no Greek?"

I rolled my eyes. "Let me get your door."

Jumping out of my truck, I jogged around to the passenger side and opened her door.

"Such a gentleman."

She wouldn't be saying that if she knew the things I was thinking about doing to her right now.

The place was packed like always. When it was finally our turn to order, Gabi got a Chicken Pesto Melt and I got the Reuben.

Gabi snagged a table outside while I grabbed our drinks.

"Their desserts looked heavenly," she said as I set her Diet Coke in front of her.

"I have an in with a bakery in Old Colorado. She makes the best panna cotta this side of the Mississippi."

She cleared her throat and raised an eyebrow so I added, "In the whole country, honestly."

"I have a confession."

The waitress brought out our two sandwiches. "Anything else?"

We both said no.

I took a bite of my Reuben and asked, "What's your confession?"

That sweet face of hers turned a shade pinker. "I made you something last night. I couldn't sleep after . . . well . . . after you left."

There was no way I could stop the wide grin from moving over my face. I knew I left her horny as hell, but the idea of her finishing herself off without me pissed me off. "I'm sorry about that, agapiméni."

Her eyes lit up. "What does that mean?"

"Sweetheart."

She pulled the corner of her lip in between her teeth. "I like that."

"You'll like it even more when I whisper it in your ear while making love to you."

Her mouth formed a small "O" as she stared at me with a dreamy face. She whispered, "What are you doing to me?" Our gaze was locked on one another as we sat for a moment in silence.

Reaching across the table, I took her hand in mine and lightly placed a kiss on the back of it. "I could ask the same thing of you. Because I don't make love, Gabi."

Her brow lifted. "You don't?"

Slowly shaking my head, I replied, "I fuck. Hard and fast. But with you, I want so much more."

She softly whispered my name. "Nic."

My chest ached. "I want to kiss you so badly right now."

Her face blushed, and she took a quick look around.

"My brother Thano's house isn't too far from here. Feel like meeting some family?"

Her mouth dropped open. "Ah, um, o-okay."

Laughing, I took another bite of my sandwich. "I needed to move us in another direction or we were about to have public sex."

Gabi laughed.

"They won't bite, I swear. You'll love Kilyn and she is going to *love* you."

She worried her lower lip and I could see the sheer fear in her eyes.

"I haven't seen my niece Kira in a few weeks. I promised Thano I'd stop by and visit with her and we're so close."

Gabi grinned. "Sounds like fun."

"Yeah?"

Nodding, she replied with a giggle, "Yeah."

GABI RUBBED HER HANDS OVER her pants and took in a deep breath.

"If you don't want to go, we don't have to stop."

Turning to me, she smiled. "No. It's just . . . you know."

"Family on the second date?"

"Yes!"

Laughing, I ran my finger along her jawline. She was so beautiful. And the way her body shook with my touch was a fucking turn on if ever there was one.

"We won't stay long. I promise."

"I'm enjoying myself and I'm sure I'm going to enjoy meeting your brother and his family."

I leaned over and kissed her cheek quickly before jumping out and jogging over to her side. The moment she stepped out of the truck, I laced her fingers with mine. If I knew Kilyn, she was already watching everything.

Heading to the front door, it flew open before we reached it.

I knew it.

Kilyn's face was lit up like the fourth of July. "Oh. My. God. The heavens did answer my cries of mercy!"

Gabi's smile faded a bit before she plastered it back on.

"Forewarning, Kilyn may be a little excited to meet you."

"Um, why?"

"Oh, you'll find out in about five seconds."

And right on cue, Kilyn rushed out and took Gabi into her arms. "You are an angel sent straight from God." Pushing her out at arm's length, she looked her over. "You're not Greek."

Gabi laughed. "Nope."

Kilyn looked up at the sky and mouthed, thank you. Focusing back on Gabi, she nonchalantly shook her head. "I've finally got another normal person on my side."

"Um . . . yay?"

Kilyn hooked her arm with Gabi and lead her into the house. "I know I sound crazy, but give me thirty minutes and I'll have you all caught up on the crazy. Also known as, the Drivas family."

Gabi looked back at me with wide eyes. "Better you know now than after we have sex and you fall in love with me."

She snarled her lip at me while Kilyn dragged her off.

"So, she's pretty," Thano said as he walked in as the girls walked out of the room.

Turning to Thano, I smiled. "She's fucking beautiful."

He laughed. "Are you trying to scare her off?"

"No, why?" I asked giving him a confused look.

"Kilyn is going to fill her in on everything. Mom. Dad. The family."

I waved him off. "Nah, Gabi won't be scared off. Besides, I don't plan on the family meeting her any time soon."

Thano laughed. "Yeah, good luck with that. Mom has some weird sense for these things. I'm telling you, she'll find out and when she does, all hell's gonna break loose."

"She likes Kilyn."

Handing me a beer, Thano nodded. "She does. But do you remember that shirt dad used to wear all the time?"

"Which one? He has a ton of them."

"The one that said Italian food is just like Greek food . . . except with less flavor."

I laughed. "Oh yeah."

"You know how Mom and Dad feel about Italians after that whole incident with Thad. Add in the fact that Gabi owns a bakery and I'm guessing she likes to cook."

My beer stopped at my lips. "Fuck. I forgot Thad dated an Italian girl."

"Whose mother tried to steal away Mom's middle son."

"The shit's gonna hit the fan."

"Yep," Thano said before taking a long drink.

"Gabi's different. She has no parents, and she's a simple girl. Mom will love her."

My brother raised a brow and said, "You keep telling yourself that. All I know is that if things work out with you and this girl, my wife is getting a major break from Mom."

I chuckled. "Then let's toast to things working out."

"Hell yeah."

Our beers clinked together. "Nic, I'm glad to see you dating someone. You deserve to find love."

"Don't get all emotional on me, little brother. We're having fun, that's all."

He stared at me for a few seconds before smiling. I knew he could see right through me. I didn't have fun by dating one single girl. I had fun by fucking a different girl every other week. Here I was sitting in his house with the girl I'd only been on two dates with chatting it up with his wife.

I tried like hell to ignore the feeling deep within my chest. The one I'd never experienced before, but grew more and more with each passing moment I spent with Gabi.

"I'm not looking for love, Thano."

He nodded and lifted his hands up. "If you say so."

I downed my beer. "I say so. Now where's my niece?"

twelve

Gabi

SITTING IN A STUNNED SILENCE, I stared at Kilyn. "You had to have a Plan B birthing plan?"

She nodded. "Yep."

"Wow. I thought my family had issues."

Kilyn laughed. "For as much of a pain in the ass they are, there isn't a damn thing they wouldn't do for me or Kira. I know that with all my heart. But, if things do turn serious for you and Nic, be prepared to not only have Nic's immediate family in your life, but all the family. It's like a package deal. At Kira's birthday party a few weeks ago, this entire back yard was filled with Thano's family. I woke up three nights in a row in a cold sweat with dreams of people yelling out Opa!"

I covered my mouth to hide my laugh.

"Well, we're just getting to know each other. It's only our second date."

She scrunched her nose up. "And here you are, sitting on my back porch talking to me."

My hands wrung together nervously. When Nic mentioned meeting his brother and family, I panicked internally. Meeting family is huge. That means more people in my life, more of a chance of someone wanting to dig into my past.

"May I be honest with you, Gabi?"

"Yes, please do."

I held my breath. She was going to tell me Nic was all wrong for me. That I was not Nic's type and that after he had his fun with me, I'd be another notch in his belt.

"I've been in this family for over five years and I have never seen nor heard of Nic dating anyone. He's never brought a girl home to meet his brothers or parents before. He really likes you, Gabi. I saw the way he looked at you, the same way Thano looks at me."

I swallowed hard. "I really like him too. He brings out feelings in me I've never experienced before."

She smiled. "I love Nic and the last thing I'd ever want was for him to get hurt."

"Is that why you told me about the family?"

"Yes, and I wished like hell someone had warned me."

I giggled. "I haven't dated anyone seriously in a long time, Kilyn. I've pretty much lived a quiet, non-existent life. But when he walked into my bakery, my entire world felt like it has been woken up. Not just my body, but my heart as well."

Chewing on her lip, she leaned in closer. "Okay, something else I have to tell. Greek men, well, you know what they say?"

With a roll of my eyes, I replied, "I've heard a rumor or two."

Her cheeks flamed. "They are possessive. In and out of bed. It's more of a gentle possessiveness. There isn't anything Thano wouldn't do for me."

Now it was time for my cheeks to heat. "Well, we're taking things slow, but he certainly knows how to rev up my engine."

Kilyn covered her mouth and giggled. "Oh, I can imagine. And Nic slow? Wow. I'm impressed. Hang on tight girl, if he is anything like his brother, you're in for a ride. And I do mean *ride*."

We both lost it laughing. It was nice to have someone other than Charity to talk to. Not that I didn't love her like a sister, but talking to Kilyn was fun and different. I'd surrounded myself with only Charity the last four years, and having another girl to talk to was a nice change.

"What's so funny?"

I glanced up and nearly fell out of my seat at the sight of Thano walking up.

"I know. Wait till you see Thad. I don't know what their mother did, but she produced three crazy handsome boys."

Kilyn stood and wrapped her arms around her husband. After a quick kiss, she faced me. "Gabi, this is Thano."

I stood and reached my hand out for his. He pulled me to him and kissed me gently on the cheek. "It's nice to meet you, Gabi. I'm not sure what you did to my big brother in there, but keep doing it. I haven't seen him this relaxed in a long ass time."

Not sure what to say, I simply smiled. The next thing I knew, a young girl in curls ran out the door screaming.

"Uncle Nic is going to get me . . . save me!"

She stopped on a dime when she saw me. Her sweet blue eyes lit up and she pointed to me. "You are *very* pretty. Who are you?"

Nic was by my side, kissing me gently on the cheek. "This is Gabi, squirt. Gabi, this is squirt. Otherwise known as Kira."

I bent down and offered my hand to her. "It's so nice to meet you, Kira."

She wore a wide smile. "Are you Uncle Nic's girlfriend?"

Opening my mouth, I wasn't sure how to answer that.

Nic answered for me. Scooping up the little girl, he threw her over his shoulder. "She is, but you'll always be my number one girl."

Joy danced through my heart at Nic telling Kira I was his girlfriend. Even though it was only our second date, the declaration felt right.

Squeals of delight came from her mouth. "Yay!"

My heart melted as I watched Nic play with his niece. He'd make a wonderful father. A slow ache began to build. I'd never really longed for a family of my own. In that moment it was all I could do to not dream of that with Nic.

Too. Soon.

These feelings were happening way too fast. Peeking over to Kilyn and Thano, they were gazing at me like I was the best thing since apple pie.

"Gabi! Gabi! Come play hide and seek!"

I quickly made my way out into the yard with Nic and Kira.

"Okay, well you guys have fun. I'm taking my wife inside for a bit."

Kilyn giggled and let Thano led her into the house. My mouth fell open. Turning, I looked at Nic.

"Are they?"

He tossed his head back and laughed. "I guess they saw an opportunity and took it."

I couldn't help but chuckle. "I guess so!"

NIC OPENED THE DOOR TO his condo and motioned for me to go in first. Following, I gasped when I saw the view before my eyes.

"Wow. Why in the world would you want to move with a view like this?"

He set the three bags of groceries down on his kitchen island. "I don't know. A change would be nice. I figured I'm almost thirty-one, buying a house seemed like the next step."

Walking to the wall of glass, I looked out at the sun dipping below the mountains. This was why I decided to stay in this city. I was ready to put my past behind me and start dreaming about the future. And Nic was the person I wanted to do that with. But could I start a relationship with someone I was so drawn to on a lie?

He spoke and I jumped. "And if you hadn't backed out of the bidding war, I might not be talking about the little blue house I'm closing on in a month."

I laughed as I spun back around and helped him take out the fixings for lasagna. "I did love that house, and I'm sad I let it go."

"I happen to know the new owner. I bet he'd let you come and have a sleepover."

My lower stomach pulled. "Hmm . . . tempting offer."

Sparks seemed to ignite the air as we both stood and stared at one another. I finally broke the stare down. "Are you sure you want me to make lasagna?"

"Hell yes I'm sure," Nic said as he pulled out the long loaf of fresh Italian bread we had just bought. I laughed when he took a bite off the end of it.

"If we were at my house, you'd be eating it with fresh pasta."

Nic sauntered over to me, placed his hands on my hips, and pulled me to him. "If we were at your place, Charity would be pushing us to the bedroom and probably telling me the correct way to use my dick."

Laughing, I hit him on the shoulder. "You're so bad, right, but bad."

He quickly kissed me on the cheek. "I'll put some music on and you get to cooking dinner for me, woman."

Colbie Caillat's soft voice came through the speakers and I couldn't help but smile. "I love her!" I called back over my shoulder.

I felt him before he touched me. The hairs on my neck stood and my lower stomach dropped as his hand moved around and rested on my stomach. He pulled me back against him and I rested my head on his massive chest.

His hot breath tickled my skin while he teased me with his lips.

"I've been wanting to tell you all day how heavenly you smell."

I could only respond with a, "Mmm."

"So good, I've been fighting the urge to explore your body to see if every inch of you smells just as divine."

"Nic," I whispered in a needy voice.

He placed a soft kiss under my ear before moving his hand up to my breasts. He rubbed his thumb over my nipple and I could feel it straining against my bra. "I'm going to make you come so hard you'll see stars."

My legs went weak and his grip on me tightened.

"Yes," I gasped. I didn't even care how needy that made me sound. I couldn't stop thinking about his touch. Dreaming of what his face would feel like between my legs.

He turned to me. "I want to touch you now, Gabi. Hear my name fall from your lips as you come."

"Touch me, Nic. Please."

Before I even knew what was happening, I was in his arms and he was walking us to his bedroom. My heart started beating faster.

"We won't do anything you don't want to do, but I want to see that pretty Italian pussy of yours."

My face buried into his chest as it burned with embarrassment. Nic stopped walking.

"Look at me, Gabi."

I did as he asked. "Don't ever be embarrassed by your body. It's perfect in every single way."

Chewing on my lip, I craved to do anything I possibly could for this man to make him happy.

"I promise I won't be," I softly said as I gazed into his beautiful hazel eyes.

His eyes turned dark as he headed into his bedroom. Gently sliding me down his body, he smiled a smile that knocked me out of my socks. "Tell me what you want me to do, agapiméni. I want to hear it from your lips how you want me to make you come."

My cheeks heated again. This man was going to kill me.

"I . . . I um . . ."

Closing my eyes, I shook my head. I'd never been open with a man before. Telling them what my fantasies were. I certainly couldn't do it with *him*.

Warm hands cupped my face. "Look at me."

My eyes snapped open and looked deep into his. His stared deep into my soul while he slowly spoke. "Tell me . . . how you want . . . me to make . . . you orgasm."

I swallowed hard. I knew exactly how I wanted him to do it.

"Start with your hand and then . . . then—"

My eyes drifted down to his mouth. The left corner slowly rose into the sexiest smile I'd ever seen in my entire life. "Keep talking, baby."

Chewing on my lip, I dug deep down inside and said the words I'd been thinking. "I want you to use your mouth."

A full-blown knock-me-the-hell-over smile spread over his face.

"That's my good girl. I think the lasagna is going to have to wait a few more minutes."

I let out a nervous chuckle. Nic dropped to his knees but kept his eyes on me. When his hands grabbed my waist, I gasped. He slowly pulled my yoga pants down. He moaned when he saw the baby blue lace panties I had on underneath.

"Blue just became my new favorite color."

Smiling, I fought the urge to reach for my own breasts. The heat of his stare alone was beginning to start the buildup.

I stepped out of my pants and Nic tossed them to the side. When he pushed his face into my panties, I moaned and dug my fingers into his thick dark hair. His long intake of air caught me off guard and caused my lower stomach to pull with a desire I'd never in my life experienced before.

"Jesus," I whispered.

"Damn, baby, you smell so fucking good."

I couldn't pull my eyes off of him. The way he was worshiping my body had me trembling with anticipation. All I could smell was Nic. Everywhere. My eyes quickly searched his room.

Dark grey covered the walls. The furniture was beautiful. It looked antique and had an old-world charm to it. I instantly loved everything about the room and I had a feeling I would love it even more when Nic was finished with me.

I gasped as his finger traced along the top of my panties. My heartbeat increased tenfold when he slowly pulled them off. I stood there, my entire lower body exposed to this man. A man I'd only known for a few days.

"So fucking beautiful. Lay down on the bed, agapiméni. I want a better look at those pretty pink lips of yours."

Oh. My. God.

I was going to explode the moment he touched me. I walked backward until Nic jumped up and pulled me to a stop.

"I need to see all of you."

He lifted my T-shirt over my head and moaned when he saw the matching baby-blue push-up bra.

"You're going to kill me, Gabi."

I couldn't help the smile that spread over my face. I'd never been treated like that before. Like I was his everything.

Nic stepped closer. My breathing increased as he reached his one hand up and traced his finger along my cleavage. The other hand moved to my back and like an expert, he had my bra undone and falling to the ground. He took two stumbled steps back.

"Goddamn, I've never seen anything so beautiful in my life."

I stood before him completely naked and exposed while he raked his eyes over my body. The greedy, hungry look in them had me growing hotter by the second. I knew if I touched myself I'd be soaking wet.

"Touch yourself, Gabi."

A lump formed in my throat. Had I said that out loud? "W-what?"

His eyes met mine. "Touch. Yourself."

With a shaky hand, I slowly moved between my legs. I swept my fingers over my clit and gasped.

"Are you wet? Slip your fingers in and tell me if you're wet."

"Oh God," I whispered as I did what he asked. A long slow hiss came from my lips.

"Yes." My cheeks heated. Closing my eyes, I softly said, "So wet for you, Nic."

He grabbed my wrist and pulled my hand up to his lips. Opening my eyes, my mouth slacked open as he pushed the two fingers I had just had inside of me into his mouth. Closing his eyes, he moaned as he sucked and ran his tongue over my fingers.

Ohmygawd. Hottest moment of my life. I swear I'm going to come any second.

Slowly taking my fingers from his mouth, he smiled. "You taste better than I could have imagined."

"Nic, please."

A small smile tugged at the corner of his mouth. "Lay down."

I did as he asked. Almost scrambling to get on my back. The way he crawled on the bed and over me had me pressing my legs together. I needed friction. Anything to ease the ache.

And with four words whispered from his mouth, I fell from the ledge. Free falling into the most amazing moment of my life.

"Spread your legs, Gabi."

thirteen

Nic

HER BODY TREMBLED AS SHE spread her legs open for me. I almost dropped to the floor when I saw that beautiful sight before me. Lips so soft and pink they were begging for my tongue to tease them. A pussy so wet it glistened with her desire.

Fuck if I didn't want to bury my cock so deep inside her she would feel me for a week.

Slow. This is for her. Not you.

My fingertips moved lightly up her thighs while I placed soft kisses along the path that lead to paradise.

Moving my lips closer, I blew on her clit. Her hips bucked. Grabbing her, I held her down.

"I'm going to keep sucking and licking on your pussy until your body stops shaking."

Her head thrashed back and forth as her hands grabbed at my comforter.

"Nic! God please!"

I loved hearing her beg.

"Touch your breasts, agapiméni. Let me see you play with your nipples."

She was so fucking responsive to everything. The moment her hands went to her breasts I was fighting the urge not to take her.

Then she twisted and pulled at her nipples and I about lost all control.

"Fucking hell, Gabi."

"Nic!"

Keeping my eyes on her, I moved my tongue slowly through her soft, pink lips.

"Yes!" She hissed.

I wanted to go slow, but once I got a taste of that sweet pussy, I got greedy and pushed my face into her. Sucking and licking. There was no way I would ever be satisfied.

"Ohmygawd!" Gabi cried out.

I sucked, licked, and devoured her. Something inside of me changed, and I knew I had to make Gabi mine. The thought of any other man touching her boiled my skin. I would be the last man to ever touch this body. I would own this pussy.

Her body began to tremble and I knew she was close.

Glancing up, I almost died. She was leaning up on her arms watching me. The moment our eyes met, she lost it. Dropping back to the bed, she cried out my name as her orgasm raced through her body.

When she finally came down from her high, I slowly crawled up her body, placing kisses all over her. I stopped and gave each nipple attention before moving to be face-to-face with her.

"I want to kiss you, Gabi. Make you taste how fucking sweet you are."

Her mouth dropped slightly open. When her tongue barely licked over her lips, I knew that was her answer. Pressing my lips to her, she opened up to me again. I moaned as her tongue danced slowly with mine. Hands laced through my hair as she gave it a small tug, causing me to moan into her mouth.

Fuck. I wanted this girl so damn bad. Pressing my hard dick against her, she wrapped her leg around me, lifting her hips to get more friction. The more we kissed, the more my hips moved against her and before I knew it, Gabi was calling out my name again. I couldn't wait until the day I could take her and really make her mine.

When her body stopped trembling, she opened her eyes and looked at me. Then Gabi whispered one word.

"Stars."

Her fingers ran lightly through my hair and I couldn't get over how beautiful she looked with the afterglow of her orgasms on her cheeks.

"You've wrecked me for any other man. Do you know that?"

With a chuckle, I kissed her lips. "Good. Because after that, I'm going to need to have you in my bed every single day."

Her eyes sparkled before she glanced down to the bulge in my pants. "What about you? Do you want me to . . ." Shy eyes looked back into mine.

"Don't worry about me, prinkipissa."

Her teeth sunk into her lip. Soft hands trailed down my chest. Pushing out, Gabi pushed me onto my back.

Trembling hands unbuttoned my pants while she continued to worry her lip.

We both laughed as she tried to pull my jeans off.

Kicking off my shoes, I lifted my hips and pushed them down.

With a gasp, Gabi stared at my dick before peeking back at me. "You were commando."

With a wink, I replied, "I'm almost always commando."

A beautiful shade of red moved over her cheeks before she looked back down at me. I quickly pulled my jeans off and tossed them to the side. I wanted this to be about Gabi, but hell if I wasn't a greedy bastard. I needed to feel her lips around my cock.

With a touch so soft I almost came on the spot, Gabi caressed my dick like it was a priceless piece of art.

Fuck. It was hot as hell watching her nibble on that lip while she looked down at me. I'd give anything to know what she was thinking. Just then, her eyes snapped up to mine.

"Take your shirt off," she commanded with the cutest damn smile I'd ever seen.

Fuck yes. My sweet demanding Gabi.

Sitting up, I pulled the shirt quickly over my head and discarded it to the floor. Gabi's eyes roamed over my body while her lips parted open slightly.

"My God you're perfect," she whispered as she lifted her hand and lightly ran it over my chest and abs. My entire body shook with a feeling I'd never experienced before in my life.

This woman was going to wreck me.

Focusing back on my rock hard dick, Gabi caressed it with both hands. The way she moved I could tell this wasn't something she did before. Son-of-a-bitch. How innocent is this girl?

With a shake to her voice, Gabi spoke. "I've never . . . um . . . I mean . . . I haven't ever done this before."

My heart slammed against my chest.

What in the hell did she just say?

I fought to catch my breath as those sweet innocent baby blues stared at me. Waiting for me to respond to her admission.

Sitting up, I pulled her to me and wrapped my arms around her. I'd never felt my heart pound so hard, not even on a damn raid.

"I'm sorry," she whispered.

Pulling back, I lifted her chin so our eyes met. "I'm the one who is sorry, prinkipissa. I would have never have let you do that had I known."

"But I wanted to do it, I'm not sure if I would do it right."

I wanted to tell her everything she did was right. The way she made my heart feel like it floated in my chest, or how each time she smiled at me she had stolen another piece of my soul. *Everything* she did was right. So much so it scared the hell out of me.

"Baby, I promise you the moment those lips wrapped around my dick, I was going to come."

Gabi giggled and buried her face into my chest.

Damn. I loved her innocence.

"That brings up something else we need to talk about."

She lifted her head.

"If you want me to come in your mouth or not."

She worried her lip. "I've heard Charity talk about it. She likes it. Said it makes the whole experience better."

My fingers ran lightly over her back. I could really get used to this girl being naked and lying next to me each night.

"It's up to you. Either way, I'll let you know before I do."

She grinned. "Is the mood gone? Or can I try?"

Fucking hell. I'm slayed with this woman.

"I certainly won't say no."

With a sexy as hell smile, she got up and moved over my body. The last thing I expected her to do was put that warm pussy over my cock. She lifted her brows and I grabbed onto her hips. We both stilled. Closing my eyes, I held my breath and tried like hell to fight the urge to flip her over and fuck her until she screamed my name.

"Nic? Is everything okay?"

I nodded. "You feel so damn good. I'm trying to keep my control, Gabi."

"What if I don't want you to keep your control?"

My eyes opened and my breath caught. "W-what?"

She pressed harder against me, causing every ounce of blood to go right to my dick. "I want you, Nic. More than I've ever wanted anyone or anything."

Slowly, I shook my head. "I don't want to push you."

Her hands went to my chest, leaning down, she kissed me gently. "I promise I wouldn't do anything if I didn't want to. I want to know what you feel like inside me. How it feels when I come and your moving in me."

Sitting up, I wrapped my arms around her beautiful body and slowly rolled her onto her back. I've never made love to a woman. Sure, I've always made sure they came first, but when it came to fucking, it was simply fucking. With Gabi, I wanted so much more.

I *needed* more.

My body shook, and it wasn't because I wanted inside her so damn bad. It was something else. Something I couldn't put my finger on.

Cupping her head within my hands, I pierced her eyes with mine. My heart beating so loud, I swore she could hear it.

"De exo niosi pote etsi os tora."

It was out of my mouth before I could even stop myself.

Gabi smiled as she lifted her hands and lightly ran her finger along my jaw. "What did you say?"

The tightness in my chest grew.

Do I tell her what I had said?

I could easily lie and tell her all I said was I wanted her. But this was

Gabi. The girl with the sky blue eyes and beautiful smile that made my heart stop the first time she looked at me. The woman who had me tossing and turning at night thinking about her and the next time I could see her.

I knew I had to tell her the truth. She deserved it.

"I said I have never felt like this before."

Her smile faded some, but her eyes lit up like the sky after a rain storm. She searched my face before saying, "I haven't either. You make me forget everything. I want to get lost with you, Nic."

Her cheeks turned pink again.

"I've . . . I've only ever been with one guy and I was tested after it ended."

My heart slammed against my chest.

"What . . . what are you saying?"

"What I feel with you, I never felt with him. This feels so different and I want to experience it . . . completely."

Swallowing hard, I stared into her eyes. "Are you saying you don't want me to wear a condom?"

"I'm on the pill. But if you're not ready for something like that, I understand. Or if you think you might not be . . ."

Her voice drifted off.

"I'm clean, Gabi. I've always used a condom. I've never not used one."

"Oh, okay. I understand if you want to use one."

I shook my head. Damn this girl. Shit her innocence was my undoing.

"Gabi, I've been tested. I'm clean and trust me when I say I would love to make love to you without a condom on."

A huge smile moved over her face. "Then take me, Nic, because I'm yours."

And like that, my walls came crashing down. I moved slightly, my dick pushing at her soft wet entrance. Everything was spinning in my head. Her words, my words, the way I was feeling, the longing I felt to make love to her all night long.

Nothing made sense anymore. The only thing I cared about was her, in this moment. Feeling her body fall apart with me inside her, completely inside her with nothing between.

I couldn't help myself, I pushed into her fast and hard, causing her to let out a small whimper.

Damn it. Motherfucker.

"Fuck, Gabi. I can't control myself with you."

Her legs wrapped around my body, pulling me as deep as she could. Her eyes closed, and the pain of me stretching her all at once evident her face.

"Give me one second to adjust to you. It's been a really long time."

I pressed my lips to her and begged for her forgiveness. "Baby, I'm so sorry if I hurt you. It's taking everything I have to not fuck you right now."

She opened her eyes and looked deep into my soul. "Make me yours."

fourteen

Gabi

SOMETHING CHANGED IN HIS EYES with those three words. He slowly pulled out and pushed back into me. The heavenly feeling was almost too much. My build up was already starting. He picked up the speed, and I met him thrust for thrust. I could tell he was holding back and was about to lose control. And how I wanted to feel Nic Drivas lose control.

"Goddamn it, Gabi. I'm trying to go slow, baby. You're squeezing down on me. Fucking hell."

I wanted him to fuck me more than anything. I *needed* him to. My nails dug into his back as I lifted my hips to him. I needed more. Wanted so much more.

"More," I gasped while wrapping my legs around him tighter.

Then the Nic who didn't make love showed up. He grabbed onto my hips and moved faster, harder. The pain now had slipped away and was replaced by utter bliss.

I gasped as my orgasm quickly swept over my body.

"Oh God!" I cried out as he pounded into my body, giving me every delicious promise he had whispered in my ear from the moment I first met him.

My body shook as another orgasm rolled into the last. I'd never experienced this before. I never wanted Nic to stop. Him inside of me was the most beautiful thing I'd ever experienced.

Grasping for the bedspread, my back arched as my orgasm reached to the point where I wasn't sure I could keep going on. Nic's body shook while he let out a long moan before dropping his head to my neck and calling out my name. We fell apart together as he poured himself into me. I knew nothing would ever be the same again.

When his body finally came to a stop, he was still shaking while I lay under him in a state of pure bliss. My body so relaxed all I wanted to do was fall asleep in his arms.

Nic hovered over me while he caught his breath. He pulled out of me, quickly got up, and walked away. My heart dropped as I watched him walk away without a single word.

I'd never felt so used in my entire life.

Was everything he said a lie?

Words to get me into bed with him?

Covering my stomach, I swung my legs over the bed and covered my mouth. I felt sick. Then he appeared in front of me. A wash cloth in his hand. His eyes looked tortured.

Placing his hand on the side of my face, he whispered, "I'm so sorry. You deserved so much more than that. I lost control with you, Gabi. I tried so hard not to." His head dropped. "I'm so sorry." My brows pinched together. Grabbing his face with my hands, I lifted his eyes to mine.

"That was amazing. I loved every single moment of what we just shared Nic. It was raw and real. Passionate. I didn't just see the stars, you took me to heaven."

A small tug at the corner of his mouth revealed a slight smile.

"I hurt you. I was too rough."

I shook my head. "If you had hurt me, I would have told you."

"But I lost control with you. I wanted to make love to you and I couldn't hold back."

"I didn't want you to hold back." I shook my head. "With you, I forget everything and seem to be lost in the moment."

"Is that a bad thing?"

"No," I said with a smile. "It's a beautiful thing."

Nic's lips were pressed to mine in a flash.

His whispered words against my lips caused my desire to bloom again. "You're so beautiful, Gabi. And you're mine."

"Yours," I whispered as I laid back on the bed. Moving to the middle. "Make love to me, Nic."

His eyes lit up while they roamed over my body. I was shocked to see he was already hard again.

I couldn't help but smile.

You know what they say about Greek men.

Nic's hand moved between my legs with two fingers sliding in. He moaned and closed his eyes.

"Mine. You're mine, Gabi."

I watched his face as he spoke. It was a mix of confusion and happiness. Exactly the same emotions I felt.

Swallowing hard, I knew the words I was about to speak were the truth. I wanted to be his.

For always.

"Yours, Nic. Forever yours."

fifteen

Nic

MY HEART WAS POUNDING AS I slipped slowly back inside Gabi. Her warmth spread throughout my body like the hot summer sun.

"You feel so damn good," I whispered as I buried my face into her neck. Inhaling a deep breath of her, I took every second in. This time moving slower, going deeper. I'd lost control with her the first time and there was no way I was doing it again. I wasn't even sure how my dick was hard again this soon, but I sure as hell wasn't going to argue.

Gabi moved in perfect harmony with me. We were one and the same, and I was so damn confused if I loved it or if it scared the piss out of me. There was one thing I was sure of. She was all that I wanted.

Slowly moving, we whispered each other's names against our lips. I never wanted the moment to end. I was lost to this woman and nothing else mattered but her and I.

Arching her back, Gabi cried out my name as she came. I swore it sounded as if it was carried off on the wind and wrapped around my body, drawing out my own release. My body trembled as my orgasm came and I poured myself into her.

When my body came to a rest, I stayed inside her. Cradling her head within my hands, I pierced her eyes with mine. My chest was tight, but I wasn't sure if it was the feelings I suddenly felt for this woman, or the fear that gripped me because of those feelings.

"Agapiméni. What have you done to me?"

"DRIVAS? DID YOU EVEN HEAR a damn word I said?"

I grabbed the towel off the handle and wiped my face. Turning to Cole, I asked, "What did you say?"

His brows furrowed as he shook his head. "What is wrong with you dude? For the last week you haven't been the same."

Scoffing at him, I responded, "Don't be ridiculous."

He stopped running. "Dude, you're lost in your own world half the time, you never want to go for drinks, you haven't flirted with a single chick, and I'm pretty sure you're avoiding your family like the plague. You must really have a thing for Gabi."

I stopped on a dime. "What?"

He lifted a brow then chuckled. "Don't even act like I haven't noticed it. Ever since you met Gabi."

"So I'm dating a girl, what's the big deal?"

Now Cole looked at me as if I was insane. "What's the big deal? Wasn't it you who said you'd rather die than be stuck with one pussy for the rest of your life?"

With a push of the button, I started running again. "We're having fun, enjoying each other's company, that's all."

I looked back at him, feeling the weight of his stare on me. "That's not what Charity says."

Hitting the pause button again, I shot him a look. "Charity? Have you been talking to Charity about me and Gabi?"

Cole held up his hands in defense. "Hey, she's the one who told me Gabi was walking around in a dream bubble. That it had been the happiest she'd seen her in four years."

I couldn't help the small crack of smile that formed at my mouth. "She said that?"

He laughed, "Yeah, and I'm going to have to say the same damn thing about you. Dude, you really like her."

There was no sense in denying it. Gabi and I had spent every day together. I had to lay my eyes on her at least once a day or I felt like I would lose my damn mind.

"I like her. Happy now?"

A wide grin spread over Cole's face. He slapped me on the side of the arm. "I'm happy for you dude."

With a roll of my eyes, I started running again. "Jesus, I'm not marrying her. I like her, we're having fun together."

"And the sex?"

I laughed. "I don't kiss and tell, dude."

Cole chuckled as he started up running again. "So, what do you know about Charity?"

Taking a quick peek over at him, I smiled. "You should totally go for it."

"Really? She seems a little rough around the edges."

"Nah, you two would hit it off. I'm positive."

"Huh. Well, she's already turned me down once, so I don't know," Cole replied as he put his head phones back in and ran faster.

I couldn't help but chuckle. Cole and Charity. Yeah, that would be interesting.

GABI STARED AT ME WITH her mouth dropped open. "Your whole family?"

Today was my first day off in a week and I couldn't wait to spend it with Gabi. She had adjusted her days off to match mine, but still got called in by that little prick Max every chance he could. Taking a bite of the linguine she had made for lunch, I nodded. "Yeah. Thad and Phoebe are having their baby shower so the whole family will be there."

She chewed on her lip. I could see how freaked out that made her. I was positive Kilyn had filled Gabi in on my family, and then some.

"Would you rather meet my parents first?"

Her eyes lit up. "Yes. I think I can handle that a little better. From what Kilyn has said, I shouldn't go in the lion's den first. I need to ease in."

I laughed. "Kilyn might be a good one to listen to. How about if I see if Thano and Kilyn can join us for dinner tonight at my folks?"

"Last minute like that? Will they be upset?"

This time I laughed harder. "Are you kidding me? My mother will be thrilled, especially if I tell her I'm bringing someone with me."

Gabi's expression turned to pure horror. Standing, I wiped my face and tossed the napkin to the table.

"Don't be afraid, agapiméni. My mother will love you."

"I'm not Greek."

"Kilyn isn't either."

She nodded while she wrung her hands together.

"Do you know what you need?"

She shrugged and asked, "Dark hair, skin, and a Greek name?"

Chuckling, I ran my finger along her jawline. "A kiss."

The corners of her mouth turned upright. "I do need a kiss. A long one."

I lifted my brows. "Oh yeah?"

She nodded. "Anything else?"

"Your hands on my body."

"I like where you're going. Keep talking."

"Your lips on my neck."

Drawing her body close to mine, I buried my face into her neck.

Her head fell back as she let out a long soft moan.

"Next," I whispered.

"Touch me, Nic."

"Where do you want me to touch you, baby?"

My body was on fire. I'd never been with a woman who turned me on twenty-four hours a day. I couldn't get enough of her.

"Nic," she whimpered.

I cupped her breasts with my hands and smiled. "Do you want me to touch your pussy, Gabi?"

She gasped. I knew she liked it when I talked dirty to her. It fueled her desire even more

When she didn't answer, I grabbed her ponytail and pulled her head back. Her eyes met mine. "Tell me."

"Yes. I want you to touch me there."

With a smirk, I shook my head. "Where is there?"

Her eyes closed as she whispered, "Nic, please."

"Tell me," I said with a growl.

"My . . . my p-pussy."

"Good girl," I softly spoke against her lips while my hand slid up her thigh. "I like it when you wear dresses."

When I brushed against her lips, I pulled back to look at her. "No panties?"

Her cheeks flushed. "I went commando today."

My entire body trembled. This girl was my undoing. I wanted her desperately.

Lifting her up, she wrapped her legs around me. Placing her on the kitchen table, I dropped to my knees.

"Oh God. Yes! Nic, Yes!"

"Watch me make you come with my mouth, Gabi."

She nodded while her chest heaved with excitement.

My mouth was sucking on her clit two seconds later. Her fingers dug into my hair as she pulled me closer to her. My greedy girl liked oral sex.

A lot.

"Yes!" she cried when my tongue dipped into her sweet, wet center.

I glanced up and almost died as I watched her bite down on her lip while she watched me eat her out.

Grabbing her ass, I pulled her closer to me.

Can't. Get. Enough.

"Nic! I'm coming! Oh God!"

Her legs trembled as her orgasm swept over her body. She never once took her eyes off of me.

Hot as fucking hell.

I stood and undid my pants, pushing them down.

When she looked into my eyes, my heart felt like it was about to pound out of my goddamn chest.

I was falling for her. Hard. I couldn't make myself say the words, but I knew that Gabi Mandola was the last girl I wanted to sink my cock into every again.

"This is going to be fast and hard."

She nodded.

Positioning myself at her entrance, I pushed in as she let out a hiss. I stilled long enough to ask if she was okay.

"Yes, I'm better than okay."

Those were the words that drove me into her again. Faster. Harder. Everything on the table was falling off to the floor, but I didn't give two shits. Being inside Gabi was like being in heaven. It was becoming an addiction. A drug I couldn't get enough of.

"Harder, Nic! Yes."

Fuck. Me. I've died and gone to heaven.

I pulled out and pounded back into so hard the table moved.

"Can't stop!" I cried out as I fucked her like never before.

Gabi grabbed her breasts and twisted her nipples and I swore everything from that point on went black.

sixteen

Gabi

"NIC, I'M COMING!"

I could feel Nic grow bigger as he pushed as deep as he could inside of me. My world was spinning as I fell apart along with him. Our bodies slapping against each other had to be one of the hottest sounds ever. It drove me to another wave of trembles. He moved in and out so hard and so fast the table started to move across the floor.

I'd never experienced this type of love making before in my life. It was one of the most erotic moments of my entire life.

When Nic finally stopped moving, he fell on top of me while I wrapped my arms around him.

He fought for air as he said, "Hottest fucking moment of my life."

Dragging in a deep long breath, I said, "Wow. That was . . . like nothing I've ever experienced before in my life."

Nic drew back and stared into my eyes. I wanted so desperately to tell him I was falling in love with him, but I knew it was way too soon for that. And I wasn't sure if I was confusing lust for love. There was for sure a lot of lust going on between us.

My heart stopped when he spoke his next words.

"Gabi, I'm falling so damn hard for you."

Thud.

Butterflies jumped into action in my stomach as I gazed into his beautiful eyes.

I opened my mouth to speak when I heard a key slip into his front door lock. We both turned and looked at the door. My chest squeezed at the thought of who could have a key to his condo.

"Fuck."

The feelings I was experiencing were throwing me off. Was it another woman? Why would another woman have a key to his place? Cole maybe?

"It's my mother."

Okay, I was not expecting that.

I was positive my expression turned to pure horror. Pushing Nic off of me, I dropped to the ground and frantically started to pick everything up off the floor.

"Please don't do this to me, God! Please," I chanted as Nic dropped to my side and began cleaning up.

"I changed the locks the other day so something like this wouldn't ever happen."

Stopping, I turned to him. "Really?"

A smirk appeared on his face. "Because I really didn't want my mother walking in on us while we're fucking."

My cheeks burned. "That wouldn't be a very good impression."

He laughed, "No, it wouldn't."

"Nicholaus! My key is not working!"

Nic's phone started to ring, and we both chuckled.

After getting everything looking somewhat normal, he reached for my hand and kissed the back of it.

"Well, looks like you're being pushed into the lion's den earlier than we hoped."

I tried to appear calm as I shrugged and winked. "I'm ready."

Bullshit.

I was terrified. Sick to my stomach. I'd just had sex with Nic, I was sure my hair was a mess, and I had no panties on.

This is not happening.

"I'm heading to the restroom, what will you say?" He smiled a wide breathtaking smile. He'd shaved two days ago, but his scruff was back, not enough to hide those dimples though. My stomach dropped.

"I've got this. Go on."

I nodded. "But, Nic?"

"Yeah?"

"Button your pants back up."

He looked down and quickly buttoned up while I rushed to the bathroom to freshen up. On my way, I dashed into Nic's room. Opening his top drawer, I smiled and grabbed what I needed before slipping into the bathroom right as Nic opened the door for his mother.

I had used the hall bathroom, so I heard every single word.

"Mom, what are you doing here?"

"Why does my key not work?"

I covered my mouth to hide my chuckle.

I cannot believe his mother had a key to his place.

After taking a close look at myself, I couldn't help but smile. I for sure had a just fucked glow to my cheeks. Pulling my hair up, I looked around for something to keep it up. I opened a drawer on the vanity and my heart seized as I stared at the pink makeup bag in front of me. It had a huge white S on the top of it.

How old was it? Who's was it? Why was it in this bathroom? And who was S?

Nic and his mother's voice mixed in with the questioning voice in my head.

"Who is here? Is there a girl here?"

Nic laughed. "Yes, Mama. There is a girl here, she's in the bathroom."

I should have been nervous as hell. Nic's mother was on the other side of the door, but all I could think about the bag in front of me. A woman kept a spare makeup bag at Nic's. The only good thing about it was it was in the spare bathroom and not his bathroom. But why had she left it if she hadn't intended on coming back? A random hook-up wouldn't leave her makeup bag behind unless she knew she would be back. Nic said he didn't date.

Confusion swept through my mind.

Opening the bag, I peeked through it. Whoever she was, she liked expensive makeup. Then I found a piece of paper. My hands shook as I opened it.

Scarlet,

Meet me at my place at ten. Don't wear panties.

Nic

I dropped the note and stumbled back. Covering my mouth, I turned and threw up in the toilet.

A light knock at the door startled me.

"Gabi? Are you okay?"

Tears streamed down my face, but I needed to get my shit together. I had no idea how long that had been in here. The thought of Nic being with another woman doing exactly what he had just done to me made my stomach turn again. I leaned over and threw up again.

The door opened, and I cursed myself for not locking it. Nic stepped in and looked at me, then over to the open drawer with the bag and note sitting on top of it. His eyes widened in horror.

"It's not what you think, Gabi."

Standing, I grabbed some toilet paper and wiped my mouth.

"What in the world happened in here, Nicholaus? It looks like you danced on the table," Nic's mother called out.

The only thing I knew to do was regain my composure, go out and meet his mother and then think of any excuse to leave.

I slammed the drawer shut and turned on the water to rinse my mouth. Now I was pissed. Not at Nic. At me for being like this.

"Gabi, just let me explain everything after she leaves."

Rinsing out my mouth, my thoughts started to go all over the place. I knew a part of this was my own guilt for not telling Nic the truth. But to have an ex-lover's note pop up in my face like that.

It was too much.

"I realize I'm overreacting. I need to process some things, but for right now, we're going to go out there so I can meet your mother."

When I walked into the dining area, a beautiful woman with dark hair and olive skin turned and gasped.

"I'm so sorry. I choked on bread and Nic scrambled over to help me. I was in the restroom trying to get myself back together."

Another lie.

Nic's mother stared at me. Once the shock wore off her face, I swore it was replaced by a look of pure evil. The way her eyes swept over my body made me want to run out the door and never come back.

"And who is this beautiful young woman, Nicholaus?"

Wow. I was honestly surprised by her kind words. They certainly didn't match the look in her eyes.

"Mama, this is Gabi Mandola. Gabi, this is my mother, Katerina Drivas."

I reached my hand out for hers. "It's a pleasure to meet you, Mrs. Drivas."

She forced a smile. "Mandola? Italian?" Her eyes shot over to Nic quickly before she focused back on me.

With a nod, I forced out my answer. "Yes, my mother and father moved from Italy to New Jersey before I was born."

Shit. Shit. Shit. I just told the truth. Damn it, Gabi.

Her eyes darted back and forth from me to Nic.

"Nicholaus, you didn't tell me you were seeing someone."

Nic cleared his throat. "I was actually going to call you and Dad to see if you wanted to do dinner tonight. Maybe invite Thano and Kilyn and spend some time with Kira."

Katerina's eyes snapped over to Nic. "Uh-huh. I see."

Oh. Shit.

"It turns out I won't be able to do dinner tonight," I quickly added. "I'm so sorry to run, Mrs. Drivas, but I've got an emergency at the bakery. It was so very nice to meet you. I've heard so much about you."

She forced a smile. "I wish I could say the same."

Nic reached for my hand, but I quickly pulled it away.

"Gabi."

Turning to Nic, I did my best to smile. "I'm sorry to run off."

I walked as fast as I could to the door. Opening it, I stepped outside and hustled to the elevators. I could hear the sound of his condo door shutting and Nic following me.

"Gabi. Wait. Damn it, if you would wait for one fucking second."

Hitting the down button, I forced myself to not cry.

Nic grabbed me and turned me to face him.

"It's not what you think."

A harsh laugh slipped from my lips. "Really? Because you have another woman's makeup bag in your spare bathroom and a note telling her to meet you at your place for what—a fuck fest, Nic? I see you like your women with no panties. That must have been an extra little turn on for you earlier."

Nic closed his eyes, and I had to look away or I'd start to cry.

"That's Scarlet's bag and I haven't seen her in months."

Hearing him say her name hurt more than I thought it would. I didn't even know this woman, but I knew she had shared Nic's bed and most likely more than once if she had a bag in his bathroom. Knowing that brought out a side of me I'd never experienced before.

My jealous side.

My teeth sunk into my trembling lip. Nic used his finger on my chin to pull my eyes to his. "That's not true. I see Scarlet when we go to her dad's place to eat lunch sometimes. But the only thing we do is exchange a hello. I swear to you, Gabi, I haven't slept with Scarlet since I've met you. I haven't slept with anyone but you. I don't *want* to sleep with anyone other than you."

"You . . . you still see her? When was the last time you slept with her?"

"It's been months. At least six. And yes, I see her, but it's like I said, we exchange a simple hello."

I had to force down the sick feeling I felt at knowing Nic saw his old fuck buddy often.

I finally lost the battle and let my tears fall. I hated being so weak and vulnerable, but that was what Nic did to me. He brought out emotions and feelings I'd never experienced before.

Nic cupped my face within his hands while brushing my tears away with his thumbs. A look of disappointment swept across his face. "I'm sorry you found that, and I'm so sorry you would think I would do that to you."

I shook my head, feeling foolish how I reacted. "I'm sorry I acted that way. I'm not sure what in the world is going on with me. You bring out so many different feelings and I'm so confused, Nic. I have never in my life been a jealous person, but seeing that note after what we just shared. All these images of you with another woman came crashing in on me."

His smile made my knees weak. "I swear to God I would never hurt you, Gabi." The way he gazed into my eyes, I knew he was telling me the truth. I also felt it in my heart. His lips pressed to mine. Wrapping my arms around his neck, I kissed him back.

When he finally pulled back some, he softly whispered against my mouth, "I know it hasn't even been two weeks, and I hope like hell I'm not about to fuck things up."

My breath stalled in my throat.

"I'm falling in love with you."

His words rushed through my mind like a bolt of lightning. Every hair on my body rose. I needed to tell Nic the truth. Everything needed to be out in the open before I declared my love to him. No. No . . . I was going to follow my heart and not my head.

"I'm falling in love with you too."

The brilliant smile that covered his face made me giggle.

"Please don't leave. I don't want your first meeting with my mother to be like that."

"What would we say if I came back?"

Right then my phone went off. It was Max. Nic frowned.

"Emergency at the bakery. Looks like I really do need to leave."

He nodded. Then holding up his finger, he said, "Wait, don't move. I'll be right back."

I watched as he raced back to his condo. A minute later he and his mother walked out of the condo and headed my direction. I couldn't shake the feeling I had when his mother stared at me like a bug that needed to be stepped on.

"I told my mom about your emergency at the bakery. She wants to come along."

My eyes widened in horror. "W-what? To the—the bakery?"

Katerina smiled big. "You're a baker? I love to bake. And cook."

Oh. Shit.

"Me too," I said before I realized how it sounded more like a challenge than a simple response.

She nodded. "So, let's go see this place of yours. I can hardly contain my excitement. First to learn my eldest son is dating, and then to find out she owns her own *Italian* bakery."

The way she stressed Italian couldn't be a good thing. And by the look on her face I would say she was far from excited.

When we stepped onto the elevator, she glanced over to me. "Are you recovered from your . . . choking . . . incident?"

With a wide smile, I nodded my head and tapped my hand on Nic's chest. "Oh, yes. Nic saved me. I'm sorry we had made such a mess. Things got a little, crazy."

Nic attempted to hold back a laugh.

Katerina simply smiled. As we stepped out of the elevator, she walked next to Nic and went on and on about a baby shower. I took out my phone and sent Kilyn a text.

Me: 911! Katerina showed up at Nic's right after we had sex!

She's with us now. Going to the bakery for an emergency!
She responded back within seconds.

Kilyn: This is a CODE RED. I repeat! CODE RED! You've had the forced meeting. That is NEVER good. Take deep breaths and whatever you do . . . don't tell her you own the bakery.

Oh no.

Me: Too late.

Kilyn: Oh . . . no. Okay. Be prepared. She is going to insult you in ways where she is acting like she isn't insulting you. Be ready. Smile. Don't let her know she's getting to you.

I cringed on the inside. Glancing up, I noticed Katerina stood at the passenger side door. She was giving me an exasperated look, and I winced, wondering how long she had been waiting for me to walk up. Then I noticed she was standing at the front passenger side door, making me go to the backseat.

With a smile, I slid into the backseat and started back up with my texting.

> *Me: She's making me sit in the backseat! WTF*

> *Kilyn: That doesn't surprise me. You are a bug she needs to crush. Okay, next, be ready for the challenge.*

> *Me: Challenge?*

> *Kilyn: Yes. She needs to prove you unworthy of her son and her above you, what better way to do it than challenge you in some way.*

My heart was racing.

> *Me: OMG. What kind of challenge?*

> *Kilyn: That's the tricky part. She'll throw it on you when you're least expecting it. Don't let her see your weakness!*

"Who are you texting?" Nic asked as I jumped and let out a yelp.
"Oh, um, Max."
More lies.
"Nervous little thing, isn't she?" Katerina said.
I swallowed hard as I glanced up at Nic. *What in the world am I about to get myself into?*
He glanced up in the mirror and winked. Then he mouthed, *I'm sorry,* and all my fears melted away.
"So, my oldest son has decided to go against his parents' wishes."
Don't. Show. Fear.
"Mama," Nic warned.

"An Italian," she huffed under her breath.

I'm so screwed.

> *Me: She's going to eat me up and spit me out! Why does she not like Italians?*

> *Kilyn: No she is not! Okay that's a lie. She probably is. Um, I think Thad dated one once and things didn't turn out well. Listen! You walk into that bakery and you own that bitch! Well wait, you do own it. You stand proud. And whatever you do, don't look her directly in the eye. She has a direct path to your soul!*

> *Me: God help me.*

> *Kilyn: You're gonna need more than just him.*

seventeen

Gabi

MY NERVES WERE RATTLED AS I walked into the back hallway of the bakery. Katerina's eyes were everywhere, taking it all in.

"Excuse me, I need to find Max. You're more than welcome to hang out in my office or in the bakery."

Katerina forced a smile and nodded. Turning to Nic, I gave him a weak grin and headed to find out what was going on. *Please don't let it be anything bad.*

When I walked into the bakery, I was happy to see it was pretty full. I would have died if there hadn't been anyone here.

I walked up to Max. "What's up?"

He spun around and looked at me. "The mixer won't start and we need to make thirty lemon mascarpone cakes to be picked up tomorrow evening."

My mouth dropped as my eyes widened in shock. "Why?"

"Someone called earlier and asked if we could manage it. We were slow and had a working mixer, so I didn't think it would be a problem. Charity ran an errand and I haven't been able to reach her."

"I don't understand, why would someone need that many cakes?"

Max shrugged. "I don't know. She said she had stopped by the bakery before and had some. Said it reminded her of her grandmother's lemon mascarpone cakes."

My heart stopped. *He loved my lemon mascarpone cakes. What if I'd been found?* "What did she look like?"

Max shrugged. "She called, Gabi. I have no clue what she looks like."

"Oh, right. Um, did she happen to leave her name?"

Staring at me as if I'd lost my damn mind, Max said, "Yes! But, Gabi, the mixer is not working and we need to get them made and you're worried about her name?"

I nodded. The fact that she mentioned it reminded her of her grandmother's recipe is what threw me. That recipe was my grandmothers, and I used it right down to the secret ingredient. "Right. Sorry, let's look at it. I can't imagine anything going out on it. It's only a year old!"

Max and I headed to the mixer only to find Nic was already working on it. I quickly glanced around to see where Katerina was. She was walking off, heading into the dining area of the bakery.

Focusing back on Nic, I asked, "Do you have any idea what's wrong?"

He glanced up and smiled. "Yeah, the breaker tripped." He turned on the mixer and it came to life. Relief washed over my body.

"Thank God that was it!" I jumped into Nic's arms the moment he stood. "Thank you for fixing it."

With a chuckle, he kissed me on the forehead then looked at Max. "You didn't think to look at the breaker?"

Max gave Nic a deer in the headlights look. "The breaker?"

"Yeah, Max. Somehow the breaker was tripped."

"Why in the world would I think about that? I'm a pastry chef, not an electrician."

Spinning on his heels, Max quickly set off to getting everything ready to make the cakes. I turned back to Nic. "We received a huge order for lemon mascarpone cakes. I need to stay and help."

"Where's Charity?" Nic asked.

I shrugged as I put an apron on. "Max said she left to run an errand when things were slow and he hasn't been able to get a hold of her. I'm so sorry, I need to stay and help."

Nic flashed that amazing smile of his. "Let me take my mom back to her car, then I'll come back and help."

My stomach dropped. This man was a dream come true. I felt so foolish for how I had acted earlier.

"I'd love that."

Katerina cleared her throat and we both turned to face her. "Nonsense, I'll stay and help."

Nic laughed, but when Katerina shot him a dirty look, he stopped.

"You're so sweet," I said with a smile. "But honestly, you don't have to do that."

Lifting her head, Katerina simply grinned and said, "I want to help. Now, you go out there with your customers, and I'll help Nic and . . ."

"Max," I added.

"Yes, Max. I'll help him make your mascarpone cake."

My eyes darted over to Nic who simply shrugged.

Damn. Where was Kilyn when I needed her?

"O-okay. Max knows all the measurements and such."

Katerina put her hands on my back and gently gave me a push.

"Off you go! I am the master in the kitchen."

My eyes widened in horror. Nic took my elbow and led me out into the bakery. It felt as though someone was sitting on my chest as I glanced over my shoulder and watched the scene play out before my eyes.

Katerina turned to Max, placed her hands on her hips and said, "Give me the recipe, young man. I'm in charge."

"Oh, my God," I whispered as I stopped and headed back into the kitchen.

"Katerina, honestly you don't have to do this."

She slowly turned and looked at me. "Do you not trust me?"

I let out a nervous laugh. "Well, you did just find out your son was dating me and that I'm not Greek."

Nic let out a small groan from behind me.

"Young lady, I take cooking very seriously. This is your business, and obviously my Nicholaus seems to be entranced by you. Therefore, I intend on helping you. It is not a sin to admit when you are defeated and need help."

My head pulled back. "I'm not defeated."

"Let it go," Nic whispered from behind me.

Katerina laughed. "You seem rattled, my dear. Maybe you're not used to getting a large order."

It was my turn to laugh. "I've gotten bigger."

When Katerina lifted her brow, I knew this was it. The challenge.

Oh hell no. You're not doing this on my own turf.

Nic let out a nervous chuckle from behind me. "Gabi, why don't we let Max and my mom start this. Liza is swamped up front."

Katerina narrowed her eyes at me, silently willing me to dare her. I was going to nip this shit in the bud.

"Max," I said with a firm voice, "Go help Liza. Katerina and I will take care of the cakes."

Max walked up to me. "Are you sure?"

I nodded. I tried to push down my fear about this order and brush it off as an over-reaction. "Go help her and try Charity again."

A slow smile moved across her face. This lady was good. But this time, she wasn't going to win. Not with me in my *own* kitchen.

"Are you sure you can keep up with me, Gabriella?"

Oh! oh, it's on!

"Are you sure you can keep up with me . . . Katerina?"

She smiled bigger.

Nic walked up and stood between us. "What's happening right now?"

Giving him a pat on the chest, I replied, "We're about to get our mascarpone on."

Nic looked between his mother and I with a mixed expression of both concern and amusement.

I walked over to the giant refrigerator and took out two large bowls of my always-on-hand lemon curd.

Placing them on the kitchen's stainless steel island, I looked at Katerina.

"What's that?" Nic asked.

"Lemon curd," Katerina answered with a smile.

"Because everyone knows you have to make the lemon curd ahead of time," I added.

Clearing his throat, I glanced over to Nic. He looked between his mother and me then laughed. "So, this ought to be interesting."

Katerina took one of the bowls. "Italian food is nothing but Greek food . . . but with less love."

I went to say something when Nic kissed me then whispered against my lips. "Just take her help. I promise I'll make it up to you."

My lower stomach pooled with heat.

"For you," I whispered. "I'm doing this for you."

He laughed. "Uh-huh. Okay."

It didn't take long for Katerina and I to get lost in the baking process. She was good, there was no denying it. But she was not about to show me up in my own kitchen.

Little did I know I was setting myself up for Katerina's real challenge.

———— ♥ ————

I SAT DOWN AT A table and sighed. "Thirty lemon mascarpone cakes done."

Nic grinned and squatted down. He lightly pushed a strand of hair from my face. "You look beautiful."

With a chuckle, I stared into his beautiful hazel eyes. "I'm a mess, Nic. I nearly killed myself trying to keep up with your mother."

My eyes lifted and looked behind the bakery counter where Katerina was currently trying to take over in helping Liza with customers. "Look at her. It's like she's not the least bit fazed by all that baking. She's the Energizer Bunny on crack."

Nic glanced over his shoulder to his mother. "That was nothing compared to some of the cooking I've seen my mother do."

I sat up. "Oh crap. She probably thinks I'm a lazy Italian!" Jumping, I quickly made my way through the bakery and started cleaning up. In a few minutes we would be closing up.

Nic grabbed me by the waist and turned me around. "It's your day off."

My brows rose. "Was. I have no idea where Charity is. This is not like her to just vanish and leave the bakery."

I started chewing on my thumb nail when Nic pulled it from my mouth. "Stop. Now come on, let's get my mother out of your bakery before she slips something Greek into the display."

Giggling, I nodded as he took my hand in his. "Mama? You ready to head out? I'm sure Dad is probably withering away with no dinner."

Katerina rolled her eyes and huffed. She pulled Liza in for a hug then turned to Max. I tried not to laugh when he stiffened up like a board when she hugged him.

As she made her way over to us, I couldn't help but notice how she looked completely and utterly unfazed by the fact that she just baked all those cakes.

Stopping in front of me, she smiled. "You're baking skills are there, you just need to get faster. You're very slow. And your lemon curd needs a bit of work." Her eyes wandered over me before capturing mine. "If only you were Greek . . . there might be hope."

My smile dropped and my mouth fell open.

"Oh, shit," Nic mumbled. "Mama, let's head on back to my place so you can get your car."

I stood there stunned. *Holy crap. She just insulted me in like three different ways!*

Nic stood in front of me. "Gabi?"

My eyes swung up to his. "I'm taking my mother back to my place. Did you want me to come back for you?"

His eyes looked pleading. He had nothing to worry about, the last place I wanted to be was in the car with her again. So she could insult me more.

"Yes, that's um . . . that sounds good."

Nic leaned in and kissed me on the lips quickly. He pulled back slightly and said, "I'll be back as fast as I can."

Nodding, I forced a smile. My eyes moved past him to see Katerina standing there with a look I couldn't read. Was she still bothered by Nic and I, or was she maybe getting used to the idea? No . . . she certainly wasn't used to the idea. I swallowed hard.

"Thank you so much for helping, Katerina. It was a pleasure meeting you."

She nodded. "The pleasure was mine, and I enjoyed myself. Nicholaus?"

"I'll be back soon."

I lifted my hand and waved as I watched them walk through the back hall and out of sight.

Max walked up to me and stood there, staring down the hall.

"That woman scared the piss out of me."

"Me too."

He laughed and I turned to him. "What's so funny?" I asked.

With a shrug, all he said was, "You're so screwed."

My body sank and I let out a sigh. I had a feeling he was right.

eighteen

Nic

WHEN I COULDN'T TAKE THE silence any longer, I spoke. "Tell me what you're thinking, Mama."

She sighed. "I'm thinking two of my sons are trying to kill their mother."

I laughed. "Why?"

"One girl is Irish, now the other is Italian. Nicholaus, we can find you a nice Greek girl. Why must you settle on . . . on this one. Italian? That's worse than Irish!"

The grip on my steering wheel tightened. "Because I like *this one*. Mama, why is it so damn important for you that I marry a Greek girl? Do you not love Kilyn?"

She huffed.

"Mama?"

"Of course I love Kilyn. She makes your brother very happy, and she has given me a beautiful granddaughter whom I love very, very much."

"Even though she is half Irish?"

Her head snapped to look at me. "I don't look at Kira like that!"

"Then why do you look at Kilyn and Gabi that way, Mama?"

Her eyes narrowed at me. "Why can't you find a Greek woman?

Why Italian?"

"Because the first moment I met Gabi, something happened that has never happened to me before. Never, not with a Greek girl, not with any girl."

Her look of frustration turned to a look of surprise. "What are you saying, Nicholaus?"

I pulled into my parking spot and turned to face my mother. Taking her hand in mine, I kissed the back of it.

"I'm saying that I've never felt this way before, and I really want to see where this goes. Please don't do anything to try to push Gabi away."

She swallowed hard. "You really care for this girl?"

"I really do. I'm falling in love with her."

With a gasp, she covered her mouth. Then tears formed in her eyes. "Oh, my baby is falling in love!" She looked up and started rattling off in Greek before she finally glanced back at me.

"Do you think she would take a DNA test?"

My smile dropped. "What for?"

With a shrug, she stated, "She might have a bit of Greek in her."

I rolled my eyes and got out of my truck. This wasn't going to be easy.

GABI'S FRONT DOOR WAS CRACKED open when I walked up to it. Pushing it open, I called out, "Gabi? Charity?"

I heard a voice coming from the balcony outside.

As I got closer, I realized it was Gabi's voice.

"I understand how this works. I've been doing it for six years now. No, I don't think so."

Her voice was different. Cold, on edge. Whoever she was talking to, they made her feel on guard.

"I'm just as tired of this as you are. Believe me."

Not wanting to eavesdrop, I cleared my throat and Gabi jumped then spun around. Her somber face was quickly replaced with a huge smile. Her eyes lit up like it was Christmas morning.

"That's fine. I need to let you go."

She hit End and pushed her phone into her back pocket.

"Hey," she said softly.

I walked up to her and pulled her into my arms. "I missed you."

"You've only been gone for an hour."

"That's too long."

With a giggle, she buried her face into my chest. I could feel the stress releasing from her body as I held her to me.

"Is everything okay?" I asked.

Pulling her head back, her eyes searched my face. I swore it looked like she wanted to tell me something, but she smiled and replied, "It is now that you're here."

"You seemed a little tense when I walked up. I wasn't listening to your conversation, but I could tell you were on edge."

"It's nothing. Business stuff." She tried to give me a reassuring smile, but I wasn't fully buying it. "So, does your mom hate me?"

I laughed. "Actually, she invited us to dinner again since we had to cancel."

Gabi's face fell. "On no! I never told Kilyn dinner was not happening tonight."

Cupping her face in my hands, I grinned. "I called Thano when everything happened at the bakery. I forgot to tell you Kilyn said to call her. I'm sure she'll want a play-by-play of how that all went."

Gabi laughed nervously. "That was crazy. I'm curious to see who this person is who ordered all those cakes."

The sound of the front door shutting had us both turning to look back into the living room. Charity walked by and Gabi immediately headed in.

"Where were you, Charity?" Gabi called out, anger lacing her voice.

Charity stopped walking. "What?"

I couldn't help but notice she looked a little confused. Her cheeks were flushed and her eyes seemed like she was lost in another world.

"You left to run an errand and never came back! We had an emergency at the bakery and Max had to call me."

Narrowing her eyes, Charity replied, "Max always has a damn emergency."

"Well, I just spent the last few hours baking thirty lemon mascarpone cakes with Nic's mom! Not how I really wanted to get to know the woman."

Charity glanced over to me and pressed her lips together, trying not to laugh.

"So?" Gabi asked, her hands now resting on her hips. She looked so damn cute standing there all pissed off. I wanted to drag her off to her bedroom and sink deep inside of her.

"Sooo? What?"

"Charity! Where were you?"

"I am um . . . I ran an errand and then got caught by someone I know and we got to talking and I totally lost track of the time."

"Was your phone off? We called you."

She looked between Gabi and me before focusing back in on Gabi. "I lost my phone. I must have left it somewhere."

Something was off. Charity was nervous as hell. She could hardly look at either one of us.

"I've got a massive headache, if you don't mind, I need to go lay down."

Gabi and I both watched as she walked into her room and slowly shut the door.

"Is she okay? Something didn't seem right," I asked.

Gabi stared at the door. "I'm not sure. I hope she is okay. She's never lost her phone before. It's like her safety beacon. I think she needs it to breathe."

I laughed and pulled her over to me. "So, we have the evening to ourselves. What do you want to do?"

She pulled her lip in between her teeth. "Would you be upset if I said I wanted to stay in? I'm exhausted."

Lifting my hand, I brushed her blonde hair behind her ear. "As long as I'm with you I don't care where we are."

When she smiled my knees felt weak. "How about I pour you a glass of wine and you sit on the sofa. I'll massage your feet."

Her eyes lit up. "Oh, my gosh, that sounds like heaven."

Slapping her on the ass, I motioned for her to sit down while I headed into her kitchen. I had remembered where her wine glasses were from our first date when she made me dinner.

I grabbed two wine glasses and set them on the counter. Glancing down, I saw the itinerary for her trip to Italy.

"You excited about your trip to Italy?"

Her head whipped to look at me. "What? Why do you ask?"

Jesus she was on edge. "I saw your itinerary and I know you had mentioned you were looking forward to going."

Her face relaxed and then finally her body did as well. "Oh right. I am looking forward to going back. I'll be worried about the bakery though."

Handing her a wineglass, I winked as I sat down next to her. "I'm sure Charity will take care of the bakery."

After she took a sip, she frowned. "She was nowhere to be found today. If I hadn't had been here, what would have happened?"

"Max would have told the customer it was too short of a notice, but that next time they needed something to please keep your bakery in mind."

The corners of her mouth pulled up into a beautiful smile. "You're right. If I hadn't had the lemon curd made up, we wouldn't have been able to do it, anyway."

"Right."

She took another sip. "Do you think it was sort of a test? I mean seriously . . . who needs that many cakes?"

Laughing, I shook my head and reached for her foot. She'd already kicked her shoes off. "Someone having a party, large dinner, a company. I could think of a hundred things."

We both set our glasses on the coffee table. Gabi slid down on the sofa while I took both feet and began massaging them.

"Mmm, that feels heavenly."

Her eyes closed and her lips slightly parted open. My dick was getting harder by the second.

I pushed a little harder and she gasped before letting out another moan.

"I think we should move this to your bedroom."

Opening her eyes, she asked, "Why?"

With a half grin, I replied, "Because I want your ass naked so I can give you a proper massage, that's why."

Gabi giggled and pulled her feet from my lap. Standing, I took her hand and led her to her bedroom. My heart was pounding like it always did when I was with this woman. She did crazy things to not only my body, but my heart as well.

When I shut the bedroom door, Gabi pulled her shirt over her head. My hands cupped her breasts while my thumbs rubbed her nipples through the thin lace bra.

Beep. Beep. Beep. Beep. Beep.

We both froze. "Fuck," I angrily said.

Gabi closed her eyes and sighed. "Terrible timing."

Cupping her face within my hands, I kissed her. Our tongues danced hungrily as I pulled her body closer. Deepening the kiss, we were lost in each other. If I thought I could go fast, I'd have taken her right then.

Beep. Beep. Beep. Beep. Beep.

"Goddamn it, I want you, Gabi."

Her hands moved down my back and over my ass where she squeezed me and pushed her hips into my dick.

"Come back by when you're done."

My forehead rested on hers as I pulled my pager out. "It could be hours."

"I don't care."

"You know the rule. Don't take care of yourself."

She smiled as her fingers traced along the stubble on my jaw. "I promise I won't."

I kissed her quickly again before pulling out my pager then my phone. My heart sank knowing I was leaving my sweet Gabi.

Calling in, I told Oliver I was on my way.

"There's a hostage situation happening."

Her eyes widened in fear. I kissed the tip of her nose. "It's okay, baby. I'll call and check in, but if you don't hear from me, don't worry."

She nodded, but I knew what I was asking was impossible.

"Gabi, if my job is going to—"

She lifted her fingers to my lips. "It's not. I can't help but worry and I'm sure I will always worry. But your job will never keep me away from you."

Smiling, I pulled her closer and kissed her softly.

I pulled back and looked into her eyes one more time. I asked, "Are you sure everything is okay, Gabi?"

The way she looked at me, I knew she was holding back something. I wasn't going to push her though. She'd tell me whenever she was ready, whatever it was.

"Everything's fine."

One more kiss and I was heading to my truck. I couldn't stop thinking of those sweet, soft lips pressed against mine. Or the way her hands felt moving over my body.

Shaking my head, I tried to clear my thoughts. I needed to have a clear head and couldn't afford a distraction. I made a mental note to talk to Oliver about Gabi.

By the time I got to the station and in the briefing room, I pretty much had my head clear. The only thing that still bothered me was the fact I knew Gabi was keeping something from me.

Sitting in front of my computer, I typed in Gabi's name and hit search. I wasn't sure why I did it, but I sure as hell wasn't expecting the results I got.

nineteen

Gabi

NIC HADN'T CALLED, AND IT had been over twelve hours since he left my place. I sat in the bakery at one of the tables in the back as I pored over financial stuff. Not my favorite thing to do. Liza sat down across from me and handed me a cup of coffee.

"It's calm right now, but wait until we get closer to lunch."

I smiled. "I'm okay with calm."

Every time the door chime rang, I looked up in a state of panic. I wasn't sure why, but I was on edge. It could have been my phone conversation last night with Antonio that had me more nervous than normal. Of course, Nic walking up on my conversation had me even tenser.

"Gabi? Is everything is okay? You seem really distracted today."

With a reassuring smile, I nodded. My eyes caught a glimpse of Charity. She was an absolute basket case. I'd never seen her drop things like she kept doing and fumbling around with stuff. She was currently standing behind the counter staring off into space.

Enough was enough. I needed to speak with her and find out what was going on.

"Liza, will you excuse me? I need to speak with Charity in the office."

Standing with me, Liza nodded. "Sure. I need to get some cannoli's made, anyway. I've been staling."

I chuckled as I closed my laptop and made my way over to Charity. "Hey, can we talk in the office?"

She pulled her eyes away from the front window and looked at me. "What was that?"

Tilting my head, I narrowed my eyes. She was totally off in la la land. "Can we talk in the office?"

With a smile, she nodded and said, "Sure."

I motioned for her to go first as I followed her. I was supposed to have today off, but with Nic still working, I figured I might as well come in and take care of things.

Shutting the door, I set my computer on my desk as Charity flopped onto the small sofa and sighed.

Something was different about her. She had a . . . glow to her. Oh. Holy. Shit.

"You slept with someone."

She jolted up. "What? How did you know? Who told you?"

I leaned against the desk and held up my hands. "Whoa, hold onto your panties there. It was a guess. You're acting different."

"I am not."

I smiled.

"You're glowing."

Her eyes widened in horror. "I am not fucking glowing! You're glowing!"

With a giggle, I replied, "I'm sure I am. I'm falling in love with Nic."

A huge smile spread over her face as she stood and walked up to me. Taking my hands in hers, she shook her head. "My baby girl is growing up."

Yanking my hands from her, I pushed her away. "Stop it. I'm serious. We both kind of admitted to each other we were falling for one another."

Her brow lifted. "Kind of?"

I shrugged. "Okay, we did. But this isn't about me. This is about you and how you disappeared yesterday and then came back and you're acting all weird. I just want to make sure everything okay."

She took a few steps back and buried her face in her hands and let out a small scream.

Okay. So that answers the *are you okay* question.

"Oh, Gabi, I'm so far from okay. I don't know what happened. I'm. He. I felt. Oh God!"

She flopped back on the sofa.

"I didn't get any of that, Charity. You're what? Who is he? And what did you feel?"

She covered her face again and said, "I slept with Cole yesterday."

Scissoring her fingers to peek at me, I stared at her in disbelief. "Wait. What?"

Her hands dropped to the sides of her body while she slumped over. "He came into the bakery like he always does, but for some reason I was insanely turned on by him yesterday. He was different. He didn't act stupid or try to flirt. He was . . . nice. Really nice."

I pursed my lips and gave her a *really* look.

"Don't judge. I haven't had good sex in so long I'm starting to think I need to plan a wedding with my vibrator."

I covered my mouth to hide my chuckle.

"Anyway, Cole came in acted all sweet and then he left. But I left right after to run to the store to buy more vanilla. Oh, by the way, we're very close to being out of vanilla. I never made it to the store because Cole was walking out of that little boutique a few doors down and we ran into each other. I swear to God the heat from his body lit mine on fire and I almost came on the spot.

I groaned and looked away.

"The next thing I knew, we were at a hotel and he was giving me the best sex of my life."

Wiggling my eyebrows, I smiled wide. "Really?"

"Yes. Then he did something no guy has ever done."

"Do I really want to know what he did?"

"Yes! Because I'm so confused by it I haven't had an ounce of sleep. I can't stop thinking about him and wondering when I'll see him again. My mind is racing and I keep asking myself if I dreamed it all up yesterday.

I pushed off the desk walked over and sat next to her. Taking her hand in mine, I asked, "My gosh, what did he do?"

She turned to look at me and said, "He made love to me and then stayed."

My eyes widened. "Huh?"

"He was slow and took his time as he worshiped my body and did things to me I never knew were possible. I came four times yesterday. Four! I've never had more than one orgasm with a man in my entire life." She smiled and closed her eyes as she kept talking. "My God . . . the man made sweet love to me even though he whispered in my ear that he wanted to fuck my brains out."

"Nice," I said with a snarled lip.

Refocusing on me again, she grinned. "I've never had a guy give me that much attention. It's usually more like let me rip your panties off, bend you over the table and fuck you till I grunt and come in six pumps."

I laughed. "But Cole wasn't that way?"

"No. I thought he was going to be, and I was okay with it. But when we got to the hotel and he kissed me, something happened. I know we both felt it. He took his time undressing me and then he . . . he . . ."

"He what?" I cried out.

"He kissed my entire body while he trailed his hands over me."

Her body trembled at the memory.

"I had never felt so sexy in my entire life. He whispered how beautiful I was against my skin and I swear it seared into my soul. What I thought was going to be a random hook up turned into the most amazing afternoon of my life."

My heart seized in my chest. Cole didn't really seem like the one-girl kind of guy.

"So after he made love to you, what happened?"

Her eyes widened as if she was still shock. "He pulled me into his arms and we laid there and . . . talked. About everything and he told me about his job and I told him about how we met and were like sisters. He asked me about my family and we talked about his. I mean . . . it was crazy insane how comfortable I felt with this man. I mean sure, I've somewhat flirted with him for weeks, but this side of him. It was like he really cared and wanted to know. It wasn't a ploy to get into my pants because . . . well duh, he already had and if he asked me again I'd spread wide for him."

"Oh, my gosh. You're so crude!" I said hitting her shoulder with my hand. "Then what happened?"

Her face lit up. "He asked me to take a shower with him. What started as slow and sweet turned into the best fucking of my life. I came so hard I thought I was going to pass the hell out."

I laughed. "Did you use protection?"

That's when her smile dropped.

My stomach dropped, and I felt sick. "Charity," I whispered.

Her eyes filled with tears. "We did the first time. The second time in the shower things got hot and heavy so fast we both lost control. I didn't remember until he was coming and even then it felt so good I pushed it from my head so I could enjoy the moment. Now . . . now I'm scared shitless. Gabi . . . I'm not on the pill. I stopped taking it a few weeks ago. I'm so scared."

I took her hands in mine. "Did you tell him you weren't on the pill?"

She nodded.

"What did he say?" I asked as I held my breath.

A tear slipped from her eye and slowly made a path down her beautiful face. I reached up and wiped it as I tried to imagine how she must be feeling.

"He . . . he held me in his arms and said that no matter what, he'd be there for me. That we were in this together."

My mouth dropped open.

"Cole? Cole said that?"

She nodded. "I mean he kind of freaked out at first, but then he saw how scared I was and he did the one thing I didn't think he would. He comforted me. The next thing I knew we were back in bed and he was making the sweetest love to me that I knew in that moment he had stolen my heart. Gabi! I don't do that. I don't do the whole instant love bullshit. I fuck a guy and if it's good, I make a second date! I don't give him my very soul!"

I hated to ask, but I had to. "Did you use a condom then?"

She nodded. "Yes."

It only took one time, but why give it greater odds.

"Okay. So that explains why you've been in a fog. Has he called you?"

"I think I left my phone in his car and I refuse to be one of those girls who waits by the phone . . . but damn it, I wish I had my phone!"

"Nic got called right after you came home and he had to go in for work. I haven't heard from him since he left. Maybe Cole was on call too. If he has your phone he hasn't had a chance to get it to you or maybe he hasn't seen it in his car?"

She chewed on her lip. "Yeah. Gabi, I don't want to be *that* girl. The one who falls for a guy and then pines over him if he doesn't call."

Smiling, I squeezed her hand. "It's okay to like him, Charity. It's okay to have feelings for him. It sounds like you guys had an amazing afternoon."

"We did," she said softly.

A knock on the door of my office had me jumping up. Walking over, I opened it and almost fell over.

Speak of the devil.

"Cole."

"Hey, Gabi. Max said Charity was in here with you."

The door was blocking Cole's view of Charity on the sofa. When I glanced over my shoulder, she was sitting there with a stunned expression. I knew she probably figured Cole was going to run for the mountains, so him standing here had to throw her even more.

I pushed the door open and watched as his face lit up when he saw her.

Oh yeah. Cole has it bad for Charity.

"Charity," he said with a huge smile.

"Well, if you'll excuse me, I've got something up front I need to take care of."

I stepped to the side as Cole walked into my office. Charity was standing as she nervously rubbed her hands together. In the four years I'd known her I'd never seen her act this way around a guy. When Cole walked up and pulled her into his arms and kissed her, my heart fluttered in my chest. I slowly shut the door, but not before I heard him say, "I found your phone."

Smiling, I leaned against the door and closed my eyes.

Could this really work? Cole and Charity? Letting out a laugh, I pushed off the door and then let out a small scream.

"Nic! You scared me."

He gave me a tired smile.

"Did you come here with Cole?"

Frowning, he said, "No. Cole's here?"

"Um . . . yeah. I figured out what was going on with Charity. Her and Cole hooked up yesterday."

Nic smiled. "That explains his weird behavior last night."

I wanted to tell him about the no-condom thing, but it didn't feel right to share that with him.

Walking up to him, I placed my hand on the side of his face. He leaned into it and closed his eyes.

"Have you slept at all?"

He shook his head. "Do you want to stay here? I'd hate for you to drive home if you're so tired."

Nic pulled me into his arms. Grabbing a handful of hair, he pressed his lips against mine. It didn't take me long to open up to him as our tongues danced together in a beautiful rhythm.

"I need to be buried balls deep inside of you, agapiméni. Now."

My lower stomach pooled with heat. Smiling, I whispered, "Yes."

Before I knew what was happening, I was in my bedroom and Nic was pulling my shirt over my head. Reaching behind my back, he undid my bra and pulled it off, tossing it to the floor. He cupped my breasts and squeezed them as he dropped his mouth onto one nipple. The sound of him sucking had my head spinning with ecstasy.

Tingles erupted across my body . . . the build-up already starting. Sliding my hands into his hair, I tugged on it, pulling a long moan from his mouth that vibrated onto my nipple. I gasped.

"More," I panted out.

Nic had my pants off and was pushing my lace panties out of the way as he slipped two fingers inside of me.

"So fucking wet. I want your pussy on my cock, Gabi. I want to feel you fall apart on me."

Oh. God. I was so close to an orgasm just by hearing him talk that way.

"Nic," I gasped as he continued to move his fingers in and out of me. When his thumb pressed against my clit, I nearly exploded.

Then he was gone. My breathing was erratic as I opened my eyes and saw him standing there staring at me with pure desire in his eyes. He slowly let his gaze fall, causing me to lick my lips.

"I want to fuck your mouth."

My eyes grew wide. I liked this dirty side of Nic. Even though it made me feel a little dirty myself, it also turned me on like never before.

Dropping to my knees, I took him into my mouth. I had no clue what I was doing, but I tried to remember to do what Charity told me. My hand cupped his balls as he grabbed my head and slowly pulled out of my mouth then pushed back in. He hissed when I lightly grazed my teeth down his shaft.

I sucked harder while grabbing onto his ass.

"Yeah, baby, that feels so damn good."

Glancing up at him, I moaned, causing him to jerk and pick up the speed. I loved knowing I could make him feel good. But this . . . this was a little too much for me as he went further down my throat. All I wanted to do was gag and that was quickly ruining the mood. Pulling away from him, I shook my head. Nic reached down and lifted me up. Cupping my face, his eyes looked deep into mine.

"I'm so sorry. I got carried away. I didn't mean to make you do something you didn't want to do."

"I love doing that to you, but it was a little too much."

He kissed me and I wrapped my arms round his neck. When he pulled back from the kiss, he bit my lip. "Gabi, I want to fuck you. I can't do slow and sweet. I need you."

Was he so desperate because he was tired or was it because we had both left each other horny as hell last night? Whatever the reason . . . I liked it. I liked this side of Nic and I decided I wanted more of it.

Staring into his eyes, I licked my lips and said, "Fuck me, Nic, I'm yours."

twenty

Nic

I WAS BEING ROUGH WITH Gabi and I knew I needed to settle down. But fuck, the moment I saw her in that hall, my dick instantly went hard. All I could think about was sinking inside her warm pussy and forgetting everything.

She was on her hands and knees as I ran my hand over that sweet ass of hers. I pumped in and out of her like my life depended on it.

My finger pressed on her ass and she jumped.

"Someday I'm going to take this sweet ass."

She glanced over her shoulder, teeth digging into her lip. Damn it all to hell I was close to coming. She liked it when I talked dirty to her. She was turned on even more and I loved it.

Reaching around her, I found that little nub that was begging for attention.

"Oh God. Nic!" she cried out. "I can't. I can't! No more."

She'd already come twice. Hard. This time I wanted to come with her. Together.

My hand dug into her hip. Our bodies slapping together making the sexiest fucking sounds I'd ever heard.

"I'm getting close, Gabi. I want you to come when I come."

"Wh . . . wh . . . what!" she panted out.

My balls started to pull up. "I'm so fucking close. Squeeze that pussy on me, baby."

Not five seconds later, Gabi was crying out my name as I pushed in as deep as I could and came. My release felt like heaven as I poured my hot cum into her.

When my dick was finally done, I moved in and out of her a few more times before pulling out. I got up and headed to the bathroom where I got a warm washcloth for Gabi.

I made my way back into the bedroom and came to a stop. She was lying on the bed with her blonde hair laid out across the pillow. Her eyes were closed and she wore a breathtaking smile.

Oh yeah, she was thoroughly fucked and she was basking in it.

Kneeling on the bed, I pushed her thighs open and gently washed her. She grabbed at the sheets and let out a few whimpers as I slipped two fingers inside her.

"Do you need more, prinkipissa?"

She laughed. "No. I'm very, *very*, satisfied right now. I dropped the washcloth to the floor and crawled next to her, pulling her body so we faced each other.

I kissed the tip of her nose and whispered, "That was amazing."

"Mmm," was her only response.

"How do you feel?" I asked her. Worried I had been too rough.

"A little sore, but in a delicious way."

Her eyes were still closed.

"Gabi, look at me."

Snapping her eyes opened, her blue eyes bright as all get out. My heart seized in my chest. I loved this woman. There was no doubt in my mind I loved her and I would do whatever it took to protect her. The need to tell her overwhelmed me. Life was too short. I wasn't going to waste another second.

"I love you."

Her eyes filled with tears and she sucked in her lower lip before releasing it and answering me. "I love you too."

"Someone died last night."

Gabi gasped and sat up. I wasn't sure why I blurted it out, I just did. I also knew that was probably why Cole was looking for Charity. We both needed to forget. I used Gabi and a part of me felt guilty about it. No. All of me felt guilty.

"Oh, my gosh. Who?"

"Phil."

Tears formed in her eyes while she covered her mouth. "Wh-what happened?"

I rolled over on my back. "It was a freak accident and had nothing to do with the fucking raid. Nothing. I had to be the one to tell his wife, and it about broke me."

"Nic, I'm so sorry."

She didn't ask what happened, and I was thanking God. My eyes grew heavy, but I couldn't stop my brain from working. Gabi reached over and began slowly stroking my dick and then running her hands over my balls. It was relaxing as fuck.

Pressing her lips against my chest, she whispered, "Sleep, Nic. Sleep."

GABI HAD A PEP IN her step as she entered the building. Liza was walking next to her and they were both going on and on about the cooking competition.

It had been almost a month since we said we loved each other and I still hadn't said a goddamn thing about what my search on her pulled up . . . or lack thereof. I'd talked to both Cole and Oliver about it. Both told me the same thing—talk to her about it.

My hand rubbed the back of my neck as I watched her walking. How did I ask her? Oh, by the way, I looked up your name and can find no traces of a Gabriella Mandola. I sighed and pushed it out of my head. The fear of finding out something I didn't want to find out was winning right now.

A young lady held out a sign that said welcome as she pointed to a side door. "Registration is this way please."

Gabi glanced over her shoulder at me and gave me that big beautiful smile of hers. Damn she was gorgeous. I still hadn't brought her home to the family yet. A part of me was scared shitless they would scare her away. I'd avoided my mother's calls for the last three weeks. To be honest, I was stunned she hadn't shown up at my place. I think a part of her was still pissed I'd hidden my relationship with Gabi.

We walked into a giant room that had about fifty cooking stations set up. Gabi was so excited she did a little hop. "I've always wanted to enter a cooking competition!"

I grinned as I leaned down and kissed her lips. "You're gonna kick ass."

She chewed on her lip. "I hope! It's three courses. Appetizer, main dish, and dessert."

Liza started pulling everything out of the cooler and placing it in the small refrigerator.

"What's on the menu?" I asked.

Gabi had three different menus planned and wasn't going to pick one until she got here. Before she had a chance to answer, I heard a familiar voice. All three of us froze.

"Gabriella! Nicholaus! So this is what I have to do to see you two."

With wide eyes of terror, Gabi whispered, "Please tell me that's not your mom."

My eyes swung over to look at my mother standing there with my aunt Maria and Aunt Agnes.

"Shit," I whispered.

"Oh God. This is *not* happening. This is it!" Gabi exclaimed as she covered her mouth.

I placed my hands on her shoulders and leaned in closer. In a whispered voice, I asked, "What is wrong?"

Her eyes met mine. "This is her challenge! I thought it was that day in the bakery. That was a merely a test! She's here to take me down!"

I laughed. "My mother is not here to take you down."

She slowly shook her head and asked, "How did she know?"

Then we both turned to look at Liza. She took a step away. "You didn't."

Liza's eyes were everywhere. Me, my mother, back to Gabi, back to my mother. "I might have mentioned it that day in the bakery when she was there. But she saw the registration form and asked if you had entered!

I didn't know I wasn't supposed to say."

"Nicholaus, don't be rude. Introduce your Gabriella to your Aunt Maria and Aunt Agnes."

Gabi took in a slow deep breath before turning and facing my mother and aunts.

With my hand on her back, we walked closer. "Mama, this is a surprise to see you here."

She looked taken aback. "Why? I love to cook, this is a cooking competition. Why wouldn't I be here?"

"Because you've never entered one before."

The three of them laughed. "Please. Your mama has won more cooking competitions than anyone in this room."

Gabi swayed, and I tightened my grip on her.

When my mother turned to look at Gabi, she wore a wide smile. "My Nicholaus cares for you, so that makes you a part of the family."

"Thank you, Mrs. Drivas."

"No! Katerina. That is what you will call me."

With a quick nod, Gabi replied, "Yes, ma'am."

Clapping her hands loudly, Gabi jumped. "So, with you being a part of our family, I want to make sure you come in second so I've brought you some help."

Oh for shits sake.

"Help?" Gabi asked with a strained voice.

And before our eyes appeared my cousins Sophia and Angie, and just when I didn't think it could get worse, cousin Maria walked up carrying a giant bag with some rat looking dog in it.

"Um, I don't think you can have a dog in here," Liza said.

Everyone turned and looked at cousin Maria. "Are you shitting me? I don't go anywhere without my Nikky."

Gabi looked at me and asked, "Is the dog named after you?"

Everyone laughed as my mother walked up and hugged Gabi. "I do like a woman with a sense of humor. Now, the family wants to meet you."

I pulled out my phone and sent Thano a text.

Me: Code fucking red!

Not ten seconds later, he responded.

Thano: Oh hell. What's happening?

Me: Mom crashed Gabi's cooking competition.

Thano: Seeking Kilyn's advice. Hold please.

"Gabriella, this is Aunt Maria and Aunt Agnes."
Gabi reached her hand out to theirs.
"Then you have Nic's cousins, Sophia, Angie, and Maria."
Gabi smiled. "Are you mother and daughter?" she asked looking between Aunt Maria and cousin Maria. They both laughed.
"No, why?" cousin Maria asked.
"Ahh! You made it!" my mother called out as her best friend came walking up. I couldn't help but groan.

Me: Half the fucking family is showing up. They are Maria'ing her to death!

Thano: Kilyn said she'll be praying for Gabi. That's all she's got.

I rolled my eyes. "Bastard."
"Gabriella, this is my very dear friend, Maria."
I didn't think Gabi could look any more confused. "Oh, um, another Maria! That's a lot of Maria's under one roof." They all stared at her like they didn't get it.
They fucking got it.
"All right, well now that the gang is here, Mama you should be heading on over to your station."
"You're not coming over there with me?"
Gabi's head jerked to the side to look at me. *Oh shit. What the hell do I do? I can't ask Thano . . . they're both staring at me.*
I did the only thing I knew to do. I looked for guidance from Liza. My eyes were wide as she motioned to Gabi.
Right. Right. I needed to stay with Gabi.

"Well, Mama, I was planning on helping Gabi and being here for moral support with this being her first competition and all." Gabi glared at me.

Shit, what did I do now?

Then my mother turned back to Gabi. "First, huh?" My heart dropped in my chest. That's why Gabi shot me a dirty look. "Well, I better let you get going then. Good luck."

With a full-on smile, Gabi nodded. "Thanks! You too. And may the best cook win."

Tossing her head back and laughing before looking back at Gabi, my mother said, "Oh, I will."

twenty-one

Gabi

I COULDN'T BELIEVE IT. KATERINA was here. In the competition. I was screwed. Then she made the comment about me coming in second. Then about her winning.

Oh. Hell. No.

Watching her walking away with her group of Maria's, I spun around. Pointing to Liza, I said, "Menu. Change."

"What? You can't do a menu change. Are you crazy?"

I paced back and forth as I rubbed my temples and tried to think of one of my grandmother's best recipes.

"Uncle Dimitris says Italian food is just Greek food, but with no flavor."

My eyes swung over to the dark haired beauty in front of me. Without taking my eyes off of her, I said, "Nic."

"I'm on it," he said as he walked toward his cousins and ushered them away.

Turning back to Liza, I said, "We have got to win. I want to take that woman down!"

She nodded then said, "You do know that's your boyfriend's mom? Like, this may end bad."

"Bullshit! She's challenging me, Liza. Don't you see that? She wants to test me. See if I'm strong enough. Well, I'm strong enough!"

Nic walked back over rubbing the back of his neck. He always did that when he was worried or nervous about something. It was a habit of his I picked up on early on.

He grinned. "I took care of my cousins."

I nodded.

"Okay. I've got the menu and I know we have everything." Liza smiled as she took out a pen and paper to write it down. "We're going to start with Spinach pesto bruschetta."

"Yum," Nic said with a huge smile.

"Then steamed mussels in that Italian beer we brought for Nic to drink."

"Hey!" Nic said with a sexy smile.

"Two appetizers?" Liza asked with a slight shake in her voice.

"Then, hazelnut chicken. It's a one-pot dish and will be easy to deal with."

Liza nodded. "Okay dessert?"

"Not yet, Liza. It's time to go big or go home. The other main course will be lemon and herb branzino."

"You're gonna make a fish also? Are you crazy?"

I smiled bigger. "Then for dessert, we'll have the one Italian dessert everyone loves, cannoli's."

Liza breathed a sigh of relief. They were simple as hell to make and I could whip them out like nothing.

"And . . . the olive oil sobertto with raspberry and balsamic. Gotta love Giada for that recipe."

Liza shook her head. "What!"

"The sorbetto is already made. So that is an easy one as well."

Peeking over to Nic, he wore a grin from ear to ear. "Don't you dare tell your mother I'm going double."

He pretended to lock his mouth and toss the key. "Not a word."

"Okay, now that we have a menu, let's write it up for the judges and finish getting set up. It will start soon."

As Liza and I moved about getting everything set up and ready to go, I felt confident I was going to at least beat Katerina. If I could place better than her, then it would earn me the respect I needed from Nic's family.

Nic walked up behind me and wrapped his arms around my waist. His breath tickled my ear and my heart froze as I waited to hear what he was about to whisper in my ear.

"You're so fucking sexy right now."

"Yeah?" I asked with a smile as I attempted to plug in the mixer with Nic all over me.

"Yeah. You have no idea how hard I am for you right now."

I pushed my ass slightly into him. My stomach clenched as I felt his desire.

"Fucking hell, Gabi."

Turning in his arms, I glanced over to see Liza pulling out all the sugar and flour. I looked into his dark eyes and softly asked, "Tell me what you would do to me if we were alone."

Nic swallowed hard then leaned in closer. "I'd slip my hands up that dress of yours and slowly pull your panties off. Then set you up on this counter and slowly lick your pussy."

Holy crap'ole. I wasn't expecting him to be so dirty.

A small moan slipped from my lips.

"Then . . . then what?" I asked, nearly panting.

"I'd finger fuck you while sucking on your clit until you screamed out my name and begged me to stop."

I could feel myself getting wet and I had to squeeze my legs together. Another peek at Liza showed she was talking to the lady setting up next to us.

"Then I'd spread your legs wider so I could see those pretty pink lips that my cock was dying to slip into."

"Nic. Stop."

He smiled. "Turning you on, baby?"

When his hand started for under my dress, I knew things were about to get a little crazier. Nic's hand came to a stop when he brushed his fingers across my bare lips.

With wide eyes, he stared at me. "You're not wearing panties?"

My face heated. "I . . . I wanted to . . . surprise . . . you . . . later."

I was so horny I could hardly think straight. This never happened to me before I met Nic. He quickly found a way to work me up so much I would be practically begging him.

"I need to fuck you."

I closed my eyes and mumbled, "Yes."

"Now."

My eyes snapped open. "What?"

Nic grabbed my hand and pulled me toward the exit door of the conference ballroom.

"Where are we going?"

He looked around after he nearly busted the door down.

"Nic! Nic, the competition is about to start!"

Dragging me down the hall, he looked back at me. "I don't think this is going to take long."

A zing zipped through my body at the idea of having Nic before the event started. It would relax me, there was no doubt about that.

Turning down a hall, he started checking doors until he found one open. Pulling me inside, he shut and locked it. Then he quickly pulled my dress over my head and pushed two fingers inside of me.

"Fuck. Fuck. Fuck. You're wet as hell."

"Of course I am. You were just whispering dirty things in my ear."

Nic laughed. "You like that don't you, baby?"

I wasn't the least bit embarrassed by admitting I did. "I do. It turns me on even more."

He pushed my bra up and over my breast, letting them bounce down as he grabbed one and clamped his mouth onto my nipple. Electricity raced through my body as I held onto his shoulders.

"Oh, God, Nic."

"I know, baby. I know."

He lifted me up and I wrapped my legs around his waist.

The way his eyes turned dark with desire almost had me coming on the spot.

Nic positioned himself at my entrance and pulled me down onto him in one quick movement, causing me to gasp.

"Damn it. I'm sorry, Gabi."

I gripped his shoulder and started moving my hips. So close. I was so close.

"Nic. Fuck me. Please!"

He did exactly as I asked him to do. I came almost immediately and the moment I did, he came right along with me. He grunted and then called out my name as I felt his warm seed spill into my body.

We stood there in silence, his cock twitching inside of me. I was a web of ecstasy as I slowly brought my breathing back down. Nic pulled out of me and smiled. I could feel his cum sliding down my leg and it was the hottest damn thing ever. He quickly looked around and found some paper towels. Dropping to his knees, he cleaned me gently before slipping my dress back over my head.

I went to talk but stilled when there was a knock on the door.

"Nicholaus? Are you in there?"

My eyes widened in horror. Nic and I stared at each other. He put his finger up to his mouth in a motion for me to keep quiet. I tilted my head and shot him a *really* look.

"I don't know where they went."

I mouthed, *who was that?*

Nic rolled his eyes and pulled me to him. Pressing his lips to mine, he kissed me. So deeply and so passionately I forgot that his mother was on the other side of the door. I forgot about the competition and most importantly, I forgot I was running from my past.

twenty-two

Gabi

I PACED BACK AND FORTH wringing my hands together as we waited for the judges to give their results. All I wanted was to place. And of course beating Katerina would be nice.

"Stop pacing, Gabi. You're making me nervous."

Stopping, I smiled at Liza. "Sorry. I'm going out of my mind waiting."

"What you need is another sneak away with Nic," she said while wiggling her eyebrows. My face heated and I looked past her to see Nic. He was over at his mother's station across the room. My heart dropped thinking about almost being caught by Katerina. That was twice she'd almost caught us in the middle of the deed.

"We only went for some air."

"Uh-huh. Please. I can practically smell the sex on you."

My mouth fell open. "Liza!"

With a nonchalant shrug, she replied, "What? I'm not naïve, Gabi. I see the way he looks at you like he wants to devour you. It's hot."

I chewed on my lip and grinned. "He's so amazing."

Liza laughed. "Charity said, from what she hears coming from your room, Nic surely must have a magical dick."

Now my face really felt hot. I slumped down into the chair and stared at Liza. "She did not say that."

"Oh, she said it. I think she said it in front of Max because she thinks he has the hots for you." Liza laughed. "Which is so far from the truth."

With a frown, I asked, "Why is that so far from the truth?"

With a surprised expression on her face, she pinched her brows together. "You don't know, do you? Oh. My. Gosh. Neither one of you know."

"Know what?" I asked in anticipation of what she was going to say.

"Max is gay, Gabi! He's been in a relationship with the same guy for three years."

I looked at her like she had grown two heads. Not that I cared Max was gay, but how could Charity and I miss that?

"Max is gay? How did I miss that?"

Her right shoulder lifted. "Beats me, but I can't wait to tell him this."

I jumped up to beg her not to when the host of the event spoke.

Nic walked up right then and wrapped me in his arms. "It's okay, agapiméni. No matter what happens, you're my number one."

Smiling, I reached up on my toes and kissed him. They were announcing the top five winners, staring with number five. I prayed like hell I got it.

"Our fifth runner up is, Lauren Night."

My body sank against Nic. "There are four other spots," he whispered. I smiled, knowing he was right. There was a small chance I could make fourth . . . maybe even third.

Glancing over to Katerina, she looked confident. Why couldn't I be that confident?

"Fourth place goes to Michelle Smith."

My heart was pounding in my ears.

"Third place goes to Katerina Drivas."

Closing my eyes, I fought to not cry out. Nic chuckled next to me. "Oh, she is *not* going to be happy with third."

I turned and sat down on the chair. She still won and I would never live it down.

"Second place goes to Elizabeth Rainy." Burying my face in my hands, I tried not to let it get to me.

Why?

Why did Liza have to tell her about the competition?

"And the winner of the Tenth Annual Colorado Springs Cooking and Baking Competition is Gabi Mandola."

My head jerked up as Liza and Nic both cried out in celebration. "You won! You won!" Liza yelled as she pulled me up and threw her arms around me.

Tears started to form in my eyes and when I pulled back and gazed over at Nic, I lost all control. He looked so proud of me and when he held his arms out, I nearly knocked him over when I rushed into them.

"You won, Gabi. I knew you would."

His words filled my heart with so much love it felt as if it would burst. When I pulled back, I had tears streaming down my face.

Nic smiled. "I'm so glad you're happy you won. You deserved it."

I shook my head while wiping my tears away.

"I'm happy I won, but I'm freaking ecstatic I beat your mother!"

Nic stared at me for a few seconds before he busted out laughing and pulled me in for another hug.

A voice cleared from behind me and I stepped back to see Katerina standing there. She wore a huge smile. I was terrified this would make her dislike me even more.

"Congratulations, Gabriella. I'm proud of you."

My chest tightened. "You are?"

She laughed. "Of course I am. I knew that day in your bakery you had it in you. You are a very talented young woman." Her eyes swung over to Nic. "My son is very lucky to have found you."

The room spun.

Did she say what I think I heard?

"He is?" I asked with a stunned expression. "But . . . I'm not . . . I'm . . . I'm not Greek."

Katerina shrugged. "Some of us can't all be that blessed, my dear."

I couldn't help but start laughing. I knew no matter what I did, I would always have that one thing against me that Katerina would hold over my head, but I was okay with that. As long as I had Nic by my side, everything else was a walk in the park.

———— ♥ ————

THE RED PHONE RANG AND my heart stopped.

It never rang.

Ever.

I slowly made my way to the drawer and pulled it open. With shaking hands, I reached for it and took a deep breath.

"Hello?"

"Gabriella, my sweet girl."

"Daddy? Is everything okay?"

He laughed. "It is. I wanted to make sure you had everything ready for the trip." I breathed a sigh of relief. In the last four years I'd only spoken to my father twice. Once was to tell me my aunt had passed away. Not being able to go to her funeral was hard.

"I'm all set. Are you *sure* this is safe?"

"Antonio and I wouldn't allow you to come if we didn't feel that it wasn't."

"Are they still watching the house?" I asked while I nervously bit my fingernail. My arm wrapped around my stomach to try to settle it. An image of my old boyfriend, Dante, flashed through my mind.

"Not in two years. Nor have they had anyone trail us to Italy. If you ask me, the man is an idiot. He has no clue what he is doing."

I thought I had loved him at one time.

How wrong I was.

Dante thought my family was naïve. He had no idea who Antonio really was. My brother was always at least two steps ahead of him.

I stayed silent for a few moments before he broke into my thoughts.

"Antonio said you were worried about someone last month."

Frowning, I nodded. "Yes. Someone came in and ordered a large number of cakes, but it turns out it was for an office party. It was nothing. Me being overly paranoid."

"That is what has kept you safe the last six years, Gabriella. Don't let your guard down now. The more you stay out of the public eye the better."

My stomach dropped. I wasn't sure if I should tell him about the picture or not. I decided it was probably best I do. If I'd put my life in danger last week at the cooking competition, my father needed to know.

twenty-three

Nic

*E*XHAUSTED WASN'T EVEN THE WORD to use to describe how I felt. I finally had a day off and the first place I was going was Gabi's. I didn't even care that it wasn't her day off. I needed to see her. Feel her in my arms. Plus, I needed to brief her on the family dinner tonight.

Rolling my eyes, I let out a sigh. Picking up the phone, I hit my mother's number.

"Nicholaus, it's about time you called your mother."

"I talked to you two days ago, Mama."

"How am I supposed to know you're okay if I don't hear from you?"

Pulling into the guest parking spot at Gabi's place, I put my truck in park and sighed. "No news is good news."

"Nonsense. Now, what time will you be bringing Gabriella over?"

"Why do you insist on calling her that? Her name is Gabi."

My mother laughed. "Because Gabi sounds like a stripper's name."

Scrubbing my hand down my face, I sighed. "Mama, how would you know what a stripper's name sounds like?"

She laughed. "Oh, I know."

My eyes rolled again. "It's only the immediate family . . . right?"

"Define immediate, Nicholaus?"

I groaned. "You, Dad, Thad and Phoebe, and Thano, Kilyn, and Kira."

"Yes."

Relief washed over me. The last thing I wanted was to scare the living shit out of Gabi with the whole family.

"Sounds good. We'll see you later tonight. I've got to get a few hours' sleep, I've been at a stand-off for the last twenty-eight hours."

"Don't worry, I'll make sure your father is on his best behavior."

I didn't have the heart to tell her I wasn't worried about him . . . it was her I was worried about.

"See you later, Mama. Love you."

"I love you too. Tell Gabriella the family is looking forward to meeting her."

Before I could correct her on the name and get her to explain who she defined as family, the line went dead.

I grunted as I got out of the truck and dragged my ass up the stairs to Gabi's place. I was positive she was down in the bakery, so I let myself in and headed to her room. I needed a hot shower and a bed.

Her voice drifted into the room as I came to a stop. I slowly made my way over to the balcony. The door was cracked open enough for her voice to carry inside.

She was upset.

"I understand. Yes, Antonio, I don't need a lecture from you too. I messed up. I had no idea they would do that. I'm very aware of that, thank you very much."

I frowned. Who was she talking to? There was no way this was a business call. Whoever she was talking to, she knew them personally.

"I've already received a lecture from father on this. I don't need one from you as well."

My breath stilled. *Her father? Her parents were dead.*

"I'm already beating myself up for letting this all happen. It got out of hand and I let my guard down. It won't happen again. Now, can we please change the subject?"

What in the hell is she talking about?

The glass on the door showed her reflection. She was sitting down and a slow smile moved across her face.

"I am excited about Italy. I cannot wait to see you, Antonio. You have no idea."

A stabbing pain shot through my chest.

Who in the fuck was Antonio?

"No, I just told Charity and Nic that I'm going to visit where I used to go with my family. Charity wanted to come with me, but I told her I needed to do this alone. I've told them both I have extended family in Italy. Well, of course I know that."

I stumbled back. Gabi was lying to both me and Charity. But what was she lying about?

"I love you too, Antonio and I can't wait to see you."

And there went the twist of the knife. Turning, I wanted to walk to the front door and leave, but I went to her room instead. I stripped out of my clothes and crawled into her bed. My mind was spinning, and I was too tired to even take a shower.

Who was Antonio? Gabi told me her parents died when she was in high school. Were they alive? Why would she lie?

"I love you too, Antonio and I can't wait to see you."

My chest tightened. Maybe he was an old family friend.

The door to her condo opened and closed. She must have been done with the call and headed back to the bakery. Forcing myself to get up, I headed to her bathroom and showered.

Wrapping a towel around my waist, I stared at myself in the mirror. The cold shower woke me up enough to do what I knew I shouldn't be doing.

I spun on my heels and headed out to the kitchen. Glancing down at Gabi's itinerary, I took a picture of it with my phone and sent it to Scarlett. Her best friend owned a travel agency.

> Me: *Can your friend get me on these flights and find me a hotel?*

Scarlett replied back within a few minutes.

> Scarlett: *She said if the flights are full, do you want the closest times to it?*

I dragged in a deep breath then whispered to myself, "Why don't you just ask her, you idiot?"

From the moment I'd met Gabi, I knew she was hiding something. If I asked her, she might make up a story.

No. I needed to see for myself what she was going to be doing and who she was going to be seeing in Italy.

Me: Yes. I need to be there either when this plane lands or before.

Scarlett: Gottcha. On it.

Me: Thanks. I owe you one.

Scarlett: Well, I know how you can repay me back. It's been a while, Nic.

I didn't respond. Scarlett knew I was seeing someone, couldn't believe it, but she knew.

Heading back to Gabi's room, I fell onto the bed and was surrounded by her smell. My dick instantly got hard thinking about her.

Fuck, I didn't want to believe she was lying to me or cheating on me, but something in my gut told me both might be true.

THE FRONT DOOR OPENED AND Charity came to a halt as she covered her chest.

"Fucking A, Nic. You scared the shit out of me."

I lifted my brow. Cole had told me a few weeks back about his and Charity's hook up. He'd been kicking himself in the ass about forgetting a condom and at the same time wondering why Charity hadn't returned any of his calls the last few days.

"Sorry. I was waiting on Gabi."

She flashed me a smile. "I forgot she gave you a key."

When she walked in, I couldn't help but notice how tired she looked.

"Long day downstairs?"

Charity stopped walking and turned to me. "No. I wasn't there today."

I nodded. "Why haven't you called Cole back?"

Her eyes filled with tears and I was honestly taken aback. Charity didn't seem like the type of girl who let her emotions show. When she instantly started crying, I jumped up and went over to her.

"Charity," I softly said as I pulled her into my arms.

"I'm not a whore, Nic. As much as I act like I have no problem sleeping around, I rarely do. What happened with Cole has never happened to me before and I have been beside myself ever since."

I lifted her chin up so she would look me in the eyes. "Because of the condom thing?"

Her eyes widened in shock. "He told you?" she barely said.

With a nod, I replied, "He's just as scared, but Charity, he really likes you and wants you to call."

Her eyes closed and a tear slipped out and slowly made a path down her cheek. It killed me. I hated seeing women cry.

Hated. It.

"Don't cry, Charity. I know you think he's a player, but honest to God he hasn't stopped talking about you."

Her eyes opened and with a trembling chin, she said, "Today I found out I'm pregnant, Nic."

I dropped my hold on her and took a few steps back. "What?"

She nodded.

Shit. Shit. Shit. Cole really liked Charity, but I wasn't sure how he would react to this.

"That's where I was today. I went this morning for the sonogram, I just walked around. I didn't know what else to do. I sent Cole a text and asked if we could meet for dinner. I . . . I don't . . . I don't know what to do."

Her face buried in her hands and I went to her again, pulling her into a hug and whispering that everything would be okay. I had wanted to drill her about Gabi, but now was not the time. I was going to have to figure that shit out on my own.

"I've known Cole a long time. He'll stand by you, Charity."

She stepped back and wiped her tear-soaked face with her fingers. "I know he will. The last few weeks we've spent together have been great.

It's just . . . I feel something with him, Nic. Something that has never happened before." She covered her mouth to hold back her sob. "I knew there was something between us, but I got scared. That overwhelming feeling I had when he made love to me was almost too much. Then when we realized what he had done, I really freaked."

"He freaked too, Charity, but that doesn't mean he won't be there for you."

She sunk down onto the sofa. "I don't want him to think I want money."

"He won't."

With a halfhearted laugh, she looked at me. "Really? Because I'm pretty sure most men in this situation would think that."

"The only way you're going to find out is to talk to him."

Her arms wrapped around her waist. "I've never really told Gabi or anyone this, but I come from a pretty wealthy family. I'm not worried about money. Jesus, I'm not ready to be a mother. I'm too greedy. This is my time to have fun and do fun things, not sit home with a baby."

She gasped then dropped back and covered her face and moaned.

"What's wrong?"

Her hands fell to the sides of her onto the sofa. "The Knitters are Purls."

"Your knitting group?"

The only reason I knew about the group was because Gabi dragged me there last week to meet Lou, Beth, Karen, and Nancy. Charity bitched the entire drive there and back home.

She nodded.

"What about them?"

Sitting up, she shot me a look like I was a dumb ass. "They're going to start knitting me shit! Oh my God! Blankets and baby booties."

I laughed. "Well, it could be worse, they could be knitting you a sweater like they are me."

When her face cracked into a smile, I felt a little better. "That's true," she said.

"Want a drink?" She tilted her head and scrounged her nose. "Shit. Right. Want a water?"

Laughing, she nodded her head. "Please."

After pouring her a glass of water, I sat down across from her.

"Will you do me a favor?" she asked.

"Sure."

Charity chewed on her lip. "Don't tell Gabi. I broke down with you and let it slip, but I need to tell Cole and figure out where we go from here before anyone else knows."

I nodded. "I won't tell a soul."

She smiled.

I flashed her a grin, but then let it drop. My tone turned serious. "Will you do something for me now?"

Setting her water down, she looked me straight in the eye. "Please tell me you're not breaking up with her."

For a moment I was taken aback, but then I could see how she would think that. I was waiting in Gabi's apartment, and I had just gotten serious on her.

"No. But I need to know something."

"Sure, what is it?"

I hated doing this. It felt like a dick-move. In my heart, I knew she would never cheat, but then again, I didn't really know Gabi Mandola or really anything about her past.

"Is Gabi seeing another man besides me?"

Her face dropped. The shocked look on her face turned to anger. "How could you even think that! I haven't seen her date but one other guy in the four years I've known her. Besides, she would never cheat. That's not who she is."

I nodded.

She shook her head. "Nic, where is this coming from?"

I swallowed hard. *Did I tell her? I had to.* Maybe if I said the name, it would spark something. "I'm asking you to do the same thing you asked me. If I tell you, please don't say anything to her."

Wringing her hands together, she reached for her glass and took a drink.

"Okay, I promise I won't say a word to her."

"I overheard her talking on the phone about her trip to Italy. She told some guy by the name of Antonio she couldn't wait to see him and that she loved him."

Charity gasped and covered her mouth. Then she dropped her hand. "Wait. She has family over there, Nic. Don't you think she might have been talking to a cousin or something?"

"She said something else. That she told me and you she had extended family in Italy."

"Huh? So does she not have family over there or does she?"

I rubbed the back of my neck as I processed her conversation again.

"Yeah, I'm not sure. I get the feeling she does, but she made it seem like there was a different reason she was going over there. Maybe to see this Antonio guy."

She shook her head. "No. It has to be family. I cannot for one minute see Gabi cheating. She loves you, Nic."

Deep down I knew that was true, but she was still hiding something and I was no longer able to keep pushing it aside. I was determined to find out what she was hiding.

I smiled. "You're right. I'm over reacting."

"Yes. I think you are."

The door opened and Gabi walked in. The second she saw me, she smiled.

Charity stood and shot me a quick look. I leaned over to her and said, "Forget we even had that conversation."

She nodded. "I will."

I made my way over to Gabi. She threw herself into my arms.

"I hadn't heard from you. I was worried," she said softly.

What a dick. I meant to text her when I got to her place, but then the whole thing happened with hearing her on the phone and it slipped my mind.

"I'm so sorry, prinkipissa. I was so tired and I came here but you were down at the bakery and I crashed in your bed."

Her eyes turned dark. "Well damn, had I known that I'd have taken a long lunch break."

Smiling, I pulled her to me and cupped her face in my hands. "Gabi," I whispered.

Searching my face with her beautiful eyes, she grinned bigger while holding onto my forearms. "Nic."

My lips pressed against hers as we exchanged a slow sweet kiss. When I pulled back, she winked. "I better go get ready if we want to be at your parents' place on time."

I let go of her and watched her walk to her room. Turning back to Charity, I took in her sad eyes. "Are you going to be okay?"

She nodded and inhaled a deep breath. "I think so. Thank you for being there for me, Nic. It really means a lot."

"Listen, I know Cole. I've been working alongside him a number of years. I have a feeling this evening is going to turn out very different from what you expect."

Her eyes filled with tears again, but she quickly got her emotions in check. "I hope you're right. Have fun tonight."

Walking up to me, she reached up and kissed me on the cheek then patted me on the chest. "I'm going to go check on Gabi and make sure she isn't freaking out with the whole *meeting the parents* and family thing."

Laughing, I replied, "Good idea."

As I watched Charity walk away, I couldn't help but smile. No matter what Cole said about loving his bachelor ways, he was going to be over the moon with Charity's news. I didn't know Charity well enough to know how she was feeling . . . but the sadness in her eyes told me enough.

twenty-four

Gabi

MY EYES WERE FIXED ON the string at the bottom of my skirt. I kept staring at it. Do I pull it? Leave it? Ask Nic for scissors?

Holy crap'ole. Why in the hell am I worried about a string?

The truck came to an abrupt stop as Nic said, "What in the fuck?"

Snapping my head up, I looked around. "What? What's wrong?"

He stared over at a house that had a ton of cars in the driveway and out front. My heart started beating faster.

Oh. No. Please God no.

Nic put the truck in reverse and started speaking in Greek. My insides started to swirl, and it wasn't from nerves.

Damn that was hot hearing him talk in Greek.

"Stop," I said.

He stopped the truck. Shaking my head, I added, "No, stop talking in Greek."

"Shit. Sorry, Gabi. I'm slightly annoyed and didn't really want you to hear all the things I was calling my mother."

My hand covered my mouth to hide my smile.

"It was turning me on."

Now he really stopped the truck. "What?"

Chewing on my lip, I shrugged. That's right. I was a nervous, horny Italian woman who wanted her very handsome Greek boyfriend to take me right there in his truck.

"You've got to stop looking at me like that, agapiméni."

My tongue ran along my lip. "And if I don't?"

"I'm going to fuck you in the backseat of my truck."

A small moan slipped from my lips. "Nic."

He quickly parked and before we had a chance to do anything, a knock on the driver's window caused both of us to yell out.

Turning, Nic cursed when he saw Thano standing there with a huge smile on his face.

"Let's go, Gabi. The faster we do this the better."

"Wait, why are you frustrated with your mom?" I asked as Nic jumped out and pushed Thano out of the way. Not waiting for him to come around to open my door, I jumped out.

"I could have told you this was going to happen," Thano said. He was holding his five-year-old daughter in his arms and it had to be the sweetest thing ever.

Kilyn came walking up to me wearing that sweet smile of hers. She had a flush on her cheeks and I couldn't help but return the gesture. Grinning, I gave her a hug.

"You look beautiful," we both said.

Laughing, I shook my head. "Do you have any idea why Nic would be so mad? He started talking in Greek when we pulled up to the house."

Kilyn made a face. "Trust me, you're about to find out."

As we walked behind Thano and Nic, I leaned closer and said, "That's their house?"

She nodded. "Yep."

"It's beautiful. Why are there so many cars?"

Kilyn looked at me and said, "Because Greek families don't know how to do small, Gabi. When Nic said immediate family only . . . his mother heard *invite the whole family! The more the better.*"

I laughed. "It can't be that bad."

She looked at me and flashed an evil smile. I had a feeling she was going to enjoy this.

"You came at the perfect time," she said with a giggle.

Before I had a chance to ask what she meant, the front door of the two-story stone house flew open. "She's here! She is here!"

Nic stopped and waited for me to walk up next to him.

"Whatever happens tonight, know this. I promise to give you the best sex of your life tonight if you don't run from this house screaming."

Thano laughed and hit his brother on the back as Kilyn groaned. "Nice. Promises of hot sex to smooth it over. I should have thought of that."

Kilyn hit Thano on the chest. "Hush! Your daughter is in your arms, Thano!"

They started walking up and Katerina quickly kissed the three of them before making a straight shot to Nic.

Oh no, wait . . . shit. She was coming to me.

The next thing I knew, at least twenty more people came flooding out. All of them making their way to me.

"Help," I whispered.

Nic looked at me and said, "We're past that phase, baby."

MY HEAD WAS SPINNING. AFTER being hugged by probably every Greek woman in the state of Colorado, I was ushered into the living room where Katerina promptly brought me up to a man who I instantly knew was Nic's father.

Nic took over. "Dad, this is Gabi. Gabi, this is my father, Dimitris."

The older version of Nic took my hand in his and lifted it to his mouth. He smiled then kissed the back of my hand.

"You have eyes like the color of the ocean. The deepest of blue."

I smiled. "I got them from my father."

He nodded then glanced over to Nic. "Nicholaus, she's beautiful."

"And Italian," Katerina added with a smile.

"Ah . . . Italian food is just like Greek."

I waited for him to finish the rest of it, but he didn't. He simply smiled at me and then winked at Nic. Maybe having Kilyn for a daughter-in-law made him more open minded.

Katerina took my arm and off we went with meeting the family.

"This is my sister Maria and her daughters Sophia, Angie, and Maria. This is my sister Agnes and her daughter Maria and son Nick. You've met some of them a few weeks back at the cook off."

I smiled as I met person after person. "Hello. Hello. Very nice to meet you."

My cheeks were going to cramp if I smiled any longer.

"And this is Maria and her husband, Nick. Their daughter Maria isn't here tonight."

"Lots of Marias!" I said with a chuckle. Everyone stared at me and Kilyn waved her hands in the corner for me to stop talking.

Shit.

Taking my arm, Katerina lead me over to another group of people. "This is Phoebe, my son Thaddeus's wife."

Phoebe extended her hand to me and gave me the warmest smile. I knew instantly I was going to like her. Kilyn had already told me how amazing she was. My eyes glanced down to her very pregnant belly and a tinge of jealousy raced through my veins.

Kilyn walked up and hugged Phoebe. "You look beautiful," she said with a smile.

Phoebe chuckled. "I feel like a whale."

Shaking my head, I said, "You're beautiful and glowing." That's when I turned to Kilyn. She had the same glow. My heart stopped. She was pregnant too.

I cleared my throat and pushed away my jealous thoughts. "So, have I met all the important people?"

Kilyn laughed. "No. You haven't met Yiayia yet."

"Yiayia?" I asked with a questioning look.

"Watch out. She spits," Kilyn warned.

My eyes widened in horror. "She . . . spits?"

Nodding, she added, "On you."

"What?" I asked in horror.

"They really don't do that anymore," Phoebe added. I guess that was supposed to make me feel better.

"Wait. Who is Yiayia?"

Kilyn answered. "The guys' grandmother."

"Oh." It was all I could say. "Do I have to greet her in any special way?"

Phoebe laughed. "No. Just ignore whatever it is she says to you."

My eyes swung over to Kilyn. "She's going to say something about you carrying a baby."

I swallowed hard. "W-what?"

She waved it off with her hand. "Just don't let it freak you out."

I was freaked out. Really freaked out.

My body warmed instantly as Nic wrapped his arm around my waist. "You ladies filling her head with things about the family?"

Kilyn let out an evil laugh as Phoebe simply grinned wider. "Never," Kilyn cackled.

There must have been fifty people in the house, I swear. One after another they came up to me. They all started off with the same first sentence.

"So, you're Italian."

The best one so far from was from Aunt Maria. No wait. Cousin Maria. No. Maybe it was Maria the best friend. Whoever it was pulled me to the side and asked if I was able to handle the strong arm of a Greek man. She warned me of how possessive they were with their women. I couldn't help but search out Kilyn and Phoebe. I watched as both Thano and Thad kept their arms on their wives. To me it was more of a loving thing than possessive. Scanning the room, I found Dimitris with Katerina. He pulled her into his arms and kissed her. My heart skipped a beat. Their love was evident not only with the way they looked at each other, but in the way their sons looked at the women they loved.

Glancing over to Nic, I wondered if he looked at me that way.

Nic placed his hand on my lower back and guided me toward the kitchen. "Time to eat, baby."

My stomach growled, and I realized I hadn't eaten anything all day. I was starving.

"You up for elk hunting this year?" Thano had asked Nic as we all stood waiting for everyone to file through the kitchen. The food smelled heavenly. I inhaled a deep breath.

"Sure. We haven't been in a few years," Nic replied. They were making small talk and it somehow eased my nerves. Kilyn was holding Kira and reminding her about her manners. I loved seeing her call out to her grandfather and run to him. The way Dimitris swept her up in his arms had my chest squeezing as memories of my own grandfather swirled in my head.

I jumped when the young lady next to me asked, "Have you had Greek food before?"

"Um . . . a few times. I've tried my hand at cooking a few Greek dishes."

The entire kitchen grew quiet as everyone looked over at me.

Shit. Damn it. Double damn. Why did I open my mouth?

Then I saw her. The woman who must be . . . Yiayia. She stood there holding a dish while her eyes met mine. The way she was looking at me had me swallowing hard.

"What have you tried your hand at?" she asked.

Nic chuckled. "There is Yiayia! Gabi, this is my grandmother."

I would have extended my hand, but she was holding a dish of something that looked and smelled heavenly.

"Let me take that, Yiayia! Now go sit down!" Katerina said.

Yiayia started to head toward the massive dining room. There was a large table set up, but I couldn't help but notice most of the people were heading out back or to the living room.

"Why is no one sitting at the dining room table?" I asked Nic as we moved closer to the kitchen island that was covered in food.

"That's for the family."

I glanced around. A few people nodded at me and smiled and I graciously returned the gesture. Weren't they all family?

"Nic, all these people didn't come just to meet me, did they?"

He laughed but never answered as we approached the table. My eyes scanned the endless amount of food on the table. Here I thought my family loved food.

"Wow. That's a lot of food," I whispered with a small giggle.

Before I knew what was happening, a plate was shoved in my hands and Katerina started piling on food. There was so much food on my plate I nearly dropped it.

"Now, Gabriella, you come sit next to Yiayia."

My heart froze and I quickly looked over at Kilyn. She lifted her brows and pretended to spit.

Glancing back over my shoulder, I searched for Nic.

"Don't worry, *my* Nicholaus will be sitting right next to you."

Was it my imagination or did she keep referring to Nic as hers?

As I sat down, Katerina pulled on my hair.

"Ouch!" I cried out as I turned to look at her. What in the hell?

She blushed. "Oh, my goodness my bracelet got caught on your hair. Look at that?"

Holding a few pieces of my hair, she smiled as if she had won a great victory. I, on the other hand, rubbed the area of my head where she had robbed me of precious strands of hair.

I slowly sank down into the chair as Katerina leaned over to Yiayia. "This is my Nicholaus's Gabriella, Yiayia."

The older woman turned and stared at me. I did the only thing I could think of doing.

"So, yiayia means grandmother in Greek?"

She huffed at me and I swear I saw smoke come from her mouth and nostrils.

The way her eyes took me in had me fidgeting in my seat. "So, you are Italian and you think you can cook Greek food, huh?"

My eyes widened in horror. "Oh, well I'm sure I can't cook it nearly as good as you or Katerina."

"Then how will our Nicholaus eat?"

I laughed and gave Yiayia a wink. "Lucky for me he said Italian was his favorite food."

The entire room fell silent.

How in the hell did they hear that over all this talking?

Everyone looked at me then Nic.

"Is this true, Nicholaus?" Katerina asked.

I couldn't help but notice how Thad and Thano leaned in closer . . . like their next breath depended on Nic's answer.

Kilyn looked at me with a terrified look on her face then said, "I think what Gabi meant to say was, lucky for her Nic will eat her Italian cooking."

She motioned for me to agree. "Oh, yes yes. That is *exactly* what I meant to say. Not that Italian was his favorite."

I let out a laugh and Kilyn followed with one of her own. Then Phoebe chuckled. "As if Nicholaus would like Italian food over Greek!" she said.

Nic sat there stunned. Not uttering a single word.

Yiayia laughed then everyone else laughed.

"I knew my Nicholaus would never prefer that food!" Katerina said.

In a sad attempt to keep my fake laugh up, my eyes scanned around the table until they fell on Dimitris. He sat there staring at me. A slight smile played across his lips as he reached for a glass of wine and lifted it. I followed suit. He took a sip while I downed the whole glass.

Yiayia made a tsking sound then said, "Well, we know she isn't pregnant with the way she drinks."

I started to choke on the wine. *Finally*, Nic was pulled out of the daze he had been in.

"Yiayia, Gabi isn't pregnant."

She nodded. "I'd hope not with the way she's kicking them back."

"What?" I asked with a stunned expression. "I've only had—"

Nic leaned in closer. "Let it go, Gabi. Let it go."

twenty-five

Gabi

THE REST OF DINNER WAS spent with Yiayia trying to shove every kind of Greek food down my throat.

Try the moussaka.

Eat the pastitisio.

Have you tried the spanakopita?

If I ate another thing I was positive I would throw up. The entire dinner Yiayia kept talking to me in Greek, like I had a clue what she was saying. All I could do was stare at her.

I was surprised to see most of the family had left, leaving pretty much just the immediate family and a few Maria's sprinkled in here and there.

Katerina cleared her throat and looked at me. "How long have you been baking, Gabriella?"

Nic took my hand in his and all the females in the room sighed. I'd also heard most of the night how happy they were *their Nicholaus* had found someone. Although, I did hear someone in the other room mention it was a shame I wasn't Greek.

Katerina actually looked happy to see the exchange between Nic and me, but I still felt like an outsider. If it hadn't been for Kilyn and Kira, I'd be the only person in the room who wasn't Greek.

Smiling, I replied, "Since I can remember. My grandmother taught me."

Katerina smiled big and bright. "Does she live here in Colorado?"

My hands started to sweat. I never talked about my past. Ever.

"Um, no she's passed on a few years back."

Sadness swept over her face. "I'm so sorry."

With a fake grin, I reached for my wineglass and took a hearty drink before saying, "It's okay. I was lucky to have the time I had with her."

Katerina's smile felt warm and caring. At least I wasn't lying about my grandmother.

"Are you from Colorado Springs?" Aunt Agnes asked.

"The east coast," I responded. They all waited for me to elaborate and when I didn't, Nic spoke.

"Gabi moved here a few years back."

"Gabi? Who is Gabi?" Yiayia asked.

I knew damn well she knew it was me.

Nic leaned forward to look around me and to his grandmother. He pointed to me. "Gabi. That's her name, Yiayia."

She frowned. "I thought her name was Gabriella?"

"It is. I go by Gabi though."

Her lips snarled. Oh hell.

"Why? Gabriella is such a beautiful name. It matches your beautiful eyes."

Then it happened. She spit on me. Or at the very least, made the noise and motion of spitting.

I jumped at the action. I was ninety-nine percent sure she hadn't actually spit on me. Turning to Kilyn, she raised her eyebrows as if to say, *told you.*

"Yiayia, stop it," Nic warned.

"Your parents?" Dimitris asked.

My chest was beginning to tighten up to the point where I couldn't breathe. I hated lying. It was why I never talked about my past. I knew of only one way to make the questions top. "They're dead." Blunt. To the point.

Gasps were heard across the room. Now to add in the final blow. "I was young, eighteen."

Katerina looked over to Kilyn. "You two have another thing in common."

"Another thing?" Kilyn asked.

Katerina looked at Kilyn like she had grown two heads. "Yes, both your parents passed away when you were young."

My heart ached for Kilyn, but at least the conversation was moving away from my past. I hated that I was lying and that this was actually something painful for her though.

"And what's the other thing?" Kilyn asked. Katerina stood and reached for my plate then Nic's. Thano looked over to his mother and gave her warning look. She smiled at him before looking at Kilyn and then me.

"Neither of you are Greek."

"Of course," Kilyn said with a sigh as Katerina announced dessert was coming. The buffet was long gone, and I had no idea who had actually cleaned it up as we sat and ate dinner.

Turning to Nic, I asked in a whispered voice, "Why is it so important for me to be Greek?"

He shrugged. "I don't think it is honestly. Not with Kilyn being Irish and all. She's just giving you a hard time."

"Why?" I asked in a hushed voice.

Nic flashed me a panty melting smile. His dark hair was messy and he hadn't shaved in a few days. I wanted to run my fingertips over his scruff and imagine it between my legs. My cheeks heated and Nic's smile grew bigger and sexier. "What are you thinking about, Gabi?"

Sinking my teeth into my lip, I replied, "It's probably better I keep it to myself."

"So, Dad, did you get that junker car running yet?" I was pulled out of my naughty daydream by Thano. Looking his way, he leaned back and rubbed his satisfied belly.

Dimitris stood. "Junker my ass. I'll show you what I've done. Come on, dessert can wait."

All four men stood, but Kilyn and Phoebe stayed seated so I did as well. I wondered if the other Drivas men were dominating like Nic had a tendency to be. I didn't mind it at all. As a matter of fact, I found that it turned me on.

Nic leaned down and brushed his lips across the skin under my ear. My whole body shuddered and I was positive Katerina noticed. My cheeks heated.

"I'll be back baby. Don't move from this spot."

I nodded. "I won't."

He moved and pressed his lips to mine. "Good girl." The authority in his voice had me squeezing my legs together to keep the throbbing at bay.

My eyes swung up to meet Kilyn's. Thano was whispering something into her ear and I could tell she was feeling the exact same way as me.

When they walked away, she looked at me and said in a soft voice, "Kind of hot when they act all caveman, isn't it?"

I nodded and attempted not to blush again.

Katerina walked back in with Agnes and Maria. Or was that Sophia?

"Ahh. The best part of the meal, isn't that right, Gabriella?"

"It's one of my favorites," I answered.

Dish after dish after dish was placed on the table, replacing the plates of food that had been sitting there.

"Eat! Eat up!"

Phoebe and Kilyn dug in like two hungry animals that had been deprived of food. I knew if I refused, I'd be insulting Katerina, so I grabbed a small piece of a few different desserts.

Katerina pointed to each one to tell me what they were.

"That is ekmek kataifi, those are koulourakia, and this right here is Yiayia's famous phyllo pastries."

"Hmm, everything looks so delicious."

Yiayia picked up my plate and put a piece of baklava on it. "Eat. You need to fatten up for the babies."

Kilyn groaned as did Phoebe.

"Oh, Yiayia, stop that!" Katerina said with a laugh.

"Babies?" I asked in a panicked voice.

Katerina scooped more desserts onto my plate. "Kourabiedes, also known as Christmas butter cookies."

My eyes met hers as I repeated, "Babies?"

She nodded, but didn't utter a word. It was like she was letting the old lady break the news to see if I'd run or not.

Well, she had no idea who she is dealing with. My eyes caught a familiar dish.

Smiling, I reached for the dish. "Diples. My mother made something similar around Christmas time."

"She probably made these," Katerina added.

Yiayia added to the conversation. "The damn Italians. Always ripping off the Greeks."

Katerina gasped then giggled. "Yiayia! Don't be mean to our lovely Gabriella."

Yiayia waved Nic's mom off with her hand and shoved a truffle ball of some sort into her mouth.

Kilyn cleared her throat, getting my attention. "So, Thano said you were heading to Italy."

I swallowed hard. With a slight smile, I nodded. "I am."

"How exciting!" Phoebe said. "Have you been before?"

With a wider smile, I replied, "Lots of times. My family used to go every spring or early summer."

"Do you have family there?" Katerina asked as she sat down.

I froze.

Stick to the plan, Gabi. Stick. To. The. Plan.

"Distant relatives. Family that we would see very briefly on our visits. One of them still owns my parents' bakery that they left behind when they came over to the US."

"Really? Do you speak with them often?"

The lump in my throat was growing by the second.

"No. I haven't really spoken to any of them in a number of years."

"Where will you stay? I mean if you don't have close family there."

"At a hotel not far from the bakery. I grew up spending my summers there, so I know my way around pretty well."

I felt his stare before I knew he was there. Nic stood in the dining room staring at me. I didn't like the way he was looking at me. There was something dark in his eyes, and it wasn't anything sexual. It was something else. Something I'd never seen before and it sent a chill through my whole body.

"Dad wanted to know if the desserts were on the table yet."

He never took his eyes off of me as he spoke.

"He knows it is here. Tell that old fool to stop tinkering with that piece of junk car and get back in here."

Nic nodded and turned on his heels.

I let out the breath I hadn't noticed I had been holding in. A buzzing sound came from my right. Glancing down, it was Nic's phone. My heart stopped when I read the preview of the text message.

> Scarlett: You're all set with the tickets. Let me know if you need anything else. I miss

I instantly felt sick. Why was he getting a text from Scarlett? What did she miss? Him? His call? Their friendship? Their relationship?

My mind started spinning in a million directions. Every word that was said was a blur. The only thing I could think about was the text.

Nic sat back down next to me and I tried to relax. He glanced at his phone, swiped it open, frowned, and then pushed it into his pocket.

Do I let it go?

Chewing on my lip, I placed my napkin onto the plate of desserts and stood. "I'm so very sorry, but I'm not feeling well. I think I need to leave."

Everyone jumped up. Nic, his parents, both his brothers . . . even Kira. They all came rushing over to me.

"Nicholaus, take her to the couch so she can lay down," Katerina said as she led the way.

I shook my head and called out, "No."

It came out harsher than I had intended. Nic stared at me with a worried expression.

Looking into Nic's eyes, I said, "I'd like to go home. Besides, Nic has a text I'm sure he is eager to answer."

Frowning, he looked confused. "What?"

Tears formed in my eyes.

This was my payback for all the lies.

The only thing I could do was whisper, "Scarlett." Turning, I looked at both Katerina and Dimitris and said, "Thank you so very much for dinner."

Katerina walked up to me and kissed me on the cheek then hugged me tightly. Dimitris followed her lead as she said, "Of course. Of course! I hope you feel better, Gabriella."

Kira who had been playing with her cousins most of the evening came rushing up to me. "Don't leave, Gabi! I wanted to play hide and seek with you."

Kilyn walked over to me and glanced between Nic and me. "Is everything okay?" she asked while bending down and picking up her daughter.

"It's fine," I said before spinning on my heels and quickly making my way out of the Drivas house.

I needed air.

I needed to think.

twenty-six

Nic

MY HEART WAS POUNDING IN my chest. I wasn't sure if it was from hearing Gabi say she only had distant family in Italy or the fact that she had seen a text come through from Scarlett. Who in the hell was Antonio? The uncle who owns the bakery now?

I kissed my mother, Kilyn, and Phoebe goodbye. Shaking my father's hand, I ignored my two brothers and rushed out the door to follow Gabi.

She was walking as fast as she could toward my truck. Her phone was in her hand.

"Gabi."

"Don't talk to me, Nic."

"Jesus Christ, don't do this."

She stopped and faced me. Her eyes filled to the rim with tears she was fighting to keep back. "You told me there was nothing between the two of you. Yet, she is texting you. What does she miss, Nic? Your cock?"

Anger raced through my veins. "No, I asked her to do me a favor for work. She knows someone who owns a travel agency and one of the guys needed plane tickets. I asked if she could get her friend to help out."

Holy fuck. That lie came way too easy.

Gabi's face softened. The beginning of the message must have been making sense to her as she put the two together.

"What does she miss?"

Pinching my brows together, I asked, "What?"

"In her message, she said, *I miss* . . . That was all it showed."

I knew I had to tell her the truth. One, because I didn't want to lie to her any more than I was, and if she asked to see the text, she'd see that was what it said. "She said she missed me."

"Do you miss her?" she asked in a trembling voice.

Placing my hands on her arms, I looked directly into her eyes. "No. Not one bit."

Her shoulders dropped slightly and she let out the breath she had been holding.

Closing her eyes, she softly said, "I'm sorry. I don't know how much more of this I can take. I overreacted again."

I drew her in close to me. "It means you care."

Her arms wrapped around me tightly, as if this was the last time she would ever hug me. "I more than care, Nic."

My head pulled back. I wanted to ask her what she meant when she said she wasn't sure how much more she could take, but I let it go. She was probably overwhelmed by my family. "Let's go back to my place."

She smiled. "I have to work in the morning. I'm leaving the next day for Italy and there is so much to do before I go."

My gut cramped. *Who was she talking to on the phone?* "Are you looking forward to seeing anyone in particular when you go to Italy?"

Her body tensed. "Um . . . no. Why would you ask me that?"

Shrugging, I replied, "I don't know, just wondering if there was a family member or someone you were excited to see."

Gabi forced a smile. "No. It's been so long since I've been there."

I nodded. "Gabi, if there was something wrong, you'd tell me."

She swallowed hard. Her eyes searched mine and I could see she wanted to tell me.

"This trip is about letting go, Nic. There is something I need to take care of and it's . . . it's complicated."

I could easily ask her if it was Antonio she was letting go . . . but I couldn't do it. I didn't trust that she wouldn't put up a wall.

"Let's go back to your place so I can hold you in my arms tonight."

Her body relaxed and she smiled. "I think that sounds like an amazing plan."

GABI STOOD AT MY TRUCK and gave me a sweet smile. "I'll miss you."

A strange ache filled my chest.

"I'll miss you too," I said. All I really wanted to do was pull her into my arms and beg her to tell me what was going on.

Lifting my hand, I placed it on the side of her face. "I love you, Gabi."

Her eyes filled with tears as she covered my hand with hers. "I love you too."

She opened her mouth as if to say something else, but closed it.

There was no doubt in my mind, she was keeping something from me and I was hell bent on finding out what it was.

Why couldn't I just ask her? Because I was afraid of the truth.

What good would come of me following her to Italy? Nothing, and I knew that. It said I didn't trust her.

I forced out my next words. "I should probably head out."

She nodded. I hated lying to her about having to go to work.

Leaning down, I kissed her. It started off slow and sweet, but she soon had her arms around me and her body pressed against mine.

She pulled her lips back some and whispered my name.

"Nic."

Dropping my forehead to hers, I took in a deep breath.

"I'll call you when I land," she whispered.

I nodded. "Okay. If I don't answer, I'm on a call." With a sweet innocent smile, she reached up one more time. "Have a safe trip, Gabi."

She swallowed hard. "Stay safe. I love you."

My heart stilled. She said the words and I knew in my heart she meant them. I winked. "Always, and I love you too."

Climbing up into my truck, I glanced back at her. I silently pleaded with her to tell me why her eyes looked so lost. When she lifted her hand in a wave, I did the same.

When I pulled away from her place, I took my phone out and hit Liam's number.

"Hey," he said.

"Anything?"

"Listen, Nic, I think you need to let this go."

My heart jumped to my throat. "What did you find out from your friend at the FBI?"

Liam' sighed.

"This sneaking behind her back doesn't feel right, Nic."

"No fucking shit. Neither does following her to Italy. I feel like a goddamn stalker. I want more than anything to believe she isn't hiding anything, but she is. So what did he find out?"

"There's nothing he can find on a Gabi or Gabriella Mandola before six years ago."

"Nothing?"

"No. He checked the entire east coast for a five-year span on either side of her date of birth. It came back with nothing. It's like she didn't exist but up until six years ago."

"What about her social?"

Liam grew silent.

"Liam?"

He blew out a quick breath. "When he typed it in it came back with . . . classified."

My breath stalled in my chest.

"What?"

"Yeah. He'd have to get a different security clearance to get in. I'm sorry, Nic. He hit a dead end. But he did say she could be in some sort of witness protection."

I scrubbed my free hand over my face and cursed. "What in the fuck?"

Holy fucking shit. What in the hell was going on?

"Nic, I'm really sorry. He doesn't have any other information."

I sighed in frustration. "It's alright. Listen, I've got a flight to catch so I'll be out of touch for about twelve hours."

"Dude, I really wish you would rethink this. I have a bad feeling you're not going to like what you see in Italy."

I wanted to agree with him.

"I'll see you in a few days. Thanks, Liam. Appreciate all you did for me."

Hitting End, I tossed my phone on the passenger seat. I had to hustle to get to the airport in time to catch my flight. Somehow I'd managed to get on a flight that left three hours before Gabi's. I'd beat her to Italy and get my plan laid out better.

All this trouble and what was I hoping to find out?

The truth.

The only problem was; I was beginning to think the last thing I wanted to know was the truth.

THE BALL CAP WAS PULLED low on my head as I watched people embark off of Gabi's plane. When I saw her, my breath caught. She was wearing a free flowing long white dress. Her hair was down and she looked beautiful.

She also looked nervous as hell as she frantically looked around her.

Tossing my bag over my shoulder, I started to follow her, being sure to keep a good distance back as we all walked to the baggage claim. I couldn't help but notice how since she left the gate area she had kept her head down and didn't really look at anyone.

My phone buzzed in my pocket and I pulled it out.

It was from Liam asking if I had made it and how it wasn't too late to turn this around.

I closed my eyes and cursed internally. I hated not knowing what was going on. My gut was telling me something was off . . . way off . . . and I wouldn't rest until I found out what it was.

Gabi pulled out her phone and a few seconds later, mine buzzed in my hand. I sent it to voicemail. She glanced around again and then smiled. She must be listening to my message. Dropping her head, she left me a message, hung up, then waited for her luggage.

Gabi headed out of the airport with one suitcase. I'd already had Liam's FBI buddy Jim Linde arrange to meet me at the airport. He was working over here on a case and was more than willing to help me out. We'd met earlier and he was waiting outside where all the Taxi's lined up to pick people up.

When I stepped outside, I headed quickly over to his car while keeping an eye on Gabi.

Slipping in, he asked, "Is that her?"

I nodded. "Yeah."

He frowned.

"What?"

Shaking his head, he replied, "She looks really familiar that's all."

I looked at him. "Really?"

He nodded. "Yeah. I can't place it though."

Gabi slipped into a taxi and we hung back far enough so we wouldn't add any suspicion.

"What's her name?" Jim asked.

Turning to him, I answered, "Gabi Mandola. Do you think you know her?"

He shook his head. "I'm not sure. Has she been to Italy before?"

"I believe she used to come a lot with her family before her parents died when she was in high school."

Jim simply nodded. "Where is she from?"

"New Jersey."

He looked at me and narrowed his eyes. "Huh. Interesting."

What in the fuck was that supposed to mean?

"You're staying at the same hotel as her?"

"Yeah."

"How will you know when she leaves?"

I felt like such an asshole. "I put a tracker in her purse."

He laughed. "Want a job with the FBI?"

I gave him a polite chuckle. "Believe me, had you asked me that six months ago I'd probably be all over it."

"You have military training, plus you're SWAT. Trust me, we'd be all over you."

This time I turned and really looked at him. "Seriously? Did Liam tell you I was in the Marines?"

"Before I agreed to do this for Liam, I ran a background check on you."

Now I laughed. "I can't say I don't blame you. How long have you been here, in Italy?"

"Four years. I was in our New York office prior to that"

"Wow. You ready to come home yet?"

Jim let out a chuckle. "Sometimes."

He pulled back and parked on the street. "There's your hotel."

We both watched as the bellman helped Gabi with her luggage.

I jumped when Jim started talking. Shit, my nerves were shot.

"Lynn, I've got a Gabi Mandola checking into the Grand Hotel Trieste. I need the room number and a room booked as close as possible to it."

Damn FBI. I was going to owe Liam and Jim big time.

"Right. Put it under the name Nic Drivas, but I want it a private booking."

A few minutes later he was hitting End. "She's on the seventh floor, 723."

I added the information to my phone.

"You're a few rooms down. Room 718."

"Jim, I don't know how to thank you for your help."

He smiled. "Liam told me what was going on and although he doesn't agree with what you're doing, I get why you're doing it. Sometimes there are things we have to know first, before we deal with it head on."

I nodded. "Yeah. Let's hope I'm wrong."

Reaching his hand out for me, he said, "I'm not far from here. If she leaves and you want to follow, give me a call. It will take me two minutes to get here."

I shook his hand. "Thanks, Jim. I appreciate all your help."

As I made my way into the hotel, I couldn't shake the strange feeling I had. My world was about to be turned upside, and I had no idea how much so.

twenty-seven

Nic

I SAT ON THE BALCONY and stared out over the beautiful city of Padua. No wonder Gabi's family returned here every year. It was breathtaking. A part of me ached that I wasn't able to share this with her. It was my first time in Italy and it should have been spent with the woman I loved showing me where her family was from. Instead, I was hiding out in the hotel like some creeper waiting for her to leave.

As if on cue, my phone beeped. I closed my eyes and drew in a deep breath. Was I really going to do this?

Yes.

Standing, I walked back into the room and picked up my phone. I sent Jim a text and he called me back in a few seconds.

"Wait for her to leave, then come down to the front five minutes later."

I paced my hotel room for the five minutes before I finally headed down to the lobby and out to Jim's car.

Slipping into his black BMW again, I showed him my phone that was tracking Gabi.

"She's heading into Padua."

Jim hit the gas and started following the same route.

"Any idea who she is with?"

My heart dropped.

"Why? Did she leave with someone?"

"I didn't see her walk out with anyone, but a car did pull up and she got in. I got the plates and I'm having them run."

I swallowed hard while giving a slight nod. A part of me wanted to tell Jim to turn around. That none of this mattered and that I trusted Gabi with my whole heart. The other part was screaming to stay the course. That I needed to know who in the hell she was talking to on the phone. For all I knew, she could have hired a driver.

Jesus, this was insane.

"It looks like it stopped," I said.

"Address?"

I called out the address and Jim pushed a little harder on the gas.

He turned the corner and found a parking spot. "There's the car, and it looks like she's still in it."

My mouth dropped open as I stared at the Maserati. I pointed. "She got into a Maserati?"

He nodded. "And it looks like she's waiting to get out."

"Why? What is she waiting for?"

"Or who is she waiting for?" Jim added.

Glancing his way, I frowned then glanced back to the car. "This is crazy. I trust, Gabi. What the fuck am I doing?"

Jim let out a harsh laugh. "If you trusted her, Nic, you wouldn't be thousands of miles away from home sitting in my car reaching for my binoculars to get a better look."

I looked down. My hand was out stretched as I waited for him to hand me the binoculars.

"Fuck," I whispered.

He handed them to me and I could see into the car better. There was an older gentleman in the car. Gabi was facing him, her smile big and bright.

The driver's side door opened and the older guy got out.

"Money," Jim said. "Whoever this is, he has a shit ton of it. Look at how he's dressed."

I didn't answer him as I watched the guy look around. I put the binoculars down when his eyes swept our way.

"It's like he is looking to see if they were followed or if someone was watching," I said.

Looking over to Jim, I added, "He's also carrying a gun."

He smiled. "Nice observation. Who do you think he is?"

I shook my head and looked back over at the driver. "I have no fucking clue."

"They're parked outside of Giovanni's."

"You've been there?"

"Sure, lots of times. It's a nice place, one of the nicest in the city."

The driver put his finger to his ear.

"He has an ear piece in," Jim said.

I scrubbed my hands down my face. "What in the fuck is going on? Who are these people she is with?"

Pushing off the side of the car, the driver walked to the passenger side and opened the door.

The first thing I noticed was her beautiful leg, then the other. Reaching his hand out for Gabi's the guy helped her out of the car. She had on a black dress and black high heels. A coat was draped over her arm and the driver motioned to put it on her.

"Seems to me she is used to this kind of behavior. Does she come from money?"

I shrugged. "I have no fucking clue. Gabi told me her parents died when she was in high school. She owns a bakery in Colorado Springs, drives a normal car and doesn't act like she grew up with money. She doesn't talk about her past at all, so I have no idea. She told my family she doesn't have any real close family over here, so who is this guy?"

"Maybe a family friend or distant uncle. You said they came here every summer."

"Yeah, maybe. She mentioned her parents owning a bakery over here that an uncle I think runs now."

"Giovanni's isn't a bakery, I can tell you that."

Another Maserati pulled up and parked behind the one Gabi had gotten out of. Two guys got out of the front, both looked like cops.

"Know them?" I asked as I handed him the glasses.

Jim grabbed the binoculars. "What in the fuck?"

"What?" I asked.

"Yeah, I know them. They're police officers."

"From the US?"

He shook his head. "No. They're um . . . they're Padua officers. Looks like they're working part-time or undercover." He looked over at me and gave me a look that said shit just got real.

My stomach dropped. "What? W-why . . . how does she . . . fucking hell."

The one guy opened up the back door and a guy stepped out. He was dressed in a long black coat and had his back to us.

"Can you see his face?" I asked.

Jim cursed. "No, he is looking directly at Gabi."

Gabi smiled and her face lit up so bright I felt sick. Whoever this guy was, she was happy as hell to see him.

Then it happened.

She ran to him. The smile on her face clearly showed how much she longed to be in his arms.

My heart slammed against my chest when her body crashed into the stranger. Her arms swung around his neck as his wrapped her up tight. When he leaned down to kiss her, I looked away.

It felt as if someone was sitting on my chest and I couldn't breathe. *How could she do this to me?*

This is exactly why I never wanted to fall in love.

Jim was staring at me, and I couldn't take the pity in his eyes. "Another man," he said more than asked.

"Appears to be," I said, forcing myself to look back at them. Anger and betrayal swept through my body. When he spun her around in his arms and her head flew back, my throat tightened. I couldn't take looking at them. "Let's go."

"You don't want to know who he is?"

I shook my head while trying to keep my voice from cracking. I'd never felt pain grip at my chest like it was right now. How could she do this to me? How could she lie? "Does it really matter at this point?"

The knife in my heart couldn't possibly go in any deeper.

Jim pulled out and as we drove by the restaurant he slowed, they both turned and headed into it. It was like she had sensed I was there. Glancing over her shoulder, our eyes met.

Looking away, I took in a slow deep breath. "You wouldn't mind swinging by the hotel so I could get my things and then taking me to the airport would you?"

"That's it? You see her hug one guy and you're out of here?"

A cold rush of air raced across my body. "I've seen enough. It has to be Antonio."

He cleared his throat. "What? Who is Antonio?"

"The guy I heard her talking to over the phone."

Jim ran his hand through his hair. He was deep in thought.

I stared at him. "You okay?"

"What? Are you sure you want to go to the airport, Nic? There's something I need to check out."

"I'm positive. I'm ready to head home."

"Okay, well you might have a hard time getting a flight out back to the states on short notice."

I shrugged. "Then I'll wait at the airport for a flight."

It didn't matter if I had to wait at the airport all night, or for two days. I wasn't going back to that hotel so I could watch Gabi walk in with her lover.

"Nic, you and I both know things aren't always what they seem. I've got a hunch. Let me check it out."

My head dropped back against the seat. Padua zipped by as Jim navigated through the small towns in his sports car. I should have been curious about his hunch and asking him for more details. But at that moment, I couldn't have cared less. I needed to get out of this damn country. All I could see was Gabi running to that guy.

"Well, if you find anything out, you can reach me on my cell."

"Has she given you a reason to think she'd lie to you or that she was cheating?"

Lifting my head, I stared out the window. "She's been hiding something. I've known it almost from the beginning, but decided to push it aside. Pretend like I didn't have this feeling in my gut because I'd never felt this way before."

"Hard to ignore that when you're a cop, Nic."

I looked over at Jim. "That's why I started looking her up. Trying to find out more information on her and I came up with nothing, then Liam's other friend in the FBI came up with nothing. It's like she didn't exist past six years ago."

Jim's brows lifted. "Six years ago?"

All of a sudden I was overcome with exhaustion. Waving it off, I said, "None of it matters anymore." My broken heart was clouding my other thoughts and if I didn't get out of this place soon, I'd go back to that restaurant and beat the living shit out that asshole.

Pulling out my phone, I called the airline to see if I could get on another flight. I was lucky, they had one leaving in two hours with a changeover in London. I wouldn't have cared if I had to stay in London overnight. If it meant not risking seeing Gabi again then it was worth it.

I shut the car door and thanked Jim. "I really appreciate all your help, Jim. I'm just going to grab a taxi. I'm sorry you were playing chauffer to me."

He gave me a weak smile. "It was no problem. Like I said, let me check some things out. Things might not be what you think."

Laughing, I shook my head. "This is why I always stuck with the poke and go method. Teach me a lesson to never fall in love again."

I was almost positive Jim was figuring out in his head what was going on. Maybe he'd seen Gabi and Antonio together before and didn't want to hurt my feelings. Whatever it was, I didn't care.

I was done with this game.

Standing back, I watched as Jim took off and blended right in with the other cars on the street. I walked into the hotel. My phone rang and I knew it was her. Pulling it out of my pocket, I saw Gabi's name flash across the screen. I hit Ignore and headed up to my room.

The sooner I got the fuck out of Italy the better.

twenty-eight

Gabi

ANTONIO WRAPPED HIS ARM AROUND me and ushered me into Uncle Alberto's office. I tried to remain calm, but I knew it was him.

It was Nic.

"Antonio, it was Nic. I'm telling you I looked directly into his eyes."

My brother cupped my face. "Look at me, Angelo. There are two reasons that is impossible. One, Nic is not in Italy. And two, the car was moving too fast to see who was in it."

I shook my head. "It' was him. I know it was."

"Call him."

With a shaky breath, I pulled out my phone and quickly dialed.

When his voicemail picked up, I dropped my head. "He didn't answer."

"Listen, I hired those two cops out there to keep an eye on you while you're here. Plus with Lanzo watching over you and driving you around, you're going to be safe. Lanzo's been trained well. He'll know if you're being followed or not."

I nodded. I knew my brother was right. He would never put my life in danger. I was missing Nic and thought I saw him. That was all.

The door opened and both of my parents walked in. I couldn't believe how much older they looked. Unlike my brother, who hadn't appeared to age a day in his life, my parents looked to be a lot older than what they really were. The tears I had been holding back burst out and I ran into their out stretched arms.

"I've missed you. I've missed you both so much," I cried out between sobs.

Both of my parents were crying as well.

"Nothing seemed out of the ordinary?" Antonio asked.

My father shook his head as he pushed me back and took a good look at me.

"My beautiful, Gabriella. I've missed you so."

"I've missed you too, Papà. I've missed you both so very much there were times I felt like I couldn't breathe."

My mother drew me back in. She started to talk to me in Italian and I couldn't help but laugh.

"Mamma, you're talking so fast and my Italian is very rusty. I don't understand a word you're saying."

She covered her mouth before dropping her hands to her side. "I'm just so happy to see you. Come, Uncle Alberto has the back private room waiting for all of us."

I glanced around the restaurant as we walked through it. Uncle Alberto still had my parents' old bakery, but this restaurant was his baby. It was beautiful.

The moment I stepped inside I felt a calm move over me. I was home. I was with my parents and my brother, and I knew I was safe. Dante didn't know I was alive, and he certainly didn't know I was in Padua Italy.

We spent the next two hours catching up while eating. I asked about life back home. My mother showed me pictures, I asked about my best friend Linda, we cried when they told me Jack, my puppy I got in high school, had passed away, and we laughed when Antonio told a story about trying to paint my parents' house last winter. I thought I would have been sadder hearing about my old life I was missing out on. But it was the opposite.

Antonio told me a little about his job, but with him being an FBI agent he hardly ever talked about it. The most I ever saw him was during the whole mess with Dante and how he helped me to disappear after the horrible night I witnessed at Dante's.

Glasses of wine were lifted into a toast as I held mine up. After six years I felt at home and whole again. Although there was a dull ache in my heart that longed to have Nic with me. I'd tried so many times to tell him the truth over the last few weeks. I was going to enjoy my time with my family, then tell them my plan of telling Nic the truth about everything. The only way to keep us all safe is if I stayed apart from my family. For good.

The thought hurt my heart.

Pulling out my phone, I glanced down at it. I had called Nic when we landed and he texted me back about an hour later. Since I got to the restaurant I'd called once and sent him five text messages over the course of almost three hours.

Was that him I saw?

Impossible.

I pulled up his number and hit the call button. When he answered, I breathed a sigh of relief.

"Nic," I said with a smile. "I've been trying to reach you. Where are you?"

Oh gesh. Like I wouldn't know where he was.

He laughed. "Out with the guys."

His answer was short and there was a bite of anger in it. Not to mention it hurt to know he was out, but then again, wasn't I doing the same thing in a way?

"In Colorado Springs?"

He laughed. "Well, where the hell else would I be, Gabi?"

"I um, well . . . it's just. The craziest thing happened to me earlier, and I thought I saw you." He remained silent. "Nic . . . is everything okay?"

With a loud laugh, he ended it with a long groan. "Fuck, I don't know. Why don't you tell me, Gabi? You having fun?"

My mind was spinning. What had happened from the time I left to now? In one short day everything felt off.

"Have you been drinking?" I asked as I turned away from everyone. I could feel Antonio's eyes on me.

"Yes I have. You usually get shitfaced when you lose something that was important to you."

I swallowed hard. "What . . . what did you lose?"

The silence on the other end of the line had my hand coming up to my neck. It felt like I couldn't breathe. A strange feeling moved over me and I had the urge to rush back to Colorado Springs and tell Nic everything. Tell him everything I should have told him from the beginning.

"Nic? What did you lose?"

"I think you already know the answer. I need to go, Scarlett's waiting for me. Goodbye, Gabi."

A sharp intake of air filled the silence. My eyes widened in shock as I let his words rattle around in my head.

"W-what? Nic . . . wait. What is happening?"

When the line went dead, it felt like my whole world stopped.

Scarlett's waiting for me.

This wasn't happening. It couldn't be happening.

My phone dropped to the floor, and I wrapped my arms around my waist and started rocking as I called out his name.

Antonio was by my side pulling me to him. Asking me over and over what was happening. I couldn't think straight to even form words in my head.

He left me. He waited until I left and then he went to her.

Unless . . .

TWO DAYS LATER

"GABI, PLEASE STOP WITH THIS. The guy is in Colorado Springs. I already had an FBI agent check. I showed you the picture he took yesterday."

The picture.

It was of Nic and Cole sitting at a table with a few other guys at a restaurant. Antonio had found out the girl in the picture was a Scarlett Hansen. Nic's old and what I was guessing current, fuck buddy. Her and her father owned the place. It had to be the place he told me where they went and ate.

"What if that was him, Antonio, and he saw me run into your arms? He'd have had plenty of time to get back to the states."

"Or what if he is just like all the other asshole men out there and was using you for sex, Gabi. You slept with him, didn't you? Isn't that why you let your guard down?"

Anger raced through my veins. "I didn't let my guard down! I told you I didn't know they were going to take a picture of me and post it in the paper!"

He frowned. "You pulled out of the state competition, right?"

"Of course I did," I bit back.

"Still. Of all the people to date, a damn cop. What if he tried to pull you up or do a background check?"

I flopped onto the sofa and laughed. "Seriously? Paranoid much?"

His eyes lifted to mine. "It's my job to be paranoid."

Picking up my phone, I checked it again for any voicemails or texts. Nothing.

I stood and started to pace. I refused to believe that Nic would use me. When he looked into my eyes and told me he loved me, I believed him.

Antonio's phone beeped. He opened up a message and frowned.

"What? What is it?"

"Does this make it more clear?"

Walking up to him, I snatched the phone out of his hand and stared at the picture. It was Nic and another woman hugging. I couldn't see her face, but it looked like it could have been Scarlett. The last bit of hope I was clinging onto fell right alongside my tears. I never thought I'd let someone hurt me again. This was ten times worse than with Dante. I never loved him. Nic I loved with my whole heart and soul.

"I need to get out for a bit."

"And go where?"

"A walk. I need air. I'll be back later."

Antonio stood. "I'll come with you."

Shaking my head, I wiped my tears. "I need to be alone, Antonio. Please just leave me alone."

❤

I WASN'T SURE HOW LONG I walked the streets of Padua. Lanzo walked a few feet behind me, but I knew he was there. I appreciated him leaving me alone. If I even tried to speak right now I was positive I'd end up a blubbering fool.

Coming up to the river, I leaned against the fence and looked out over it. A young couple walked hand-in-hand up the sidewalk. He whispered something in her ear and she blushed. A sharp pain hit me in the chest and I had to force myself not to start crying.

"Nic," I whispered.

My phone buzzed and I looked to see it was Charity.

"Hello?"

"Hey, how is it going over there in Italy?"

With a sigh, I replied, "It could be better. How are things at home?"

"Okay."

"Just okay? How are things at the bakery?"

"They are okay," she said with a small sigh.

I needed happy news. Not bad.

"What happened?"

"Max broke the mixer. He needs you to come back right away."

I laughed. Leave it to Charity to make me smile.

"What else is new? How are things with you and Cole?"

She chuckled then said, "They're good."

Lifting a brow, I asked, "Just good?"

"Just good. Hey, Beth and Nancy said hi."

With a gasp, I covered my mouth and shook my head. "You went to knitting club."

"Yeah well, I guess I was in the mood to knit some shit."

Laughing, I let out a sigh as my sadness quickly engulfed me again. "I should have never come to Italy."

"Why?" she asked.

"I'll tell you when I get back."

"Gabi, is everything okay? You sound so sad and I know how much you were looking forward to this trip."

The hair on my body rose as a strange feeling swept over me. I quickly glanced around.

"Gabi?"

Someone was watching me.

"It's been nice, but I may be coming home early."

Lanzo's eyes met mine and I knew that look. I'd seen it before.

"Oh, okay. Um, you're sure everything is okay?"

Motioning with his head, I started to walk toward him. "Yeah. Listen, my tour is about to start. I need to run. See ya soon and I'll keep you updated."

"Sounds good. Love you!"

"Love ya back," I said before hitting End and walking next to Lanzo.

"Someone is watching me."

"Yes. I noticed the BMW the other day when it drove by the restaurant."

I stopped walking. "Were there two men in it?"

He simply nodded.

My heart was racing and fear gripped deep within my soul.

"He couldn't have found me. Could he have?"

Lanzo placed his hand on my lower back as we picked up the pace. His silence was my answer.

twenty-nine

Nic

THE FEEL OF THE GROUND hitting below my feet wasn't enough to drive out the thoughts running in my head.

Stopping, I dropped my hands to my knees and dragged in a deep breath. "Fuck," I whispered.

My phone buzzed. Pulling it out of my pocket, I saw it was Cole.

Cole: Charity said Gabi's on her way home.

I stood up. She was coming home early.

Pushing my hand through my hair, I frowned.

Me: I did something I probably shouldn't have.

Fucking hell. *Why did I mention Scarlett when I was talking to Gabi?* Hell, I knew my answer before I asked myself the question.

I was angry.

Hurt.

Drunk.

I wanted her to feel the way I felt when I saw her run into that asshole's arms.

I dragged in a deep breath. None of it mattered because the facts were the facts. Gabi lied to me. Plain and simple. I needed to accept it and move on.

My phone rang and I let out a groan.

"What?"

"Dude, don't snap my head off."

I started walking on the trail again. "Sorry, Cole."

"What did you do to mess up?"

Sighing, I replied, "It's a long story. But I can tell you this, trust is the key in a relationship. Don't forget that."

Cole had found out a few days ago about the baby. He freaked for ten minutes he said, then told Charity he would be there for both her and the baby.

"Okay. What happened, Nic? What did you do?"

"Nothing. How are things with you and Charity?"

"Nice change of subject. They're going. Every now and then I have a slight panic attack and wonder what in the fuck I'm going to do."

"You do what you promised Charity you would do. Be there for her and then be a good dad when the baby comes."

He sighed. "That's a no brainer. But what about Charity?"

"What about her?"

"I like her, Nic. I like her a lot. But this is all moving so fast."

I chuckled. "Listen, I hardly think she expects you to drop on one knee and ask her to marry you. She just needs to know that for right now, you're there supporting her."

"Yeah. But I'm confused as hell. I never in my life thought I would be happy with one woman. Then she came rushing into my world and everything is turned upside down and the thought of her not being there scares the shit out of me. What the fuck shit is that?"

My chest squeezed. I knew exactly how he felt. "Love. That shit is love."

I stopped walking when I saw the cab pull up in front of the bakery.

"Yeah. That shit is fucked up."

Nodding, I said, "Tell me about it. Did Charity mention when Gabi would be getting home?"

"This morning."

Moving behind a tree, I watched as Gabi climbed out of the cab. She looked exhausted. My heart ached, and I fought the urge to rush across the street and take her into my arms.

When she wiped her face, my world felt like it had fallen apart all over again. She'd been crying.

"Did she say how she was?"

Cole remained silent.

"Cole?"

"She only said that Gabi sounded really upset, but that she would tell her everything when she got home. Nic, what's going on?"

"Gabi was cheating on me. I got the evidence I needed, so I broke up with her."

"What? That's fucking insane, Nic. Gabi would never."

I laughed. "Yeah, well I didn't think so either, but I saw it with my own eyes. I'll tell you about it in a bit. I've got to go."

I watched as she walked over to the door that lead up to her place. She stopped and looked over her shoulder, as if looking for someone.

"Are you sure? Maybe you misunderstood something."

My breath caught when I saw the look on her face. It wasn't sadness. It was fear.

"Listen, I've got to go, my mom is due at my place soon. Like I said, I'll fill you in later."

Not waiting for his response, I hit End and looked at Gabi.

No. That was definitely fear on her face.

Utter fear.

thirty

Gabi

THE SUITCASE SAT ON MY bed as I stood there and stared at it. A part of me wanted to run again. Leave Colorado Springs and start over somewhere else. Antonio didn't waste time when I got back from my walk. He had me on a private plane heading back to Colorado Springs. I barely had time to pack up my suitcase.

Something was off, but he wasn't telling me what it was.

"Gabi? What's going on?"

Turning, I saw Charity standing in the doorway to my room.

I swallowed hard and wiped my tears away. Her eyes widened in surprise before she rushed over to me.

"Gabi, what happened?"

"He left me."

She looked at me with a confused look on her face. "Nic?"

I nodded as I let out a few sobs before saying, "I don't know what happened, Charity. He went back to Scarlett."

"Who in the hell is Scarlett?"

"Scarlett?"

My eyes swung over to see Cole standing there. "Cole, I didn't know you were here." I quickly said. Wiping my tear soaked face, I dragged in a deep breath and forced a smile.

He stepped into my room, his expression looking sad. "Nic isn't with Scarlett. And trust me when I say that he is a mess right now. He thinks you cheated on him."

I nearly stumbled back.

"W-what? Why would he think that?"

"Oh no. Damn it, Nic!" Charity said before looking back at me. "He overheard you talking on the phone. I tried to tell him you were probably talking to family in Italy and I thought he dropped it," Charity said barely above a whisper.

My mouth dropped open "Why didn't you tell me? You never said a word about it! Why wouldn't you tell me something like that?"

She chewed on her lip. "I didn't really think it was that big of a deal. And I've kind of had other things on my mind, Gabi."

I let out a gruff laugh. "Oh, really? What could possibly be on your mind that you wouldn't think to tell me Nic was questioning his trust about me?"

Cole walked over to Charity and wrapped his arms around her. It was the first time I'd actually seen them together since their hook up that one afternoon.

"I'm pregnant, Gabi."

I gasped. "What?"

She smiled slightly and I couldn't help but notice that Cole smiled even bigger.

"You're going to have a baby?"

With a light giggle, she nodded. "Yep. You're gonna be an aunt."

A million different emotions swept around me. I was happy for Charity, sad for me, angry that she didn't tell me about Nic, and confused about the small amount of jealousy I was feeling towards her. And then finally the last emotion. Fear for her and the baby's safety.

Cole cleared his throat. "Nic would kill me if he knew I told you this, but he went to Italy, Gabi. He said he had a reason to believe you were cheating on him and he said he saw it with his own eyes. That's all I know right now."

My hands came over my mouth as I tried to steady my heartbeat.

It felt like someone had punched me in the chest. Every ounce of air in my lungs was gone. I stumbled back and hit the bed. Slowly sinking to it, I whispered, "It was him. I *knew* that was him."

"Wait. Cole, why didn't you tell me Nic went to Italy?" Charity asked.

"He literally told me earlier this morning. Then he called just now and said he fucked up by lying to Gabi. That he hurt her because she hurt him."

Charity looked at me. "Gabi, you told me you weren't meeting anyone there. You said you were going to feel closer to your parents. You lied?"

Placing my hand over my stomach, I attempted not to get sick. I looked at Cole "He said on the phone he was meeting Scarlett, then I saw a picture of him hugging a woman."

Cole pinched his brows together. "He was at the airport waiting to fly out. He was pissed, Gabi. He thought you were cheating, so he said the only thing he knew to say to make you hurt the same way he was."

I felt dizzy. Everything was a misunderstanding. Nic went to Italy. It was him I saw in the car.

"Who was the guy? Who did you meet?" Charity asked me with a look of disbelief on her face.

"My brother."

She gasped as she asked, "You have a brother?"

Cole shook his head. "I knew it wasn't what he thought."

The red phone rang.

Jumping up, I rushed over to the dresser.

"Gabi! Why did you lie to us about your family?"

There wasn't time to explain anything to Charity. Something was wrong. Terribly wrong. I fumbled with the phone for a few seconds before getting it open.

"H-hello. Papá?"

The looks on Charity and Cole's face were unmistakable. The truth that I had lied to them now out in the open.

"Gabi, it's me Antonio." I could hear it in his voice. Something was very wrong.

"What's happening?" I asked.

"Dante has found you."

Fear splintered into my heart and twisted my gut as I bit back a scream.

"One of my guys spotted him in the Denver airport late last night."

I was barely able to breathe as Antonio's words sunk in.

He found me. Dante found me.

My body trembled. Dropping to the floor, I started crying. The nightmare was beginning all over again.

Charity and Cole were by my side in flash.

"How? How did he find me?"

"I'm not sure. Maybe from the picture in the paper. Or, he may have seen you in Italy."

Tears streamed down my face. I knew I should have never have gone! I knew it!

Antonio cleared his throat and kept talking. "I got a call from an old friend of mine in the FBI. His name is Jim."

I somehow must have turned the speaker on because Antonio's voice was filling my room. I didn't care though. All I could think about was Dante finding me here with Charity.

Oh my God. The baby.

"I worked with him in the New York office when everything took place with Dante. He saw you in Italy."

Sucking in a breath, I waited for what was coming next. A part of me already knew what Antonio would say.

"Nic was there, Gabi. I'm so sorry I didn't believe you. He followed you to Italy because he thought you were meeting a man there. From what Jim told me Nic had a feeling you had been hiding something from him and was having someone at the FBI try to find out more information on you."

My eyes widened as I sat there shocked. Nic was having the FBI check up on me?

"He had reason to believe you were meeting a man in Italy so he followed you there. When he saw us, his suspicions were confirmed and Jim said Nic left for the airport right away. Jim said Nic was really upset."

My arm wrapped around my stomach in an attempt to hold the bile down.

"But Jim came back to the restaurant a few times because he said he couldn't shake the feeling he had seen you before. He thought he recognized you the first day they followed you to the restaurant. Then, Nic mentioned my name and Jim started to dig around a bit. Yesterday, when you were here saying goodbye to everyone, he saw me walking you out to the car and put two and two together. It didn't take him long to figure out I set everything up to fake your death and that you had been in hiding."

Charity fell back on her ass and covered her mouth. I reached for her hand and she took it. Her eyes were filled with nothing but questions.

"If he figured it out then Dante could as well," I barely said.

"I don't think he had any of his guys in Italy. I've been watching for four years, Gabi. But it's like Jim said, we slipped and got careless. If Dante did have someone watching the place, they would have seen you."

A chill moved through my veins and I was instantly taken back to the night that changed my life.

I squeezed my eyes closed, trying not to see the blood.

All the blood.

Dante knew I was alive, and I was positive he knew where I was.

When I opened my eyes, Charity was staring at me. Her confusion replaced with fear. "When I got home, it felt like someone was watching me. He knows where I am, Antonio. He knows."

"You have to get out of there now. You know where the closest safe house is I set up, right?"

"Y-yes."

Cole reached for the phone.

"Antonio, this is Cole Night. I work for Colorado Springs Police Department and Nic is my best friend. What do you need us to do?"

The line went dead.

"Hello?"

"He won't talk to you, Cole. He's going to be furious with me that you heard any of that."

Standing, I quickly rushed into my closet and grabbed another suitcase. Turning to Charity, I covered my mouth with my hands then dropped them to my sides.

"Oh, my God. I've put you and the baby in danger."

Cole walked up to me and placed his hands on my shoulders. "Gabi, look at me."

My eyes lifted to his, but I could hardly see through my tears welling up in them.

"I have to leave, Cole. Now."

"Let me call, Nic."

"NO!" I screamed, causing Charity to jump.

Shaking my head, I looked at him with pleading eyes. "You can't tell him, Cole. Please you can't tell him. If you do, he'll come searching for me and Dante will have him followed. He probably already knows of my relationship with Nic. Please don't put his life in danger."

"You want him to think you're really cheating? Gabi, it will destroy him."

Reaching for Charity's hands, I tried to smile. "I'll make sure my brother has someone watching the place. You and the baby will be safe. I promise."

Glancing back to Cole, I added, "You can't tell him the truth, Cole. He'll try to find me!"

The look on Charity's face was utter confusion. "Wait. Gabi, what in the hell is going on? You're in hiding?"

"Yes. I have been for six years."

"Oh my God. Why?"

My chest stuttered. "I want to tell you everything, but I can't. I have to leave. Now!"

Charity and Cole stood there and watched me frantically pack. I took only the things I needed. Rushing back to the closet, I reached up and found the bag I had stashed up there.

"What's in that bag?" Charity asked.

Without looking at her, I simply said, "Money to start over somewhere else."

"Jesus Christ! Gabi! This is insane," Charity said. "Stop for five minutes and talk to me. It's the least you could do."

Zipping up my bag, I inhaled a deep breath while brushing my tears to the side.

Slowly turning to face Charity and Cole, I said, "I can't tell you. The less you know the better. Please just know I'm so sorry I put your life in danger. I got careless and slipped up. I should have never have gone out with Nic, or did that stupid cooking competition, or went back to Italy." Rubbing my hands over my arms, I added in a whispered voice, "I should have known Dante would never stop looking."

"What about the bakery?" Charity asked.

"In the office safe is an envelope marked with the words *secret recipes*. It's paperwork that states the bakery is yours should anything like this ever happen. I had planned on writing you a note if I ever had to leave."

She laughed. "A note? A note that said what exactly?"

"That I had to leave and that the bakery was now yours."

Tears filled her eyes. "So you would have left without saying goodbye or telling me any of this?"

I slowly nodded. My eyes pierced hers and I would have done anything to take the hurt away.

When I looked over at Cole, I forced a smile. "Will you please let Nic at least know that I wasn't cheating on him? That it was my brother he saw me with. But please don't' tell him anything else."

He shook his head. "If you think I'm not going to tell Nic about this, you're insane. I already sent him a text. If anyone can keep you safe, it's Nic."

Horror spread over my face. "What?"

"He loves you, Gabi. He'll do whatever he can to protect you."

My body started to tremble. "I have to leave."

"No, Gabi please don't leave," Charity begged.

"Gabi, wait," Cole said with a panicked look on his face.

If he sent Nic a text, that was another life in danger because of me.

Pushing past both of them, I rushed to the door. "Please let me go! You have to for your own safety," I cried out as I threw the door open and rushed into the hall with the small bag I had packed. "It's for the best that I leave now."

The air surrounding me suddenly changed. I came to a stop when I saw him standing there.

I dropped everything and covered my mouth with my hands.

He stood there looking directly into my eyes. All I could see in them was love. How could I have ever doubted him? Not trusted him? Before

I had a chance to move, he was in front of me, pulling me into his arms.

"You're not going anywhere, Gabi."

Hope fluttered inside of me. Burying my face into his chest, I sobbed uncontrollably as Nic's love covered me in a protective blanket.

thirty-one

MOMENTS EARLIER . . .

Nic

MY MOTHER WALKED SILENTLY NEXT to me after I told her about me and Gabi.

"I thought you would be happy," I mumbled.

"What! Why would you think I would be happy, Nicholaus?"

I laughed. "Oh, let me see what reasons I can come up with. One, she isn't Greek."

My mother held up her hand. "That's not true. She is three percent Greek."

"What? How do you know that?"

She grinned. "Don't be mad, but I had a DNA test done."

Narrowing my eyes at her, I asked, "How in the hell did you get her DNA?"

"I have my ways."

"Who did the test for you?"

Her brow lifted. "You're not the only cop I know, son."

My head cocked to the side. "Who are you and where has my mama gone?"

"What happened?"

"I opened my heart up like a fool." Her smile dropped.

Wrapping her arm in mine, we walked down the street toward my house I had closed on recently. Gabi had been so excited I would be living so close to her. Now, I hated being so close to Gabi's bakery. The idea that she was so near to me tormented my mind.

"Opening your heart to someone doesn't make you a fool, Nicholaus."

I inhaled a deep breath. "I did something I regret."

My mother stopped walking and turned to me. "Am I going to be smacking you after you tell me?"

A light rumble came from my chest. "Probably."

She motioned for me to talk.

"I purposely hurt Gabi because she hurt me."

Glaring at me, she drew her hand back and punched me square in the chest, causing me to stumble back.

"What the hell?"

Her hand came up and slapped me on the back of the head.

"Jesus Chr—"

Her eyes went dark.

"Why are you hitting me?"

"Because you're stupid."

Dropping my mouth open, I stared at her. "How do you know Gabi wasn't being the stupid one?"

"Because she is a tormented soul. You can see it in her eyes. She harbors a secret, Nicholaus."

I laughed while rubbing my chest. "Yeah. Her lover in Italy."

"I don't believe that for one second. I've seen the way that girl looks at you."

Before I had a chance to say anything else, my phone rang. I narrowed my eyes at the number.

"Hello?"

"Nic, it's Jim Linde, FBI in Italy."

"Yeah, right of course."

He sighed, "Listen, do you have a minute?"

Glancing over to my mother, I motioned for her to head up the steps to the house. "I'll be right in, Mama. I need to take this call."

She nodded her head and entered the house.

"Is the FBI that hard up for guys you're cold calling now?"

He laughed. "No, I wish it was that, but this is more important. It's about Gabi."

My heart dropped. I knew she was safe, I'd seen her arrive home today. "What about her?"

"Are you sitting?"

Fuck.

"Do I need to be?"

"Probably."

I sat on the steps of my house. "All right. Go."

I heard a door shut and footsteps before hearing another door shut.

"Listen, what I'm about to tell you is highly classified. I'm actually putting your life and your family's life in danger if I keep talking. Do you want me to continue?"

What in the fuck?

"And this had to do with Gabi? Gabi Mandola?"

"Yes."

Rubbing the back of my neck, I looked around. "Tell me."

"All right, first her name isn't Gabi Mandola. It's Gabriella Rossi. She is the daughter of an extremely wealthy Italian immigrant. Her brother, Antonio, is an undercover FBI agent."

I sat there numb while I tried to process everything that Jim was saying.

"Wait. Antonio is her brother?"

"Yes. That was the man she ran to in Italy and hugged. She hadn't seen him or her family for six years. Not since her brother had secretly arranged for her death . . . or pretend death I should say."

Everything started to sway as I tried to regain my balance.

Fuck, I'm sitting down not standing.

I closed my eyes and took in a few deep breaths. "Wait. You're throwing some serious shit my way with no explanations."

"Eight years ago, Antonio and I were undercover in New Jersey. We were working to bring down Marco Du Luca, an Italian mob boss. In the process, Antonio and I befriended the guy's son, who we didn't think was a part of the mob. His name was Dante De Luca. He hung around with us, did everything with us. So much so, I was beginning to have my suspicions that he was undercover himself. One night, he met Gabi. He really took to her and they started dating. I never got the feeling Gabi was as into Dante as he was to her. He asked her to marry him and she was going to tell him no, but Antonio ended up telling her about the opt. He needed Gabi to get closer to the family so we could bust them."

My stomach turned. "He used his sister to get closer into a mob family?"

"Believe me, he hated himself then and even more when Gabi witnessed Dante killing his own father."

It felt like I hit a brick wall.

"What?"

"Yeah, she of course freaked and immediately told Dante she wouldn't have anything to do with this life. He threatened her. Told her if she ever left, he'd kill her."

"And where in the fuck were you and her brother when all this went down?"

"About to bust a drug deal Dante's father had set up for that night. This was the deal we had been waiting for. The one that was going to take the family down. Gabi had called Antonio freaking out. He left right before the bust went down, so Dante never did find out that Antonio was FBI because he wasn't there when it all went down. News spread quickly that Marco had killed himself. That he didn't want to spend the rest of his life in jail. The body though was never found."

I sat there stunned. Listening to Jim speak.

"Two days later, I got a call from Antonio saying his sister had died in a car accident. I had no idea she had witnessed the murder, fuck I had no idea about the murder until Antonio had told me. He didn't trust the FBI with his sister, and he certainly didn't trust Dante. The guy is a nut case. He wanted his father dead so he could have control of the family."

"It was staged? Her death was staged?" I asked.

"Yes, but at the time I didn't know it was. Antonio did it all on his own without the FBI's help. He felt like he couldn't trust anyone."

"Not even you? His partner?"

Jim laughed. "If that had been my sister, I wouldn't have told him. Anyway, once I started to piece it all together, I went to Antonio in Italy. Told him I had seen Gabi and that you had been in Italy. That's when he told me the truth. That Gabi was alive. I told him if I had put two and two together, it wouldn't take long for Dante's guys to figure it out. Antonio put someone on Gabi when she left Italy and Antonio's had someone planted in with Dante the last six years. Dante's in Colorado. He's coming after Gabi."

I dropped my head and scrubbed my hand down my face. "Son of a bitch."

"Yeah. I'm not convinced they saw her in Italy though and neither is Antonio."

"Why?"

"Dante is a smart guy. I don't doubt that he hasn't believed that Gabi has been dead all this time, but he isn't a very trusting guy. I'd bet a year's paycheck he's been scanning all the major newspapers still for Gabi to slip up."

The cooking competition.

"Oh holy shit. The cooking competition. They put her picture in the Denver paper."

"That's what Antonio thinks. Anyway, he was contacting Gabi and telling her to move on to the closest safe house."

I shook my head, trying to make sense of the massive information Jim had just laid out on me. Then it hit me.

"Dante's here in Colorado?"

"Yes. And he knows her name, Nic. Antonio has someone following her."

"Why are you telling me this, Jim?"

He paused before answering. "I saw the way you looked at her that day and I knew you were destroyed thinking she was cheating. I didn't want you to go the rest of your life wondering what happened. If Gabi leaves, you'll never see her again."

Standing, I attempted to calm my heart down. It was pounding in my chest.

"Then I better make sure I get to her before she leaves."

"Hey, Nic. Can ask one favor of you."

"Anything," I said as I raced into my house.

"You didn't get any of this information from me. Right?"

With a grin, I put my side arm holster on. My mother stood there staring at me as I checked my gun and slipped it into the holster.

"What information?"

Jim chuckled. "If you ever want a job . . ."

"I'm actually pretty damn happy where I am."

"I thought so. Take care and please, don't try to be the hero. Dante De Luca isn't someone to mess around with."

I smiled. "Neither am I, Jim. Neither am I."

thirty-two

Nic

AFTER HANGING UP WITH JIM. I got a text from Cole.

Cole: Nic, I need you at Gabi's place. STAT

I could run to Gabi's place faster than I could drive, so that's what I was going to do.

"Mama, I need to get over to Gabi's."

The look on her face told me she knew something was wrong.

"What is happening, Nicholaus?"

Kissing her on the cheek, I grabbed my other phone for work. Just in case.

"I can't go into it right now, Mama. I'll call you later."

"Is Gabriella okay?"

Stopping, I turned back to look at her. "I really hope so."

She nodded. "Then go to her. Be careful, son. I love you."

"I love you too, Mama."

Racing down the street, I said a prayer I wasn't too late.

I hit reply on Cole's text and tried to type the best I could as I ran.

Me: I'm on my way.

Antonio had a guy on Gabi, so I knew the moment I got to her place he would alert her brother. Fine by me. I had no fucking intentions of letting the woman I loved leave me. Her days of running were over if I had anything to say about it.

A half a block away from her place, I dropped my jog down to a walk. I didn't want to bring attention to myself or alert Dante's people of anything.

Lifting my phone, I pretended to be on it, but what I was really doing was trying to look around. I saw a black car parked on a side road. It had a perfect view of Gabi's bakery. There was no way that was the FBI guy. He wouldn't be that obvious.

No. That was Dante's thugs probably. Lifting my phone from my ear, I called Liam.

"I need a favor."

"You're going to owe me a shit ton of them, do you know that?"

"I know. Listen there's a car parked on Twenty-fifth just up from Colorado Ave. I'm pretty sure it's the mob."

Liam chuckled, then grew quiet. "Wait, are you being serious right now?"

"Never been more serious."

"Does this have anything to do with Gabi?"

"Yes, and I'll tell you when I can."

He let out a groan. "Fuck. All right, I'm on it."

Crossing the street, I made my way around the building. I was going in the back, which I knew meant the guy Antonio had on Gabi would know I was there.

Rushing up the steps, I stopped when I saw Gabi coming out of her place with a suitcase.

"It's for the best that I leave now."

Cole was on her heels and they both stopped when they saw me.

Gabi gasped and dropped her things. Covering her hands with her mouth, I knew she was trying to hold back her emotions, just like I was. So many things had happened over the last few days. The last time we spoke I said things I regretted. The pain and confusion I had felt hours ago vanished looking at the fear in her eyes.

We stood there for a few moments staring into each other's eyes before I made my way over to her.

I pulled her into my arms. "You're not going anywhere, Gabi."

Her body instantly melted into mine as she buried her face in my chest and cried. I was practically shaking at the idea of her taking off all on her own.

Lifting my eyes to Cole, I said, "There was a black car parked on Twenty-fifth. See if a black and white is there with it."

He nodded and quickly made his way back inside Gabi and Charity's place.

"I'm so sorry," Gabi sobbed. "I wanted to tell you the truth, but I was so afraid."

Cupping her face in my hands, I kissed her lips and softly said, "It's okay, agapimé. I'm here now."

She shook her head as tears streamed down her cheeks. "You don't understand, Nic. I have someone after me. He's dangerous and I'm putting all of your lives at risk."

I kissed her again. Her arms wrapped around my neck as she held onto me as if her life depended on it.

"Let's go back inside, Gabi."

Drawing back, her eyes widened in horror. "Nic, I have to leave. I can't tell you why, but—"

"I know everything, Gabi. I know Antonio is your brother, I know about Dante. I know everything."

"W-what? How?"

"It doesn't matter, all that matters is keeping you safe, let's go back inside."

Gabi shook her head, her body trembling in fear.

"I wanted to tell you so many times! I couldn't betray my family or risk putting you and them in danger."

My arm wrapped around her as I reached for her bag and handed it to Charity. "Let's go back in and figure all of this out."

When we walked in, I looked over at Cole. He motioned to the balcony. "Things are getting interesting."

"How so?" I asked.

"There is more than just one black and white. If I had to guess, I'd say FBI is there as well."

I walked over to the sofa and sat Gabi down on it. Charity instantly sat next to her and wrapped her arm around her.

"What's going on?" Gabi asked.

"Hang tight, baby."

Taking out my phone, I called Liam. "Talk to me."

"Turns out you weren't the only one interested in that car. When I called it in, the Feds must have heard it. Drake Handley said when he pulled up behind the car, it was instantly surrounded by FBI agents."

My heart started pounding as I stepped out onto the balcony. "Any word from your friend over there?"

"I've got a call in, waiting to hear back."

One of the feds walked up to the guy thrown over the hood of the car and said something to him that caused him to look directly up at me and Cole.

"That's him," I mumbled.

"Who?" Cole asked.

Turning to look at Cole, I said, "Dante."

His eyes widened in shock as he leaned in closer to me and asked, "How do you know?"

Forcing my eyes back to the asshole who was now being cuffed, I slowly shook my head and shrugged.

"Call it a gut feeling. But I think I know the person who knows for sure."

The fed watched as they walked Dante and two other men to the back of a black SUV. He then turned and looked up at me.

"Antonio," I whispered.

thirty-three

Gabi

*E*VERYTHING WAS SPINNING. NIC WAS here. Dante was coming after me. I needed to get to the next safe house.

I turned to look at Charity. She was my best friend. Like a sister to me and I had to leave her. If I didn't, I'd be putting her and her unborn child in danger.

"Why didn't you just testify against Dante, put his ass in jail?"

I swallowed hard. Shaking my head, I knew I shouldn't even be still here, let alone talking to Charity about this.

"The first person I told was Antonio. He was working undercover to take the family down. By the time Antonio had gotten to where it happened, everything had been cleaned up, the body moved. He had no proof Dante had killed his father. It was my word against his."

Wrapping my arms around my body, I glanced out onto the balcony. "Dante threatened me and said if I told anyone, he was going to kill me and my family."

"That had to have been terrible."

Nodding, I whispered, "It was. The FBI promised protection, but Antonio decided it would be safer if he faked my death and only my father and he were in on it. They didn't tell my mother right away because they needed her to act like her only daughter had just died."

Charity gasped.

"The last six years my brother has been waiting for Dante to screw up. And Lucas would be there to get it all."

"Whose Lucas?"

I was telling Charity way too much information, but God it felt good to get it all out.

"Lucas was the inside guy Antonio had planted with Dante. Not FBI, an old friend of his that pretty much buried himself into the family as a payback for my brother saving his life. He was there waiting for Dante to slip up."

"Holy shit. This feels like a damn movie."

With a soft laugh, I stood. "Yeah. A horror movie."

Nic and Cole were both looking down at something going on.

"What are they doing out there?"

"Nic mentioned something about a car sitting out there." She took me by the arms and faced me to her.

"Let me make you something to drink or eat."

Frantically shaking my head, I replied, "I have to go, Charity. If I don't leave soon . . . something . . . something terrible could happen." My voice cracked.

Strong arms wrapped around my body.

"Nothing is going to happen," Nic whispered in my ear.

My head dropped back to his chest. Oh, how I wanted to believe him.

"I'll make something to eat for us all," Charity said as she glanced over to Cole.

"You don't understand, I have to leave before . . ."

The knock on the door had us all frozen in place. Nic placed his finger on my chin. "Baby, breathe. I think it's just going to be your brother."

My brows furrowed. "What?"

Nic motioned for Cole to come stand next to me. Cole grabbed Charity's hand and pulled her with him as he stood in front of both of us. My head peeked around his body as I watched Nic head toward the door. My breath caught in my throat.

He looked out first, then reached for the door handle.

The pounding of my heart in my chest was almost unbearable. "Nic! Don't!" I cried out.

My knees almost buckled when I saw my brother standing in the doorway.

"Antonio?" I gasped.

His eyes found mine.

"Gabi, are you okay?"

Rushing around Cole, I ran to my brother. "What's going on? Why are you here? What's happening?"

Antonio laughed then wrapped his arm around me. "Christ, Gabi. Catch your breath and invite your brother into your house."

I stared at him like he had grown two heads. "Not more than an hour ago you were telling me to leave. Now you want me to show you the place?"

He nodded. "Yes. But first, I think you need to introduce me to someone."

All I could do was stand there and look at him. He finally took me by my arms and said, "Gabi, it's over. Dante will never hurt you."

The air left my lungs and I had to reach for his arms to steady myself. "What do you mean it's over?"

His eyes swung over to Nic, then back to me.

"Let's sit down. I'll explain everything."

I SAT WITH MY HAND in Nic's as Antonio explained everything to me. How Lucas had alerted him to Dante finding my picture in the Denver paper and how Dante had been having someone follow me since he found out where I was. He even knew I went to Italy. Lucas had secretly recorded Dante's plan to kidnap me.

My entire body shuddered.

"Is that why you had so much security in Italy? You thought he'd show up?"

He nodded. "I knew I was risking things, but it was the only way to get Dante to come to you."

My stomach churned as a wave of nausea hit me. "Come to *me*? You *wanted* him to find me?"

"Once I found out Dante had found you and was crafting a plan, I went to the FBI and got them involved."

My mouth dropped open. "You said you couldn't trust anyone in the FBI. That's why you came up with this whole plan to keep me away."

"The plans changed. I needed them. Needless to say, they weren't very happy with me not bringing you to them immediately, but I pleaded my case. Brother worried about his sister . . . I played that card."

Numb. My entire body was numb as I sat there and listened to my brother. I drew in a shaky breath and waited for him to keep talking.

Pushing his hand through his hair, he closed his eyes then looked back at me. "The FBI had been watching you since your picture went into the paper."

"What?" The pounding in my head was getting louder. The ache growing stronger. "You've had the FBI watching me? And you said nothing!"

I'd never been so angry with my brother in my entire life.

"I know, Gabi. I know you're angry with me. I needed you to believe that you were safe. That everything was good. If for any reason I would have thought your life was in danger, I'd have gotten you out. But Lucas gained Dante's trust a few years back and has been his number two guy. Dante just started talking more and more, I needed to make sure everything we got down was done legally. I needed him to confess about his father's murder and the only way to do that was with him finding you. That picture was actually a good thing. Once Dante saw it, he started spewing out everything about his father's murder."

I dropped Nic's hand. My fingers came up to my temples were I massaged them gently. "So you knew Dante had found me weeks ago, and you said nothing. How could you do that to me?"

"I knew Nic was around and he was a cop. I really felt like you were safe. Plus the FBI has been watching you."

Standing, I pointed to Antonio. My entire body shook with anger. "You used me as a damn pawn, Antonio! Again! And to make matters worse, you put the lives of people I love in danger."

His eyes turned sad.

"I did what I thought was right, and in the end it all worked out."

"How do you figure?" I shouted.

Antonio looked over to Nic. "Does she know about Jim?"

Swinging my head over to Nic, I asked, "Jim? Who is Jim?"

Nic groaned. "Jesus, this is starting to get overwhelming, Antonio."

"Angelo, sit down."

"NO! I'm not sitting down. Jim, Lucas, FBI agents. Was I the only one who didn't know what was going on?" I spun around and looked at Nic. "And when did you find all of this out?"

"About thirty minutes ago."

My body relaxed. "Oh."

Nic stood and took my hands in his. "Let's let Antonio finish and then you and I will talk."

When my eyes caught Charity's I smiled weakly. "I'll take that drink now."

thirty-four

Nic

WE ALL SAT AND LISTENED to Antonio explain how once Jim had notified him about figuring out that the girl I had gone to Italy to follow was Gabi, he had used me to help out in their plan to get Dante.

"So you told Jim to call me and pretend like he was giving me this info without you knowing. Why?"

"Because if my hunch about how much you loved my sister was right, I needed you to know the truth. I needed you to go to her. What I was really wasn't banking on was that you would be smart enough to look for Dante's men. So when you had your friend call a black and white to the scene, I knew we had to rush in and grab him."

"You knew he was there?"

"Yes. Lucas was in the car recording everything. Dante knew we had figured out he was on to Gabi. He was waiting for her to leave because he knew I would tell her to go to the next safe house. What he didn't know was that we knew he knew."

"My God. I'm so flipping confused," Charity said with a sigh.

I shook my head. "So wait, you told Gabi to leave because you *wanted* Dante to try to get her?"

"Yes. We were there as well. Waiting for when it happened. So in a way, you seeing the car kind of fucked up the plan."

I cringed. "Sorry."

Antonio laughed. "It's okay, because with you being there . . . going to Gabi, it pissed Dante off. He sort of lost it in the car and started talking about the night he shot his father. He confessed to everything and we got it all. When we intercepted the call for the black and white, we had to move in a bit earlier. It would have been nice to have attempted kidnapping, but we do have him talking about the plan to do it so hopefully that, along with his murder confession, will be enough to put his ass in jail for the rest of his life."

"But you got his confession on tape? Is this all over? Do I have to keep hiding?" Gabi asked.

"Yes. It's over, Gabi. He'll never be a threat to you again. Under Dante's leadership the family has fallen apart and no one is loyal to him. Truth be told, they'll probably be happy to see him sent to jail."

She covered her mouth as a loud sob slipped out. "I can go back to being me? No more lies? No more running?"

I could see the devastation on Antonio's face. He hated that his sister had been running scared for so long. "No more running, Angelo. It's over."

Gabi's body melted into mine. It didn't take her long before she broke down in another round of crying.

Glancing up, I looked at Cole. He lifted his brows and mouthed, holy shit.

I drew Gabi closer to my body and nodded. My attention then focused on her brother. I wasn't sure if I wanted to hit the asshole or shake his hand. Right now, I was leaning toward hitting him.

CHARITY WALKED OUT ONTO THE balcony and handed me a cup of coffee.

"She still asleep?"

I nodded and took a drink. "Yeah. I'm sure she is emotionally exhausted."

Chewing on her lip, she looked away from me. "It's not really over, is it?"

Blowing out a deep breath, I replied, "No. She'll have to testify."

"So all that running, the lies, it was all for nothing?"

I smiled. "I wouldn't say that. If she hadn't gone on the run, we'd have never have had her come into our lives. Plus, like Antonio said, no one is loyal to Dante. Even if he tried to put a hit out on Gabi, he wouldn't find anyone to do it."

Charity sighed. "That's true. She wouldn't have been brought into our lives and I wouldn't be debating on what baby blanket to knit in our Knitters are Purls club."

With a laugh, I sat down next to her. "Crazy last few months, huh?"

She stared straight ahead. "Yeah. Crazy."

"Cole handling the baby okay?"

Charity turned to me and winked. "You would know better than me, you're his best friend."

I smiled as she continued on.

"At first I think he was freaked. Then with everything that happened yesterday with Gabi, I noticed he never left my side. He stayed last night and it was probably the most amazing night yet."

I lifted my hand. "Spare me the details or I may throw up in my mouth."

She giggled. "No, it's nothing like that. We stayed up most of the night talking."

"Talking, huh? Doesn't sound like the Cole I know and love."

I got another chuckle from her. "I don't know who else to say this to, so you're the lucky one again."

"Hit me," I said.

She looked into her cup nervously. I already knew what was coming, but knew she needed to say it out loud to someone else before she even thought of saying it to Cole.

"I'm in love with Cole. And I'm so scared because what I feel for him is unlike anything I've ever felt before. I knew he was a player that day I hooked up with him. But something happened when we were together and maybe it was the baby. I don't know. I don't want to pressure him or scare him, but I feel like I need to be honest with him about how I feel."

I reached for her hand. "I think if we learned anything over the last few days, it's that honesty is the way to go."

"Yeah," she whispered. "But it's scary. If I tell Cole I love him, I may be pushing him away."

"Or pulling me closer."

Charity and I both turned to see Cole standing there. A huge smile was spread over his face. My heart never felt so happy as it did seeing my best friend standing there with that goofy-ass look on his face that said *I'm head over heels in love.*

"I thought you left!" Charity said as she stood up.

Cole walked up to her, took her coffee cup and handed it to me. Reaching down, he picked up Charity and headed back into the house and to her bedroom.

"Make sure you remember we're here!" I shouted out to them.

Gabi walked around the corner grinning. "Well, I see those two are really bonding."

I nodded. "Cole overheard Charity telling me she loved him."

Stopping, Gabi's mouth dropped open. "What?"

My eyes scanned her body from top to bottom. She was wearing a white flowing skirt and a yellow top. Her blonde hair was pulled up into two pigtails and she had not an ounce of makeup on.

She was the most beautiful woman I'd ever laid eyes on.

I stood. Cupping her face in my hands, I looked deep into her eyes. "I'm so sorry, agapiméni. I should have trusted you."

Her eyes glistened. "I should have trusted you with the truth. I was so scared and confused."

Brushing my lips across her cheek, I took in a deep breath. "The thought of losing you . . . it destroyed me."

"Nic," she whispered as she leaned back and captured my gaze. "You'll never lose me."

"And you'll never lose me. I promise."

When she smiled, I knew everything would be okay. But first, we had a bit of additional making up to do.

Taking her hand, I said, "We're going to my house."

Her eyes lit up as she lifted her brows. "I like that plan."

Grabbing her hand, I practically dragged her back into the house. Quickly getting my phone and wallet, I pulled her out the door, down the stairs, and to her car.

"We can walk ya know."

I laughed. "No, because if I don't get what I want soon, I'll end up fucking you in someone's front yard."

Gabi laughed. "That would probably be bad for my business."

Making it to my house in record time, I parked Gabi's car out front. I couldn't focus on anything. The only thing I could think about was my cock inside her warm pussy. And it was driving me fucking nuts. I just wanted to forget the last few days. This last week.

Opening the passenger side door, I took her hand in mine and nearly jerked her up the steps to my house.

"Nic!" she said with a giggle. "Where is the fire?"

"In my damn pants."

Gabi giggled. "I've missed you."

Unlocking the door, I slid my hand behind her neck and pulled her lips to mine. I kissed her like I'd never kissed her before. The soft moan rushed through my body and made my dick harder than ever before.

She reached for and found the door handle, opening the door. We stumbled in, nearly falling over boxes in the process.

"Nic," Gabi said as she tried to pull my shirt over my head.

Breaking our kiss long enough to pull our shirts off, we both tossed them to the floor and slammed our mouths together again. My hand was up her skirt, pushing her lace panties to the side.

"I need you now, Gabi. I'm sorry. I need my cock buried in your . . ."

A voice cleared from behind us and everything instantly came to a stop.

Looking past Gabi's shoulder, I saw my mother standing there.

Holy fuck. I just said I needed to have my cock buried in Gabi and my mother heard it.

"Please . . . *please* tell me it's not your mom," Gabi whispered as I looked back down at her.

"Um," was all I could get out as I looked back up. Aunt Maria, Aunt Agnes, and cousin Sophia were all standing there now, smiling.

"I see you two made up. Wonderful! Get dressed and let's eat, we'll have a celebration!"

"Opa!" the other's all cried out.

Gabi's eyes widened in horror at the sound of more than one person shouting out. "Oh. My. God. There are more people here?"

I nodded. "This is my family, Gabi. There is always more than one person."

Her head dropped to my chest. I thought she was crying when her body started to shake, but when I lifted her chin to look at me, she was laughing.

"Are you ready?" I asked.

She shook her head and let out another chuckle before asking, "Ready for what?"

"To spend the rest of your life in this crazy-ass Greek family of mine."

Her smile dropped and tears quickly filled her eyes.

She looked so damn cute when she nodded. "There's nothing I want more in this life than to deal with your crazy-ass Greek family."

Leaning down, I brushed my lips across hers. "Good."

Gabi and I quickly pulled our shirts back on. Before walking into the kitchen where everyone was, I pulled Gabi to a stop.

"There is one little thing I do have to tell you about."

Her brows pulled together with a concerned look. "Besides that your mother overheard you just now."

I groaned. "Yes, besides that."

"Okay, what is it?"

"My mother kind of did something insane. Like *really* insane."

Gabi stared at me. "What did she do?"

"She took your hair and had a DNA test done to see if you had any Greek in you."

It was like she was staring straight through me she was so stunned. "Gabi? Hey, are you okay?"

Waving my hand in front of her face, she didn't even blink.

"Gabi, she didn't mean any harm. Hey, talk to me, prinkipissa."

Her eyes lifted to mine. "Oh. Oh. I know *exactly* when she got my hair sample!"

"You do?" I asked with a shocked voice.

She laughed then looked at me with those beautiful blue eyes and asked, "What did the results say?"

I jerked my head back. "Huh?"

"The results. What did it say?"

"You're not mad?"

With a shrug, she answered. "I mean, I'm not going to say that I don't find it a little odd, but then again, I don't find it strange at all. It's weird."

I laughed. "It said you were three percent Greek."

Gabi covered her mouth and chuckled. "No way!"

Nodding, I said, "It did."

She laughed. "Nick, that is impossible. I've done my family tree back for hundreds of years. I'm full-blown Italian."

He winked. "Let's just let her believe." I wrapped my arm around her shoulders and guided her into the kitchen.

"She's going to expect me to fall in love with Greek food now."

I tossed my head back and let out a roar of laughter before I said, "Hell, she's going to expect you to give up Italian cooking for Greek."

Moaning, she dropped her head against my shoulder.

"Welcome to the family, baby."

thirty-five

FOUR MONTHS LATER

Gabi

WHAT DO YOU MEAN YOU'RE making Irish desserts?"

Glancing over to Katerina, I stared at her for a few seconds. By now, I was starting to figure out Nic's mother. She was a hard nut to crack, but I was somehow making my way in and learning how to maneuver around in this family.

It was the pretend three percent Greek in me.

"Well, Kilyn is Irish, so I thought for her baby shower, a few Irish desserts would be fun to do."

She stood there staring at me with her mouth gaped open. "What is wrong with baklava or katifi?"

Shrugging, I replied, "Nothing."

"Most of the guests will be Greek!"

"Probably," I said with a chuckle.

"Then why not make a Greek dessert. Something everyone would enjoy?"

I was having a hard time holding back my smile. "Katerina, you're more than welcome to make the desserts if you'd think everyone would prefer Greek."

Narrowing her eyes at me, she forced a smile and waved her hand around. "No. Kilyn specifically asked for you to handle the desserts."

I smiled. "Besides, it will be fun for everyone to try something new."

Katerina huffed.

Going back to reading Kilyn's and Thano's baby registry, I couldn't help but notice Katerina glancing around the house.

Peeking up, I watched her walk over to one of the kitchen cabinets and open it. Any other woman would have been pissed, but I knew this was part of the *Nic package*. And I knew that privacy was something his family didn't do. I learned that the day Nic practically had sex with me in front of his mother and aunts when they decided to come over and cook him some meals so he didn't starve.

"Did Nic get new mixing bowls?"

I fought to roll my eyes.

"Nope. Those are mine."

Another cabinet opened. "He bought new plates?"

"Those are my plates."

Grunting, she looked through a drawer then another cabinet.

"Your pasta bowl?" she asked.

"Yep."

She shut the cabinet. "Have you officially moved in, Gabriella?"

Her eyes shot right to my left hand.

"I guess you could say I have since I'm here every night."

"What about your place above the bakery?" Katerina asked as she took a seat at the kitchen island.

"Charity is living there. With the baby coming, she needed the extra room."

Katerina smiled. She loved babies, and I knew she was counting the days until Kilyn had her second child. It killed her Thano and Kilyn hadn't told anyone the sex of the baby.

"How nice of you to do that. It's the Greek in you."

I smiled. "Don't you think it is strange, Katerina, that I'm ninety-seven percent Italian, and three percent Greek?"

"No. Someone in your family history had the good sense to sleep with a Greek man." She wiggled her eyebrows. "We both know how well they are in bed."

Dropping my mouth open, I gasped. "Katerina!"

She brushed me off with her hands. "Oh, don't pretend you are shy and innocent now, Gabriella. I've heard my Nicholaus and how he talks dirty to you."

I wanted to crawl under a rock. I'd never live that moment down for as long as I live.

"If my Nic makes you as happy as my Dimitris does, I know why someone in your family went Greek. You know what they say about Greek men."

Grinning, I asked, "No, what do they say?"

"Once you've had Greek, you can't walk for a week."

I could feel the heat on my cheeks as she sat there and stared at me with a deadpan face.

When she lifted her brow, as if to challenge me, I closed my eyes and wished for a time machine to go back an hour and not answer the door.

My phone beeped, causing me to open my eyes and glance down at it. "It's Max."

Katerina chuckled. "It's always Max."

I couldn't argue with her on that.

Standing, I knew she was waiting. "Would you like to drive over there with me?"

A smile exploded on her face. "I'd love to."

Katerina and I talked a little more about Kilyn's baby shower on the way to the bakery. It was a short drive. Less than five minutes. I was lucky enough to find a parking space right out front so we walked in through the front door.

My eyes immediately went to the display cabinets.

Oh. No. She. Did. Not.

Snapping my eyes up to Charity, she was making a face like she tried to stop it, but failed.

Katerina walked in and started greeting patrons at their tables as I stood there and stared at the foreign desserts.

Leaning closer, I whispered, "Kataifi!"

Sweeping my eyes across I saw baklava, phyllo pastries, kourabiedes, and kariokes.

I turned on my heels and stormed past Katerina who was asking a lady how she liked the baklava.

"It's delicious, but I thought baklava was Greek?"

Katerina chuckled. "It is."

"I thought this was an Italian bakery."

I held my breath as I stopped and faced them.

"You know what they say about Italian cooking. It goes for baking as well. It's simply Greek food with no taste."

The older lady's eyes widened in shock before she giggled.

Ugh! This woman is going to drive me insane!

Max and Charity started walking next to me as we made our way down the hall and to my office. Once in, I slammed the door and glared at them both.

Charity put her hands up in defense. "First off, I'm pregnant and trying to argue with that woman is exhausting. I need to harness all my energy for sex. Have I mentioned how good Cole is in bed?"

Max and I both groaned.

"Seriously. Shut up, Charity." My eyes shot over to Max. "How? How did she get that food in my bakery?!"

"Stop yelling at me, Gabi! It makes me nervous."

I closed my eyes and took in a deep breath before forcing a smile and looking back at him.

"Max, would you mind telling me how Katerina was able to put at least five different Greek desserts in my bakery."

He rubbed the back of his neck. "Well, she came in about two hours ago."

"More like an hour and a half," Charity added.

"And she carried them in, walked around the counter and just kind of . . . well she . . . she kind of . . . she . . ."

"Oh my gosh, just say it!"

"She started putting them in with the other desserts! Charity asked her if you had said she could and all she did was laugh and replied with *what do you think, Charity?*"

Charity nodded. "And what I really wanted to say was I think she would say fuck to the hell no, but then I got scared."

I shook my head. "Why did you get scared?"

They both shrugged. "She's scary," Charity whispered as Max nodded in agreement.

Pointing to Max, I said, "Take them out."

"R-right now? With her here?"

"Yes."

"Why do I have to do it? Make Charity! She's pregnant and Katerina won't do anything to her."

"Ah, hell no, Max. She told you to do it."

I pulled out my phone and hit Nic's number.

"Hey, agapiméni."

"She's gone too far."

Nic was silent for a few seconds. "What did she do now?"

"She put Greek desserts in my bakery. My *Italian* bakery."

"Wait. She did what?"

I sighed. "She walked into the bakery, went behind the counter and started to put Greek desserts in with mine."

Max held up his finger. "Oh, she kind of took some of yours out and gave them away to customers."

If looks could kill, Max would have been on the floor.

"Nic, I've got to let you go. I need to throw out some Greek food."

"Wait! Did she happen to make any kariokes?"

Pulling the phone out, I looked at it before putting it back to my ear.

"I can't even with you right now, Nic Drivas."

Hitting End, I pushed past Max.

As I reached for the door and opened it, he softly spoke to Charity. "I think she's gonna do it. We'll live to see another day."

"Ugh!" I cried out.

I knew I was on edge. Hell, anytime Katerina was around she put me on edge. But I had to give a deposition on Monday regarding Dante and the night he shot his father. All I wanted to do was put that life behind me.

Making my way back into the bakery, I watched as Katerina sat down at a table with an older couple.

I shot her a dirty look and wished I had the power to shoot daggers at her.

The bell to the bakery opened and Kilyn walked in. She saw Katerina sitting at a table and her eyes widened in surprise. Then she turned and saw me. Walking up to me, she plastered an *everything is okay* smile on her face.

"Hey, I see you and Katerina are hanging out."

Glaring back over at her, I tried not to growl.

"Or maybe not."

Focusing back on Kilyn, I said, "She put Greek desserts in my bakery."

She frowned. "Huh?"

I motioned for her to walk to the end of the counter. Leaning down, she gasped.

"Oh. No."

"Yes. And they are all going in the trash."

Kilyn jumped up. "What? There is some good stuff in there. I'll take it home! Don't throw it away."

I narrowed my left eye on her and she took a step back. "Or you could throw it all out."

"Max!" I called out.

"Yep, right here."

"Will you package all of this up for Kilyn, please."

She smiled and licked her lips as she watched Max reach in for the Greek desserts. Katerina looked up at me. Pointing to her, I motioned for her to meet me in the back.

"What are you doing?" Kilyn asked.

"I'm going to set her straight."

Max, Charity, and Kilyn all gasped.

"It's about time," Liza said walking up tying on an apron.

I looked at her as she shrugged. "Sorry, but this has been going on for too long. This is your turf. She can't mess with you on your turf."

"Yeah!" Kilyn said as she lifted her fist into the air. Slowly pulling it back down, she turned to Max. "If you've got that ready, I'll just be leaving before the shit hits the fan. Later, guys."

"Chicken," I called out. Lifting her hand, Kilyn gave it a quick wave and was out the door with her goodies.

And to think I'm planning her baby shower.

Spinning around, I made my way to my office where Katerina was already sitting behind my desk.

I shut the door and took a seat. Before I had a chance to even start talking, she went first.

"Don't be upset, Gabriella. I only meant it with good intentions."

Breathe. Stay calm. You've got this.

"Katerina, this is my bakery. My business, my livelihood. My dream. You cannot come in here and act like you are a part of it. You especially cannot come in and bring food. For one, it is a health violation. I could get in trouble."

Her face dropped. "Oh, Gabriella, I wasn't even thinking about that."

"Well, honestly Katerina, you weren't thinking at all. You're walking around putting down my baking to my customers. How do you think that makes me feel?"

She only stared at me, but didn't respond.

"You are to never bring food into this bakery again, and if for any reason you think there needs to be a dessert here, talk to me about it first. Maybe we can have a Greek day or something."

I don't think in the six months that I have known Katerina Drivas I have I ever seen her speechless. Standing, she smoothed out her hair and smiled.

"Well, it appears I've been put in my place."

Sighing, I dropped my head. When I glanced back up at her, she was moving around the desk. "I'm not trying to put you in your place. I'm simply asking that you not interfere with my business. I've worked very hard to make this bakery what it is. I know you wish I was Greek, and I'm sorry I'm not."

She smiled. "You're three percent."

Slowly shaking my head, I smiled softly. I could tell her the test was false, but what good what it do.

"I'm very proud of my Italian heritage, just as you're proud of your Greek. I'm very passionate about my cooking, like you're passionate about yours. It's okay to be different. It's okay if Nic loves an Italian dish.

Because no matter what I cook or what I bake, you'll always be his mother and he will always love you with every ounce of his heart and soul. I'm not competing with you on that, Katerina. We both love the same man, but in two totally different ways."

Katerina glanced away for a few moments while she cleared her throat before focusing back on me.

"You are a strong woman, Gabriella, and I see why my Nicholaus loves you so."

Smiling, I walked up to her and kissed her on the cheek. "You raised an amazing man, Katerina. I'd be lost without him."

With a quick pat on my arm, she stood up straighter. "Now, if you'll bring me back to my . . . er . . . Nicholaus's house, I will get my car and head home. I have some planning to do for the shower." Narrowing her eyes, she flashed me an evil smile. "Kilyn thinks she snuck in the bakery today without me seeing her, but I saw her. I also saw her taking all the desserts! I knew that girl loved my kariokes."

I covered my mouth to hide my smile as Katerina marched out of my office.

With a deep exhale, I looked up and said a quick prayer. As I made my way out of my office, I couldn't help but chuckle. Life with Katerina Drivas was going to be interesting.

Exhausting.

But very interesting.

thirty-six

Gabi

"THIS WAS SUCH A BAD idea," I mumbled to myself while I climbed up one step at a time.

Swinging my leg over the ladder, I stepped up onto the roof. Smiling, I let out the breath I'd been holding.

"Oh, wow."

The view was breathtaking. Charity was right. This would be the perfect place. Reaching for my phone in my back pocket, I pulled up her name.

> Me: I can see the mountains perfectly.

> Charity: Told you!

> Me: This was a great idea!

> Charity: LOL. I'm surprised you got up there.

I stared at her text like it was a snake about to bite me.

"Oh God."

I closed my eyes and sank down onto the roof. Pulling my knees to my chest, I dragged in a deep breath. This was my karma. Coming back to me for the way I snapped last week at the bakery when Katerina put the Greek desserts in. I quickly typed my response back.

Me: OMG! Charity. I'm on the roof. I'm on the damn roof.

Charity: Okay. I thought you had already made that clear but . . .

Me: No! I'm ON THE ROOF. I'm afraid of heights.

My phone rang.

"H-hello?"

"You didn't go all the way up alone, did you?"

"Well of course I did! I had to see what the view looked like."

"I said, put the ladder up and climb up as far as you can and look! I didn't tell you to go on the roof."

I gulped as I looked around.

"I'm so high! Oh, my gosh. I'm going to die!"

She laughed. My jaw dropped open as I pulled my phone out to stare at it. Putting it back to my ear, I huffed. "You're laughing?"

"Yes. You're barely one story up. Just climb back down."

Standing, I walked over to the edge of the roof. My knees instantly hurt when I peeked over.

"I can't do it. I can't!"

"Lord almighty. Do I need to come over and help you?"

"No! You're five months pregnant. You can't be climbing a ladder."

"I climb onto Cole every night."

Gagging, I shook my head to erase the image. "Throw up. In. My. Mouth."

Charity giggled. "Oh stop. I'm only trying to make light of your freak out moment. Just hold onto the ladder, swing your leg over it, and step down."

"It is not that simple, Char."

"Really? I'm pretty sure it is. Christ, I'm on my way over."

She hung up before I could argue with her.

I pushed my phone back into my pocket and slowly backed away from the edge.

"Hi, Gabi!" Mrs. Hawk yelled from her front porch across the street.

Waving, I called back, "Hey, Mrs. Hawk."

"What are you doing on the roof dear?"

How do I explain I came up here to see if it would make a good picnic spot for me to surprise Nic with the news that I didn't have to testify in Dante's case? He had confessed to killing his father in exchange for some deal the FBI made with him. Antonio was pissed, I was pissed, but relieved at the same time.

"Checking something, that's all."

She smiled and waved again before going back into the house.

Sighing, I sat down and pulled my knees up to my chest again.

Okay, you've got this, Gabi. You are a strong, independent woman who owns her own business. You can do anything you set your mind to. All you have to do is take one step down. That's it.

I stared at the ladder peeking up over the roof.

"I am so fucked."

Charity popped her head up, making me scream. "What in the hell are you doing? You're pregnant! Cole will kill you if he sees you on a ladder."

She stepped up and flashed me an evil little smile. "I had to come show you what a baby you're being. If I can get up here and get back down with a belly, then so can you."

"You're not even that big," I said, my eyes wandering down to her little tummy sticking out.

Rolling her eyes, she reached for my hand. "Shut up. Come on, we'll be late for knitting club and Nancy is showing me the yarn she got for the baby."

I tried to hide my smile as I followed her back over to the ladder. "Why do you go? You don't even knit and the bet has long since been over."

Charity shrugged. "I like it. Sue me."

When she stopped at the ladder, I patiently waited for her to show me how to get off. But she didn't move.

"What's wrong?" I asked.

"Um. Nothing. I just need a second."

I nodded. "Okay. Is anything wrong though?"

Glancing back at me, she gave me a nervous smile. "No."

With a lift of my brows, I asked, "Are you sure?"

She nodded. "Uh-huh. Yep. I need a moment."

My shoulders dropped. "Please don't tell me you're afraid to get down."

Charity turned to face me. "Oh, you have no right to judge me! You were sitting up here in a fetal position!"

I huffed. "It was not a fetal position."

She quirked her brow. "Really?"

I waved my hands around like a crazy person. "It doesn't matter. How are we going to get down?"

"Girls, are you okay up there?"

We both turned to see Mrs. Hawk standing out from the house looking up.

"Yes."

"No!" Charity cried out.

Hitting her, I smiled. "We've just hit a bump in the road. That's all."

"What bump is that, sweetheart?" Mrs. Hawk asked.

"We're too afraid to get back down!" Charity cried out.

Reaching for her phone, Charity said, "I'm calling Cole!"

I grabbed it. "Are you insane? If he finds out you crawled up on the roof, he is going to be pissed. Then he'll be pissed at me because I'm the reason you're up here."

"Damn it. Well, who do we call? Kilyn?"

Laughing, I rolled my eyes. "So we can get her stuck up here?"

"She's seven months pregnant, I don't think she would climb up here."

"And you're five months pregnant. I didn't think you would climb up here either, but here you are."

With a frown, she mumbled, "Touché."

"Don't worry, girls, I called for help."

Charity and I both froze. "Holy shit. Who would she have called?" I asked.

Pressing her hands together, Charity started praying. "Please don't have called 9-1-1. Lord, please."

I glanced back down. "Oh, that wasn't necessary, Mrs. Hawk. You can call them back. We're perfectly fine."

She looked up with a sweet smile. "Katerina said she knew what to do."

My stomach dropped.

Dear Lord above, please no. No. No. No. No.

thirty-seven

Gabi

CHARITY GASPED. "DID SHE SAY she called…oh…my…God… please tell me she didn't say what I think she said."

Covering my mouth, I tried to keep the bile I instantly felt down.

She called Katerina. How does she even know her?

My hand dropped to my side as I called down, "What did you tell her, Mrs. Hawk?"

"That you and Charity were both stuck on the roof and couldn't get down."

Charity crawled on her hands and feet to the middle of the roof and sat down. Her arms were wrapped around her legs and she had her eyes closed. "This is bad. This is so very bad. Go to a happy place. Go to your happy place, Charity!"

Rolling my eyes, I said, "Who's in the fetal position now?"

She stuck her hand up and shot me the middle finger. "Fuck you, Gabi. Fuck. You."

I turned back to Mrs. Hawk. "You can call her back and tell her we're fine. We're about to come down."

Staring up at me, she shook her head. "Sweetheart, if you could get down, you'd be down by now. Katerina is bringing Dimitris, he'll help."

"How do you know Katerina?" I asked.

Laughing, she said, "We met when Nic moved in. Such a nice woman."

My shoulders dropped and I made my way over to Charity. Dropping down next to her, I put my head on her shoulder and looked out to the mountains.

"It's a pretty view, isn't it?"

Charity sighed. "Yeah. It's beautiful."

I wasn't sure how long we sat there staring out to the west before we heard Katerina's voice calling up at us.

Dropping onto my back, I let out a long groan. "I'm never going to live this down. Ever."

Suddenly, a loaf of bread was thrown up on the roof. Turning our heads, we stared at it.

Charity turned back to me and asked, "How the fuck long does she think we've been up here?"

Laughing, I got up and walked over to the edge, but not too close. "Oh. No."

"How many people are with her?"

I glanced back over my shoulder to Charity. "There are at least three Maria's, Aunt Agnes, cousin Angie, and Phoebe. With the baby!"

She covered her mouth to hide her laugh. "It's not funny!" I stated as I giggled myself.

"So much for keeping this from Nic," she chuckled.

"Eat the bread! It will give you energy!" Katerina called up.

Focusing back on the group, I said, "Katerina, we've only been up here for a little bit. I think we're good in the food department."

"Charity needs to eat! For the baby!"

"Oh, dear God she's screaming out my name for the whole world to know!"

My breath caught in my throat when I saw Dimitris and Thad pull up. Jumping out of the car, Thad looked up and started laughing. I shot him a dirty look and walked back over to Charity.

"The whole family is showing up."

Her eyes about popped out of her head. "What do you mean?"

"I mean Thad just showed up with Dimitris. Nic and Cole have to know by now."

As if on cue, both of our phones rang.

"I'm not answering it!" Charity cried out.

"Oh, stop being a baby. Answer it because if you don't, Cole will be here next."

We both answered at the same time and said the same exact thing.

"Hey, babe. What's up?"

I covered my mouth to hide my laugh as Charity rolled her eyes but smiled.

"I don't know. You tell me what's up?"

Shrugging, as if he could see me, I replied, "Not much. I'm sitting here chatting with Charity."

"Uh-huh. That's it?"

Thad popped his head up over the ladder and grinned like a silly fool.

"Hey, girls."

Lifting my hand, I answered, "Hey, Thad."

"I see my brother made it up to you guys."

With a sigh, I responded, "Is *nothing* kept a secret in this family?"

Thad lost it laughing as did Nic.

"Put Thad on, baby."

I handed Thad the phone. He winked and started talking to Nic.

"Yeah. Right. I know. I will. Okay. Well, things were looking okay until the news showed up."

"The news!" I practically screamed.

Thad chuckled. "I'm kidding. They're not here. Yet."

Charity had a look of pure horror on her face.

"Cole, I need to go. I love you."

She pushed her phone back into her pocket, marched over to the edge of the house, grabbed the ladder, and before I knew it, she was heading down.

"How did she do that?" I asked.

Thad handed me my phone back. I mindlessly put it in my back pocket. "Nic's still on the line."

"Oh shit!"

"Nic?"

"Thad's going to help you down."

Chewing on my lip, I shook my head. "I don't think I can do it, Nic."

"Yes you can. He's going to help you. I promise if you got up, you can get down."

I took in a shaky breath. "O-okay. I love you."

"Love you too."

It wasn't lost on me I could hear the smile in his voice. He was laughing at me.

"I'm going to go do this now."

"Okay. Be careful. See you soon."

Nodding, I said, "Kay. Bye."

"See ya later, agapiméni."

I hit End and looked at Thad. "I can't do it."

"Yes you can."

Peeking over the edge, I asked, "Can I just like jump into the bushes. Or maybe you can hold my hands and help me get to them."

For as long as I live, I would never forget the look on Thad's face as he stared at me with disbelief.

"You want me to drop you into the bushes rather than help you down the ladder?"

My arms wrapped around my body. "It's the swinging my leg over. I can't do it."

Thad took my hand in his and led me over to the ladder.

"Look at me, Gabi."

I did as he asked. "I'm going to put your hands on the ladder, and you're going to hold onto the ladder, but I've got a hold of you. Then you're going to back yourself up and simply slide to the left and step on the ladder."

My entire body was shaking. I was positive my face was white as a ghost. I did what he said.

"Now move your left foot out and put it on the ladder."

"You can do it, Gabi!" Charity called out from below.

"Great . . . my own personal cheerleader."

Thad laughed. My foot felt for the ladder and I started to panic when

I couldn't find it. Once I did, I set it down slowly.

"I can't move," I panted out.

Thad looked down below then back up at me. "You've got one foot on the ladder and one on the roof. You're halfway there."

My legs felt like lead. Pulling my right leg to me, I placed it on the ladder.

"I'm on!" I cried out.

"Now move on down."

Ever so slowly, I moved each foot down until I was on the ground and in Charity's arms.

"We almost died! We need to go shopping!"

I laughed at her then realized there was a plethora of people staring at me.

"When did all these people get here?" I asked as I looked around to see the Marias', cousin Angelo and his wife Christine. Their daughter Marianna was holding out her little camera and taking pictures.

Great. The family documenter.

Aunt Agnes was ushering everyone over to the back of her SUV where she had some food out if anyone was hungry.

Cousin Sophia stood next to Katerina who was informing Mrs. Hawk I had officially moved in with Nic, but there had been no formal engagement.

Pressing my fingers to my temple, I groaned. Thad bumped my shoulder. "It's not that bad."

My hands fell to my sides. "Not that bad? Thad, the entire neighborhood is out and your Aunt Agnes is feeding everyone out of her SUV. Where in the hell did she even get all that food?"

He chuckled and Phoebe walked up carrying little Michael. "Man, Kilyn will be so tickled to hear this one."

I shot her a dirty look. "I'm not babysitting for y'all this weekend."

Thad jumped into the conversation. "She takes it back! Take it back, Phoebe! Take it back!"

My brows lifted. "I guess someone needs a night out."

With a sigh, he nodded. "You have no idea."

The pain of jealousy ripped through my chest. "No, I don't."

Phoebe tilted her head and looked at me. When I smiled, she returned one, but I knew she saw the hint of my jealousy.

The next three hours were spent with the entire Drivas clan entertaining my neighbors. At one point, I looked over and saw Charity sitting on a chair chatting to Phoebe as if they were at a damn family reunion.

Finally people started leaving, and the questions about why I was on the roof finally stopped. The only two people left were Katerina and Dimitris.

I stumbled into the house, exhausted from the day's events. Katerina immediately headed to the kitchen.

"I'll whip up a dinner for Nicholaus to have when he gets home." I didn't have the energy to stop her. I had made fresh pasta this morning for linguini with my lemon pesto sauce, but I could make it tomorrow.

By the time Katerina and Dimitris were ready to leave, I had four different meals put in my freezer, Dimitris had fixed the door that creaked and had installed the new light I bought for over the kitchen island. Katerina had made arrangements for her and I, and I'm sure at least three Maria's, to go get our nails done the following afternoon, even though I told her I was working at the bakery. Her response was, "You're the boss! Take time off!"

As I walked them to the front door, Katerina turned back to me. "You had some pasta that looked a bit old, so I tossed it out for you."

I balled my fists and took in a deep breath. "I made that this morning."

"Really?" she asked pinching her brows together. "Huh."

And like it wasn't a big deal, she breezed through the door and was gone.

After I shut the door, I leaned against it and whispered, "Bath. Hot. Bath."

Making my way to the bathroom, all I could think about was how I needed this day to end.

thirty-eight

Nic

THE SOUND OF RUNNING WATER caught my ear as I made my way into the bedroom looking for Gabi. From what Thad had said, there had been a lot of action here today, and with the evidence of my mother in the refrigerator, I was sure Gabi was spent.

Peeking in the bathroom door, I smiled at the sight before me. Gabi was sitting in a tub filled with bubbles, a glass of wine in her hand, and her eyes closed.

My dick instantly grew hard while my eyes roamed over the barely exposed skin. The bubbles hid those perfect breasts of hers as did her long blonde hair that fell over her shoulders. My mouth watered. I wanted a taste of what was mine.

"You're home," she softly said without opening her eyes.

Smiling, I quickly stripped out of my clothes. "I am. How did you know?"

A gorgeous grin graced her face. "I felt you."

Slipping into the hot water, I pulled her legs to me as she wrapped them around my body.

"You're really going to feel me now."

Her stunning blue eyes opened and I swear they caught every beam of light in them.

"Rough day?" I asked with a wink.

She giggled. "You have no idea."

Drawing her closer to me, I leaned back while she crawled on top of me. Her fingers traced my jaw.

"You haven't shaved."

I'd been gone for three straight days. We had a standoff that lasted nearly twelve hours and two felony warrants we had to serve. To say I needed this as much as she did was an understatement.

"Been a crazy few days."

Smiling, she brushed her lips over mine. "I've been lonely without you."

My hands grabbed her ass while she pressed that sweet pussy against my cock. I moaned and said, "Sounded like you had a house full."

She looked into my eyes and shot me a look.

Laughing, I pulled her sweetness closer to me.

"I haven't touched myself since you left. I'm aching for you, Nic."

Fucking hell. I wanted to fuck her senseless, but I needed to take my time and enjoy her. We both needed an escape and being with each other slowly was the ultimate escape.

Her breasts pressed against my chest and I could feel her hardened nipples. It drove me bat-ass crazy. I wanted her mouth on mine.

"I want to be buried deep inside you, but first, I want your lips pressed to mine, Gabi."

Without hesitation, our lips collided in a beautiful dance. Her tongue keeping pace with mine. Slow at first, then hungry for more.

Gabi lifted her hips. Guiding my cock to her entrance, she slowly sank down on me. Both of us letting out a moan until she had taken all of me.

Her head dropped back and I gave each nipple the attention they deserved. Sucking and biting on one while I twisted and pulled the other with my fingers.

"Oh, Nic, yes don't stop."

Her body slowly rocked against mine. The feel of the hot water moving over us as we slowly made love was fucking heaven.

"Goddamn, Gabi. I need to be deeper."

Her hands gripped my shoulders as she lifted slightly and ever so slowly sank back down over my cock.

"Yes," she hissed.

Gabi leaned forward, her lips inches from mine. Those blue eyes sparkling as they looked deep into mine. Her body rocking so slowly I thought for sure I would come from the pure ecstasy I felt from being inside her.

My chest squeezed as our gaze locked. I loved this woman more than anything. She was the reason I breathed in and out. My heart was full of nothing but love for her.

I needed her.

Desired her.

Craved her.

She was mine and I needed her to know.

Lifting my hands, I cupped her face. Our eyes so drawn to each other that nothing else in the world mattered but this moment.

"Marry me, Gabi." Her body stilled. Tears filled her eyes and she slowly smiled.

With a nod of her head, she whispered, "Yes."

I lifted my hand up and pushed her wet blonde hair away from her gorgeous face.

"When?"

Giggling, she replied, "I'd marry you this very moment if we could."

My brows lifted. "A wedding?" I asked, hoping like hell she would say no. The last thing I wanted was a dog and pony show for a wedding.

"No. I love your family, Nic, honest to God I do. But if we get married, I want it to only be the two of us."

Relief swept across my body as my heart raced in my chest. If someone had told me six months ago I'd be whisking a woman off to marry her, I'd have laughed in their face. But for the last few weeks it was all I could think about. Watching Charity and Cole, and Thad and Phoebe, as well as Thano and Kilyn, I knew I wanted that life with Gabi. There was no doubt about it. I wanted to watch the sunrise as the moon set for the rest of my life with this woman.

"I agree. I took vacation this week so we could paint the house. We could blow that off."

Excitement danced across her face. "What are you saying, Nic?"

"I'm saying, after we get done fucking in the tub, I'm taking you to Lake Tahoe, making you my wife, and spending the next four days buried inside of you."

With a concerned expression, she asked, "What about the bakery?"

"For once I don't want to care about anything. The only thing I want to think about is the fact that I want to marry you. I want to take you away and spend every minute of the day with you." My fingertips traced her jawline. "I want to make love until we can hardly move."

Her mouth rose in a sinfully sexy grin, causing me to smile.

"Gabi, I want to make a baby."

I watched as her eyes went from happy, to shocked, to pure bliss. A sob slipped from her mouth as she started to laugh while tears slid down her face.

"I . . . I want . . . I want that too, Nic. So badly!"

Slipping my hand around her neck, I drew her mouth to mine. "Then we better get to starting."

Our mouths crushed together as Gabi picked up the pace. The sound of the water sloshing was hot as damn hell. Neither one of us gave two shits it was getting everywhere. Our sweet passion turned into a lust I couldn't describe. If I thought I could crawl into her body I would, and I knew she felt the same.

"That's it, fuck me faster."

She did what I asked. Her tits bouncing as the water went everywhere.

"Nic. I'm going to come," she cried out. Her hands splayed across my chest when her orgasm hit her, causing her entire body to tremble and her pussy to squeeze around my cock.

"Jesus," I cried out as we came together. My warm cum pouring into her body. Heaven on earth.

When she collapsed onto me, I wrapped her up in my arms. The once-hot water now seeming cold as Gabi shivered.

I reached for the drain and sat there holding her while the water level slowly fell. Reaching for the towel that was on the stool, I wrapped it around her.

She sat up, my cock still inside of her, jerking and trying to make another go at it.

When she smiled, my heart filled with love and contentment. For a quick moment, it was hard to fill my lungs with air as she gazed at me.

We both stood. I stepped out of the tub first, then reached for her hand and helped her out. Reaching for another towel, I put it around my waist then bent down to start drying off Gabi. She never took her eyes off of me while I dried off every single inch of her body.

With a grin, she said, "I love you."

Standing, I cupped her face within in my hands. "And I love you. More than anything."

Gabi covered her mouth and giggled. Her towel dropped to her feet and my eyes swept over that perfect body.

"Are we really going to elope, Nic?"

"Fuck yes we are, if you're down for it."

She nodded. "We have to tell someone though."

"Cole and Charity. I don't trust anyone in my family."

"Absolutely. Even Thano and Kilyn can't be trusted. She's been binging on your mother's desserts. Who knows what she would say to get more kataifi."

My hand was itching to touch her body. Pushing my towel down, I watched her eyes turn dark while taking in my naked body.

"When . . . when are we going to go?"

With a smug grin, I drew her body to mine, sliding my hand between her legs. I slipped my fingers inside her, moaning at how ready she was for me again.

"After I fuck you here in the bathroom. Then we'll figure it out."

"Yes," she responded breathlessly.

Lifting her, I pushed inside her and did exactly what I said I was going to do.

thirty-nine

Nic

"YOU'RE DOING WHAT?" COLE ASKED.

I watched as Gabi packed up a small suitcase, a huge smile playing across her gorgeous face.

"We're heading to Reno then up to Lake Tahoe."

"You're eloping? Are you fucking insane! Not only will you have to deal with your mother, but we're *all* going to have to deal with Charity!"

Laughing, I shook my head. "Gabi will call her here in a bit, unless you want to tell her."

Cole huffed. "I'll pass on that invite. Are you sure this is what you guys want to do?"

"Positive. My family is in our business so much, and Gabi would really like for this to be something we do together. Alone."

"Is it something you want to do?"

"Yeah. It really is."

"Then all right. I'm happy for you, Nic."

With a chuckle, I pushed the back door open and stood on the porch. "A year ago, would you have imagined our lives to be like this? You have a baby on the way, me getting married. Crazy what happens when you meet the right person."

"Yeah, I was thinking about that earlier when I was watching Charity baking in the kitchen. She was humming and looked so damn happy. I was pissed at the little stunt she pulled earlier by getting on the roof, but when I realized why I was so mad, it didn't freak me out. A weird warmth spread through my chest."

Nodding, I replied, "I get that feeling a lot when I'm with Gabi."

"We're lucky bastards, I can tell ya that."

"So what about you?"

"What about me?"

"You ever think of asking Charity to marry you?"

He was silent for a moment. "All the damn time. I think I'm going to wait until after the baby is born."

I could hear the smile in his voice. "Sounds like a good plan."

"Oh hell, I think Gabi called Charity."

"Why?"

"I just heard her scream *you're doing what?*"

Laughing again, I walked back into the house. Gabi was standing there holding the phone out with a frown.

"We'll call you guys when we land and then after the deed is done."

Cole chuckled. "Sounds good. Have a safe trip."

Gabi shook her head and smiled. "She's listing all the reasons why we can't elope."

I lifted a brow. "Any good ones?"

She shook her head. "They're all about her! She needs to be the bridesmaid, she has to throw me a shower because she's always wanted to throw a shower and a bachelorette party."

Covering her mouth, she whispered, "Oh, this is the best one. We have to wait until she has the baby so she can fit into a sexy bridesmaid gown."

"While you have made valid points on a few of your arguments, I'm still leaving on a flight tonight to Reno," Gabi said.

"I know you want to be there, but how about you throw us a shower when we get back?"

She rolled her eyes. "We both know that is a promise I can't make, but I'll try. If you want to close the bakery, you can since I'll be gone. You sure? Okay. I love you too, Charity. Please don't work too hard. We will. Bye."

Gabi let out a long sigh. "I have a feeling that was a preview of what is to come with your mother."

I tossed my head back and let out a roar of laughter before focusing back on her. "Baby, that is the calm before the storm."

Gabi giggled then looked at me with a questioning look. "Are you sure?"

Pulling her into my arms, I ran my thumb over her lips. "I've never been so sure of anything in my life."

She smiled and my heart skipped a beat.

"Did you leave your birth control pills here?"

Her cheeks turned a beautiful rose color. "Yes," she softly said.

"Good. We need to get in some serious practice on making a baby."

Gabi put her arms around my neck. "I like the sound of that."

Leaning down, I kissed her gently on the lips. *If I wasn't careful, I'd take her again here in the living room.*

"You ready to head out?"

She chewed on her lip then grinned wide. "Never been more ready!"

LAKE TAHOE IN SEPTEMBER WAS beautiful. The warm afternoon sun shined down on us, keeping things comfortable as we stood on the beach.

"We never usually have openings, but it looks like you lucked out."

My eyes swung over to the wedding planner from the Hyatt and I grinned. "I'd say we did for sure."

We had flown in last night, stayed in Reno and got our marriage certificate in morning before we drove out to the lake.

Gabi smiled as she looked out over the crystal blue lake. "I am going to owe Charity big time."

My arm slipped around her waist. "She did good."

Charity had called ahead to the Hyatt to see if the beach location would be available for a wedding today. Totally last minute, minimal wedding she told the wedding planner. Of course, it didn't hurt that Charity's family had been coming to this hotel for years and she had attended a few weddings here. We were walking in blind, but Charity had taken care of everything for Gabi. It was her way of being a part of the wedding.

"So, Ms. Rossi, would you like to see the bridal bouquet that Ms. Evans had designed?"

I wasn't used to hearing people call Gabi by her real last name. Each time it threw me.

Gabi turned to the wedding planner. "No, I think I'll be surprised."

The older lady smiled. "Well, the ceremony is scheduled for seven. The sun will be setting at seven eleven this evening."

"That's perfect!" Gabi said with a little excited hop.

Glancing between the two of us, the wedding planner asked, "Will you need any help with anything?"

I turned to Gabi. She shook her head. "No, thank you. I'm going to take care of my makeup and hair."

The older lady nodded. "Well, you should have something delivered to your room by now. A gift from Ms. Evans."

Gabi looked surprised. "Oh, okay thank you."

"Now, if you'll both be down to the reception area at six fifty. You may want to come a few minutes apart if you don't want to see the bride before the ceremony, Mr. Drivas."

I laughed and replied, "Yes ma'am."

"You have my number. If you need anything, we are here to help. We want this to be the perfect day for you both."

Gabi laced her fingers with mine and said, "It will be, Mrs. Mitchell. Thank you."

With a nod, the wedding planner excused herself and started back to the hotel. Gabi and I faced each other and smiled.

Biting on her lip, Gabi asked, "Are you nervous?"

I chuckled. "Not in the least bit. You?"

She squeezed my hands. "A little. There is a little dress shop up the road, I'm going to head over there and look for a dress after we get settled into the room."

I agreed. We had driven straight here, checked in and went straight over to the wedding coordinator's office. When we landed last night, Charity had sent a text saying she had set up the wedding for today as her and Cole's wedding gift to us. I had to admit, it was nice having the plans already made, and I knew Gabi felt the same way. We were totally going to fly by the seat of our pants and no matter what would have happened, I knew it would have been perfect. This plan of ours was insane, but at the same time it was perfect for us. Knowing that we were going to be able to spend something so special with just each other made it feel more magical.

We made our way back into the hotel and up to our room. When we opened the door, Gabi gasped.

"Holy shit," I whispered. The only thing you could see was a wall of windows and the lake in front of us.

"This is stunning. Hell, we could have gotten married here with this view!"

Gabi chuckled. "This room is amazing, Nic!"

Smiling, I drew her to me. "Well, if we're in Lake Tahoe for our wedding and honeymoon, we had to stay in the honeymoon suite, right?"

Her lips found mine and we quickly got lost in one another. Then she pulled back and looked past my shoulder. Her eyes widened in shock. "She didn't."

Turning around, I saw two garment bags hanging up. One white. One black.

"I think she did," I said.

Gabi raced over and grabbed the white bag. "Turn around, Nic! Let me open it!"

The excitement in her voice made my heartbeat pick up.

I could hear the zipper and then a loud gasp. "Oh. My. Goodness. It's a dress! Nic, it's a dress!"

"What's in the black bag?"

Another zipper. "A tux!"

With a chuckle, I asked, "Can I turn around?"

"One second, let me take this in the bathroom and try it on."

The sound of the bag rustling was followed by the bathroom door closing.

"Okay! Make sure the tux fits!" Gabi called out.

I did what she asked and tried it on quickly before she came back out.

"Fits like a damn glove. How in the hell did she do this?" I asked while walking over to the bar and pouring a small amount of bourbon into a glass.

"I'm not sure," Gabi answered.

I walked around the giant suite taking everything in. There was a king-size bed that faced the wall of windows. A small living room area where the bar was at, and a small kitchen. Hell, we could order food and never leave the room. It was like a mini apartment with a killer view.

The bathroom door opened and Gabi stepped out. Her eyes were red and swollen. My heart seized in my chest as I put the drink down and made my way over to her.

"Gabi, what's the matter?"

She shook her head then buried her face into my chest. Shit. I was hoping she wasn't having second thoughts.

Pushing her out so that I could look at her, I wiped the tears from her face.

"Gabi?"

She smiled and shook her head. "The dress . . . it's perfect. It's beyond perfect."

I gently placed the strand of hair hanging in her face behind her ear. "That's wonderful, baby."

"Charity thought to take care of everything, and a small part of me feels guilty she isn't here."

My heart ached. "Do you want to wait?"

"No!" she said as she grabbed onto my shirt. "This is exactly what I want."

Kissing the tip of her nose, I added, "Good, because it's what I want too."

We leaned our foreheads together.

"Ya know, since I don't have to go dress shopping, we could do some baby making practice."

My dick jumped in my pants. Reaching down, I picked up Gabi as she let out a small yelp.

Tossing her onto the bed, I slowly crawled over her, leaning down so that our lips were merely inches apart.

"How much time do you need to get ready?"

The grin that spread across her face had heat surging through my body.

"Two hours."

"Good, until then it's practice, practice, practice."

Gabi giggled as she lifted my T-shirt over my head.

I slowly undressed my future wife and took full advantage of the hours I had before she would slip into the other room and get ready.

Life couldn't possibly get any better than this.

forty

Gabi

STOOD BEFORE THE FLOOR-LENGTH mirror and stared at my reflection. A slow smile moved across my face and I couldn't help the butterflies in my stomach.

"Nic is going to die when he sees this."

"He sure as shit is!" Charity agreed.

I'd propped up my phone and facetimed Charity as I got ready. That small part of me longed to have her here, but I was glad it was only Nic and I.

"Make sure you spray your hair again before you go out."

Nodding, my eyes swept up and down the beaded lace gown. The sweetheart neckline showed the perfect amount of cleavage and the dropped waist in the back left little to the imagination. I wasn't sure how Charity got a dress to fit me like a glove, but this dress did. All that and more.

"If this dress went any further down in the back you'd see my ass crack."

Her laughter came through the phone.

"How in the world did you do this?" I asked as I turned to see the back. There was lace at the lower portion of my back, but with wide gaps, just enough to show it dipped low . . . very low.

"My ass looks perfect in this dress!"

"So, you know how I said we went to Lake Tahoe all the time when I was growing up?"

"Yeah," I said as I touched up my lipstick.

"Well, a girl I practically grew up with lives there. Makes wedding dresses for a living. You guys are practically the same size. I told her I needed a sexy as hell wedding dress that was in her size."

"And she just happened to have one?"

"Yep. She models a lot of her gowns, so most are in her size! It was pure luck."

Shaking my head, I turned and picked up my phone. "Charity, thank you. For all of this. You've made this day so special."

"Well, when you told me what you were doing, I felt like I needed to at least be a part of it somehow. Don't worry though, you can pay me back with babysitting."

"Sounds like a plan," I replied with a lighthearted laugh.

Her smile faded some. "You scared?"

"No. It's weird, really. I'm not really nervous at all about the wedding. It's after the wedding that is giving me butterflies."

Charity let out a roar of laughter. "Cause you know that man is going to devour you!"

"We've been in bed nearly all day. Nic's stamina is like no other."

"You know what they say about Greek men."

I had told her what Katerina had said to me about Greek men and not being able to walk for a week. With a chuckle, I sighed. "Well, I guess I should head down there. Nic was going to go to the bar for a bit after he got dressed then come down after me."

I watched as her eyes filled with tears. "You're getting married."

Blinking rapidly, I was thanking God I used waterproof mascara. "I know."

"And in a few hours, you'll be a part of that crazy-ass family!"

My hand came up to mouth as I laughed. "I know!"

"I love you, Gabi."

"Love you too, Char. Rub the baby for me."

She grinned and moved her phone down to show me she was rubbing her belly. Lifting it back up, she blew me a kiss. "Go get married for Christ's sake."

Nodding, I fought to find the words to speak.

"See ya later," I softly said.

She lifted her hand and waved. "See ya."

The call ended and I stood there staring at my phone before I drew in a deep breath and exhaled. Leaning in, I looked at myself in the mirror and smiled. My blonde hair was done up in a French twist with curls hanging down to frame my face. I'd done a very light, natural eye makeup followed by a pink lipstick. Not too much, but just enough.

Closing my eyes, I counted to ten before opening them again. I was marrying the man of my dreams. My fingers came up to my mouth as I smiled at the thought.

Today was my wedding day. No more secrets, no more running, only happiness and hope from this day forward. The thought made me dizzy with happiness.

I took in a deep cleansing breath and made my way down to the reception hall that would lead out to the beach. I carefully looked around me as I made my way, making sure I didn't run into Nic. Person after person smiled at me, each telling me I looked beautiful. I thought I would have been sadder when the actual moment arrived. Ten years ago I would have wanted a huge catholic wedding, now all I wanted was Nic and I holding hands and vowing our love to each other.

The door opened and Mrs. Mitchell wore a wide grin. "You look stunning, Ms. Rossi."

"Gabi, please call me Gabi."

She nodded then handed me a beautiful bouquet of white and red roses. The smell immediately hit me.

"Charity," I whispered. This was her small way of having a piece of her with me. Roses were her favorite.

"Did you need a few moments or are you ready to make your way down to the beach?"

I gulped. "Nic?"

"He's already down there."

Laughing, I rolled my eyes. "Of course he is. He was probably here at six thirty."

Mrs. Mitchell chuckled. "He was. I had to give him a shot of whiskey to calm his nerves."

My hand landed on my stomach as I tried to calm my own set of nerves. It felt like every nerve ending was tingling.

Lifting her brows, she asked, "Ready?"

I nodded. "Never been more."

My head was spinning. This was crazy! Insane! Twenty-four hours ago we were making love and now we're getting married. I couldn't stop the giggle if I had wanted to.

"Is that a nervous chuckle?"

Holding onto my bouquet of flowers tightly, I slowly shook my head. "No. It's a joyful chuckle. I don't think I'll ever be this happy again."

Mrs. Mitchell smiled wide and then she winked. "Trust me, you will be, if not more."

I chewed on my lip.

A baby.

Following Mrs. Mitchell down to the beach, I was totally lost in thought. Nic wanted a baby. I'd dreamed for years of being a mom. Teaching a little girl how to bake and cook like my mother and grandmother did for me.

Katerina popped into my head and I couldn't help but smile. After the family had found out about Dante and that whole mess, I thought for sure they would tell Nic to drop me like a hot plate. But they didn't. It was the opposite. I was welcomed into the family with such love and affection. Sure. They drove me crazy, but I loved their kind of crazy. Even Kilyn loved it . . . as much as she pretended not to.

The music started and my breath caught in my throat.

"It's time," Mrs. Mitchell said.

With a nod, I took in a deep, long breath and pushed it out. "Let's do this."

forty-one

Nic

SHE WAS THE MOST BEAUTIFUL sight I'd ever seen.

Gabi appeared to be floating on a cloud as she walked down the white carpet to where I was standing on the beach. My eyes took in every ounce of her perfection.

The dress was captivating, and as amazing as it looked on her, all I could do was picture me taking it off of her.

As she drew closer, I could see the tears in her eyes. She was nibbling on that lower lip, causing my dick to twitch in my pants.

"She's stunning," the pastor said.

I agreed. "Yes, she is. Incredibly stunning."

When she finally came to a stop in front of me, I let my eyes soak her up.

"You. Look. Beautiful."

Her cheeks turned the same shade as the pink lipstick she wore.

Leaning closer, I pressed my lips against her ear. "I can't wait to slowly take this dress off of you."

She giggled. "Charity had one more surprise. It's under the dress."

I swallowed hard and almost had to reach down and adjust my dick as I took a step back. The pastor cleared his throat and began to talk.

Gabi's blue eyes picked up the color from the lake and I was totally captivated by them. The color of the setting sun against her skin was a picture I never wanted to forget. She smiled and cried as she repeated her vows. My voice shook, and I fought like hell not to shed a tear, to which I lost the battle when I said the last vow.

When it came time for the kiss, I moved slowly. The need to burn this memory into my mind was strong. My hand lightly landed on the side of her face while the other hand brushed a curl back from her face. The reds, pinks, and yellows in the sky cast the most alluring light around us. It was magical.

"I love you, Gabi."

Her shaking hand covered mine. "I love you, Nic."

"You may kiss your bride," the preacher said with a chuckle.

And kiss her I did. It was slow and sweet. Gabi wrapped her arms around my neck as I picked her up and held her tightly against me. When our lips parted, her eyes captured mine.

"You're mine now."

The sparkle in those baby blues was a fucking turn on, but what she said next left me utterly breathless.

"I've always been yours."

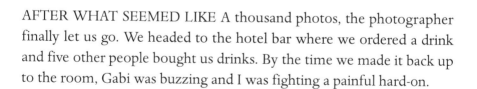

AFTER WHAT SEEMED LIKE A thousand photos, the photographer finally let us go. We headed to the hotel bar where we ordered a drink and five other people bought us drinks. By the time we made it back up to the room, Gabi was buzzing and I was fighting a painful hard-on.

When the door shut, Gabi slowly walked backward away from me. A come hither look in her eyes.

"That's a beautiful dress, prinkipissa."

Her eyes lit up and she licked her lips.

"Did you know you call me prinkipissa when you're about to fuck me, and agapiméni when you make love to me?"

I laughed. "I never thought about it."

She nodded.

"What do you want me to do to you right now? Fuck you. Or make slow, passionate love to you?"

Her mouth parted open slightly. "What do *you* want to do?"

"Fuck you. With your wedding dress on. It's too beautiful to take off just yet."

Gabi moaned.

"Keep your shoes on. And let me see the other surprise under that gown."

With a full-blown smile, Gabi slowly pulled up the dress, one painstaking inch at a time until the only thing showing were her sexy ass legs and a baby-blue see-through lace thong.

"Fuck me."

"I believe I'm supposed to say that to you."

Quickly walking up to her, I dropped to my knees, pushed the thin panties to the side and buried my face in her pussy. Gabi's hands pulled at my hair as she started to rock her hips into my face.

"Oh God. Yes. Nic. Yes."

Her body started to trembled and I pulled back, leaving her on the edge of an orgasm.

"What? Why did you stop?" she panted.

Standing, I quickly started to take off my tux when she stopped me.

"No! Don't. You look so damn hot in that tux, it makes me even wetter."

My heart slammed against my chest. With a smirk, I said, "My new wife likes to talk dirty, does she?"

She slowly nodded.

I unzipped my pants and pulled out my cock. Slowly moving my hand over my shaft, I watched her as she stared at me working myself.

"You like that, baby?"

"Yes," she hissed.

My other hand went between her legs. Slipping two fingers in, I about dropped back down to my knees. She was dripping wet.

"Turn around and put your hands on the table, Gabi. And don't let go."

She quickly did as I said. With my fingers, I leisurely pulled the barely-there thong down her legs and tossed it to the side. Using my foot, I pushed her legs apart then cupped her tight sweet ass. My eyes lifted to her hair twisted up. Reaching over, I took the pins out until her long blonde hair fell around her shoulders. Grabbing it, I held onto it with one hand while I moved my cock into position.

Gabi pushed her ass back against me, silently begging me for more. One quick push and I filled her completely, causing her to cry out in pleasure.

Wrapping her hair around my hand, I pulled gently. When she moaned I couldn't help but smile.

"Hang on, baby, this is going to be quick so you better come fast."

It didn't take Gabi long to cry out my name as she fell apart with each pounding movement. As soon as she grew quiet, it was my turn. Her pussy tightened around my cock as she pulled every ounce of cum out of me when her second orgasm hit.

Slowing down, I stayed inside her and leaned against her back. Fuck this gown was sexy as shit. I placed light kisses on her bare skin as my cock twitched and jumped inside her.

"That. Was. Amazing," she panted.

I stood and slowly pulled out of her. Watching my cum trickle down her leg was the hottest fucking thing I'd ever seen. I ran my fingertips along her bare back as she stood. Glancing over her shoulder, she flashed me a sexy smile. The rest of the night was going to be about loving this woman. Showing her how happy she had made me and whispering how much I loved her.

forty-two

Gabi

MY BODY WAS TANGLED UP in Nic's as I laid there and stared out the windows while my fingers lightly brushed over his arm.

I gently sighed as contentment settled in. Glancing down, I smiled as I looked upon Nic sleeping so peacefully. His head laid on my stomach and his arms and legs were wrapped around my body like a pretzel.

It was crazy insane how much my life had changed since he came into it. I used to live in fear of being found by Dante, now I lived with so much peace and content in my heart I had to pinch myself to make sure I wasn't dreaming.

Lifting my eyes, I watched the sun dance on the water. Last night had been amazing. Nic showered me with attention in every possible way imaginable. The things he whispered to me while he made love to me still had my stomach fluttering and my heart racing.

I closed my eyes only to snap them open when Nic's phone vibrated on the side table . . . again. Last night he had silenced it, refusing to answer his mother's texts. Pulling my lip in between my teeth, I glanced over at the phone. It buzzed again. I carefully untangled myself and reached for his phone.

"Ignore it," Nic mumbled while grabbing me and dragging me back over to him. I couldn't help but giggle.

"You should probably answer her, Nic."

He crawled over my body, planting soft kisses as he moved up toward my lips.

When his gaze met mine, I inhaled a deep breath. He was so damn handsome. His dark hair and hazel eyes were just the icing on the cake. Nic had a body to die for. Rock solid muscles that knew how to hold me perfectly, whether he was making love to me or being a little rougher.

The scruff on his face had me moaning as it brushed against my hypersensitive skin.

His mouth sucked on a nipple, causing me to gasp and arch my body up for more.

Finally making his way to my lips, he whispered, "I'll call her after I make love to my wife."

Slowly sinking deep inside me, we were soon lost in a world of utter bliss. A world where it was only the two of us. Soft sweet kisses, whispered words of *I love you*, and touches that were sure to set my body on fire.

Heaven.

This was heaven.

❤

SIPPING MY COFFEE, I PULLED my knees up to my chest and took in view. The beautiful blue water of Lake Tahoe was calming. Nic couldn't have picked a better place to get married. I hated Las Vegas. I'd only been once, but the idea of going there and getting married would have made my skin crawl.

I could hear Nic talking on the phone. From what he was saying, I was going to guess Katerina wasn't very happy.

I'd already called my parents yesterday when we arrived and told them we were eloping. It killed me to hear the sadness in my mother's voice. She'd missed so much the last six years, and in a way it was selfish of me to deny them this. But it was only fair. If I didn't want Nic's family here, I couldn't have mine here. I promised her we would fly back home and do something special.

"Mama, will you stop acting like you're crying," Nic said as he stepped out onto the balcony.

My fingers went to my lips in an attempt not to laugh.

He sat next to me and rolled his eyes.

"It was last minute. No one knew. Well, Charity and Cole knew."

Peeking back out over the lake, I silently wished we could stay here forever.

"We'll do something when we get back. Yes. We can have a reception. I'm sure Gabi would love to invite her family out for that."

Smiling, I nodded.

"See, she just said yes. Wait, what are you doing? Dad, what is she doing?"

Oh no. This could only mean trouble.

"How does she have the number? Dad, will you please stop her?"

Nic covered the phone then said to me, "Code red. Call your mom. My mother is about to call her and plan the reception."

I nearly fell out of the chair. "What?" I cried out as I raced back into the room.

My hands fumbled around with my phone before I was finally able to dial my mother's number.

"Hello, sweetheart. How is the honeymoon?"

"Good. It's good. Mom! Listen! Katerina is going to call you and—"

"Oh, she's buzzing in right now."

"NO! Don't answer it!"

"Why on earth not, Gabi?"

"She's going to invite you to a reception for us in Colorado Springs."

My mother called for my father. "How exciting!"

I shook my head. "Mom, you don't understand Nic's family. They are overwhelming, to say the least."

"Nonsense, Gabi. I'm looking forward to meeting them. Now, let me listen to her message and call her back. Oh, this is going to be fun! We can plan it together. The menu, the desserts. How exciting!"

I groaned as I sat on the sofa. "Mom, Katerina will take over. It will be a Greek festival when she is done planning it."

Silence.

Nothing.

Not even the sound of her breathing. Then, finally, she spoke.

"Is that so?"

Oh. Shit.

"We will plan something for there at home. Nic and I can fly out and—"

"No no. Let's do this. I think it will be more . . . interesting."

"For who?" I asked chewing on my thumbnail.

She laughed so evil I had to pull the phone away to make sure I still had my mother on the line.

"Don't worry, Gabi. I'm positive I can hold my own next to Katerina. Besides, everyone knows what they say about Greek food."

I held my breath. Dear God no. Please no.

"It's just Italian food, but without the flavor."

Relaxing back against the couch, I sighed.

"I'm not going to talk you out of this, am I?" I asked with nothing but defeat in my voice.

My mother laughed. "Enjoy your honeymoon! Talk soon."

And just like that, she was gone. Probably dialing Katerina's number right then. I covered my face with my hands and groaned. "This is not going to end well."

Dropping my hands to my sides, I turned to see Nic walking in. He sat on the couch and said, "She let me go. Said your mom was calling."

He looked at me. "You know what this means, don't you?"

I nodded. "Food wars."

With a slow smile, he fist pumped. "Yes!"

Sitting up, I looked at him like he had two heads. "Are you crazy? You want our moms to compete?"

Now it was his turn to look at me like I was crazy. "You're kidding, right? Italian food, made by your mother. Have you tasted her food?"

Laughing, I nodded. Nic and I had flown back to New Jersey a couple months ago so I could properly introduce him to the family. He never left my mother's kitchen.

"Yes, but you know your mother won't let you take a bite of Italian food."

He brushed me off with a gruff laugh. "I'm not worried." Standing, he pulled out his phone again.

"What are you doing?" I asked.

"Texting your mom. I'm going to see if she'll make that pasta with artichoke in it."

I watched him walk out onto the balcony as he typed away on his phone.

Shaking my head, I leaned back against the couch.

"This ought to be interesting," I mumbled.

forty-three

Gabi

I T WAS THE BEGINNING OF October and the weather in Colorado Springs was perfect for Kilyn's baby shower.

I'd gotten to Thano and Kilyn's house early this morning to do some last-minute baking. Kilyn had given me the house key and told me to come anytime. The house had been quiet until I heard Kira up and running around.

Kilyn walked into the kitchen and smiled. Her hand rested on her very pregnant belly.

"Hey, how are you feeling?" I asked with a wide grin.

"Like a beached whale. I am so regretting pushing the shower off this close to my due date."

"It doesn't bother me any and I'm sure it won't the guests. You're the one who is about to pop out a baby."

She rolled her eyes. "He is all over the place this morning."

Kilyn and Thano had decided not to tell anyone the sex of the baby. It was their little secret to hold on to and I totally got it. Each day Kilyn would either call the baby 'he' or 'she'. She alternated. It was kind of evil how it threw Katerina off each time. But I also knew Kilyn got her kicks from driving Katerina insane.

"Who has a baby shower two weeks before her due date?"

I laughed. "A mom who is busy."

She chuckled. "I finished my last house design yesterday. I'm off for ten weeks. It's going to feel like heaven."

"I bet," I replied.

"Tea?" Kilyn asked as she filled a kettle up.

"Sure."

Turning back to my work, I started back up at frosting the oat flapjacks.

"Oh. My. God. Is that apple cake?"

Peeking over to the table with more desserts on it, I grinned. "Yep."

"Where is the custard sauce? I remember my grandmother making a custard sauce!"

Laughing, I pointed to the refrigerator. "It's in there."

Kilyn was soon dipping her finger into the custard sauce and moaning in delight.

"What's going on in here?" Thano asked as he walked in with Kira in his arms. She gasped as her little eyes looked at the kitchen island filled with different desserts.

"Your wife is getting a little frisky with the custard sauce."

Thano laughed as he put Kira down. "So, where are all the whiskey cakes? Don't the Irish put booze in almost everything?"

I chuckled. "Pretty much. I've got some barmbrack sliced up on that plate. It's like a fruit cake, but ten times better. The fruit is soaked in Irish whiskey and tea, so be sure to cover it up when you're done."

Thano reached in and took a piece out. He practically melted on the spot when he put it in his mouth. "Damn, that's moist."

"Just don't eat too much of it," I said with a wink.

"Mommy, can I have pancakes?" Kira asked.

"How would you like to eat traditional Irish pancakes?" I asked. Kilyn beamed.

Crinkling her nose, Kira asked, "Are they good?"

I shrugged. "Depends. Do you like strawberries and chocolate?"

Nodding her head, Kira replied, "Do I ever!"

Laughing, I motioned for her to follow me over to the stove.

"You know how your mommy likes to make crepes?"

Kira nodded.

"These are kind of like that."

"Oh," Kira said.

Kilyn laughed. "They are that!"

Leaning in, I whispered, "Don't listen to her. The Irish pancakes are special."

Kira's eyes grew wide. "Why?"

I looked around as if to make sure no one could hear me. "They have magic in them."

"Cool! What kind of magic?"

"Good luck magic."

Kira was entranced. I loved having her help with the pancakes. It reminded me of when I used to help my mother make breakfast sometimes. Plus it gave Thano and Kilyn a little bit of time to enjoy breakfast on the back porch, just the two of them.

Kira sat at the kitchen island and ate her pancakes as I went back to work.

"Have you always liked to cook, Aunt Gabi?"

My heart seized in my chest. *Aunt Gabi.* I loved being called that!

I nodded. "Yep. When I was your age, my grandmother used to teach me everything she knew about cooking. Baking is what I really loved to do though, so we would make the most amazing Italian desserts. She hardly spoke English, so I had to learn Italian to be able to speak to her."

"That's cool! Can you still speak Italian?"

"I can. Not as well as my parents, but I can hold my own."

She laughed and finished eating her pancakes while I finished up on a few other things. Phoebe would be by later with the cake she had decorated.

"Do I get to stay for the baby shower?" Kira asked.

"I think so. Your Mitera and Pappou will be here. Plus Yiayia."

Kira smiled with delight. It warmed my heart to see how much she loved her grandparents. It also made me sad knowing they were all she had since Kilyn's parents had died.

The doorbell rang and Kira jumped down to get it.

Kilyn came into the kitchen with a confused look on her face. "Who could that be? The shower isn't for another three hours."

"Mitera!" Kira called out.

My hands went to my hips. "Why is she here?" I asked.

Kilyn tilted her head and gave me a dumfounded look.

Katerina walked in with her best friend Maria, Aunt Agnes, and Aunt Maria. I would never get used to all the Maria's in this family.

"What are you guys doing here so early?" Kilyn asked.

Katerina glanced over to me and smiled. "We came to help Gabi of course."

I added the last touch to one of the desserts and stood tall. "Done. Everything is ready to go."

All eyes landed on the desserts.

"Everything looks amazing!" Aunt Maria whispered. I could feel my chest stick out a little bit more as pride raced through my veins. Even I had to admit everything looked amazing.

Katerina walked over and stared down at the cake. "You baked all of this, Gabriella?"

I nodded. "Yes."

"It all looks amazing."

Smiling, I said, "Thank you, Katerina."

She eyed the other desserts then turned to the other Greek women in the room.

"All right, ladies. Let's get everything set up and we can start bringing in the food."

"Food?" Kilyn and I both asked at once.

Katerina glanced over her shoulder at us. "Yes. You can't expect people to eat only cake and ice cream."

My jaw dropped open and I took a step toward her, my finger in position to tell her off. Kilyn stepped in front of me, blocking my move.

"Um, Katerina, I thought we decided to only do desserts. That was the plan."

She waved her hand to dismiss Kilyn.

"Nonsense. People need food. A good Greek salad and some meat will do them wonders. You can't live on desserts alone."

Kilyn turned to face me after Katerina left the kitchen. "I'm so sorry."

I was still glaring at the spot where Nic's mom had just retreated.

"Oh. Oh, it's on now," I mumbled.

The rest of the day was spent with me and Katerina trying to shove desserts and food down people's throats. In the end, it turned out to be a beautiful baby shower and Kilyn had a wonderful day. So, that was all that mattered.

Sitting back in the chair, I kicked my feet up onto the other chair and smiled. Thano came walking in.

He stopped walking and looked down at me. "If that isn't a victory smile, I don't know what is."

Blowing on my knuckles, I rubbed them against my chest. "Not one piece of dessert left. Nothing. Nada. Zero. But there is a shit ton of food left. I won!"

He laughed. "I wasn't aware there was a contest going on."

"Neither was I until your mother showed up with her gang of Maria's and tried to take over. Well, not today! Victory was mine!"

Thano stood there with a shocked look on his face. "You do know this isn't healthy. If my mother thinks you're competing with her, she won't stop."

I folded my arms over my chest. "I won't either."

"And to think when Nic first told me about you I was worried."

With a wink, I stood and started to clean up the kitchen. "Don't worry about this, Gabi. I'll take care of it all."

"Gabi!"

I jumped and turned to look at Kilyn. She had a look of pure horror on her face. "What's wrong?" I asked in a panicked voice. Thano kept going about his business cleaning up.

"We need to enact Plan D."

I jerked my head back in surprise. "Huh?"

Thano rushed by me and was in front of Kilyn. His hands cupping her face. "What? No! Not now, Kilyn. There are still people here."

"Wait. What is happening? What's Plan D?" I asked. Then it hit me. The story she told me about Plan B! She was in labor!

"I know, Thano. Do you think I want to be going into labor right now with a houseful of *your* Greek family!"

My stomach dropped. "W-what! You're in labor?"

Thano and Kilyn looked at me and both said, "Shh! No one can know."

I nodded. "Okay, well wait. What happened to Plan C?"

Thano rolled his eyes. "It's a long story. But we need a distraction, Gabi."

"A distraction?"

"Yes, Claire is here which is good. We're going to use her car to head to the hospital. It will be hours before anyone figures out we're gone."

I frowned. "Um. It's your baby shower. I'm pretty sure people will notice the parents of said baby are missing."

Thano looked at me and grinned. "Gabi, you've been around this family long enough now to know they won't notice we're missing for at least an hour and a half. Especially if you throw them off."

I wrung my hands together. Damn it. I wish Nic hadn't had to work today. "Okay. Claire knows?"

"Yes. She was standing next to me when the first contraction hit."

I paced back and forth. How was I going to cause a distraction? Then it hit me.

"I think I can buy y'all a few hours at least."

Furrowing her brows, Kilyn asked, "How?"

Smiling, I walked up to them and ushered them outside. "Leave it to me. Where is your hospital bag?"

"In the car already. Thano kept panicking about it," Kilyn said with a giggle.

"I'll grab it, but we forgot something else. Kira."

I waved him off. "I've got her. Don't worry. As soon as Claire or I get the all clear, one of us will bring her."

Kilyn grabbed my hand. "Thank you, Gabi. Someday, I'll do the same for you." My heart jumped into my throat, and I was once again reminded of how much I wanted to have a child with Nic.

I gave her a gentle grin. "Go. Go have your baby in peace!"

forty-four

Nic

WALKING INTO THE KITCHEN, I came to an abrupt halt. Gabi and my mother were each holding up a spatula like a weapon at each other.

"Um . . . as interesting as this is . . . what in the hell is going on?"

"She tricked me!" my mother said as a slow smirk moved over Gabi's face.

"I don't know what you're talking about."

Mom jerked the spatula causing batter to hit Gabi on the forehead. Her eyes widened in shock. "You threw food at me!"

"Tell me where they went! My sons get married and start hiding secrets."

"Who are we talking about?" I asked while I looked between the two of them. "And where is everyone?"

"Everyone left after I won the cook off."

My brows lifted. "A cook off?"

"Yep. I challenged her to see who could make the better moussaka."

I clutched my chest. Had Gabi gone insane? "You did what?"

"We did a blind taste test and Gabi cheated. She thinks she won."

Gasping, Gabi flung her spatula at my mother, spraying white batter all over her face. "I did not cheat, Katerina! Admit it. Everyone liked my moussaka. None of the Maria's could tell the difference!"

My mother moaned. "Traitors! They're all traitors."

I closed my eyes and shook my head while asking the Lord for strength. Looking back at Gabi, I said, "I knew from the beginning you knew what you were getting into with my family, but baby. I never dreamed you'd turn into my family."

Gabi's phone went off. Narrowing her eye at my mother, she said, "I'm watching you!"

Her eyes dashed down to read a text. When she looked up, she was grinning. When she looked back up, a tear was rolling down her face.

"Well now sweetheart, don't cry because you know I'm the better cook."

"Mama!" I said as I made my way over to Gabi. Brushing the batter covered string of hair away from her face, I lifted her eyes to mine "Hey, what's with the tears?"

"Kilyn and Thano are asking everyone to come meet there their new baby."

My mother dropped her spatula. "What? They had the baby? How? Why?" Then she covered her mouth with her hands. "You were Plan D, weren't you?"

Gabi laughed. "Yes, Katerina. I don't think I was originally part of Plan D, but I helped execute it."

My mother started to cry as I wrapped the two women I loved more than life in my arms. "You're both nuts do you know that?"

Pushing away from me, my mother was on the phone and running out to the living room to the few people still here.

"Thano had the baby! The baby is here."

"Opa!" was cried out by everyone in the living room.

Gabi shook her head. "She does know Kilyn was the one who actually *had* the baby?"

Chuckling, I said, "She knows. Hey, where is Kira?"

"Claire took her up to the hospital while I kept everyone occupied with the cook off. Thano and Kilyn wanted it to be just them for a bit."

I drew her closer to me, my lips inches from hers. "That was brilliant by the way. The whole cook off thing."

She shrugged. "I'm slowly figuring out how to manage your mother."

Our mouths crashed together in a slow sweet kiss.

When Gabi finally pulled back, she gave me an evil little grin. "By the way, Aunt Maria said she liked my moussaka better than your moms!"

"You better take that secret to the grave with you."

Laughing, she said, "I promised her it would stay between the two of us."

"Come on, let's go meet our new niece or nephew."

She pulled my arm back to stop me from walking then whispered, "It's a boy, but I wanted your mom to be surprised."

My heart squeezed in my chest at her words. I knew my mother could be a royal pain in the ass. But that small sweet gesture by Gabi just showed how much she cared for her.

Then I realized what she had said. Thano has a little boy. Damn, I'd never in my life been jealous of one of my brothers before, but with them both having kids now I was finding I was more and more jealous of both of them.

"Awesome. Then let's lock this place up and go meet the next Drivas heartbreaker."

♥

GABI AND I SAT IN the waiting room and played with Kira while a steady stream of family came in and out of Kilyn's room.

"She has to be exhausted, Nic. This is insane. Why won't she tell your mother enough already?"

I shrugged. "Dad even tried to get everyone to leave."

Gabi stood up. "We haven't even had a chance to really look at Alec. I want to hold him before Kilyn passes out."

The resolve to do something was already in full swing. I stood and took Kira's hand. "Let's go see your baby brother."

Kira clapped. "Yay! Once Mitera came in, I couldn't get to him anymore."

I laughed as I scooped up my niece and followed a very determined

Gabi to Kilyn's room.

When we walked in both Kilyn and Thano looked exhausted. My mother was standing over the baby telling Aunt Agnes how Alec meant men in Greek. Yiayia was sitting in the corner watching TV with Dad. Well, Dad was actually asleep. Cousin Sophia was talking to Claire about setting her up with a nice Greek boy to which Claire declared she'd rather die an old maid.

Gabi cleared her throat loudly then spoke loudly. "I'm going to have to ask everyone to leave now."

All talking ceased and every head turned to look at my wife.

"What?" my mother asked with a half laugh.

"It's time for everyone to leave. Kilyn is exhausted, and the nurse needs to do a few tests on Alec, so I think now would be the perfect time to say goodbye and let everyone rest. Besides, Kira would really like to spend some time with her baby brother and her parents without someone trying to take the baby from her."

"Yeah! What Aunt Gabi said!" Kira piped in.

Thano was smiling at Gabi and Kilyn looked as if she was about to burst into tears of joy when she saw people gathering up their things and heading out. Each person stopped to look at the baby one more time.

Everyone was telling Thano and Kilyn how beautiful Alec was.

When Yiayia walked up, she leaned over and took the baby in. "Don't spit on him, Yiayia!" Kilyn cried out.

Gabi turned to me. "I didn't think the Greeks still did that silly superstition anymore."

I was about to answer her when my mother walked up and said, "You will make a wonderful mother someday." She moved her lips and fake spit on Gabi. To which Gabi yelped and jumped back. Then they all followed my mother's lead as they passed Gabi by.

When it came to Yiayia, Gabi cringed and closed her eyes. When Yiayia placed her hand on Gabi stomach she smiled. Gabi opened her eyes and gazed at my grandmother.

"Soon. Very soon. You better start eating or the child will starve."

Gabi's mouth fell open as she watched Yiayia walk out the door.

"Okay, first off, there is no way that woman can tell if I'll be having a baby soon and they all spit at me!"

"Well, they didn't really spit at you." I said.

"Oh, I'm pretty sure Sophia let a real one fly!"

Kilyn laughed. "Thank you so much, Gabi. I was so ready for everyone to leave a few hours ago."

Thano had sat Kira on the couch and placed Alec in her arms. The way she looked at him tugged on my heartstrings. Then she started to sing to him and I'm pretty sure the four of us were all crying like babies. I was too busy watching Gabi's face to pay attention to Thano and Kilyn. The way she was looking at the scene before us was like she was wishing with everything she had that that would be us soon.

Once Kira was finished with her song, she asked Gabi to hold Alec while she went and snuggled with Kilyn.

"I'm more than happy to do that!" Gabi said. She sat in the rocking chair and rocked Alec as she traced her finger gently around his face and head.

I glanced over to Thano, he smiled at me and I returned the gesture.

I walked over to him and stuck my hand out. "Congrats little brother. He's beautiful."

Standing, he pulled me into a hug and then asked in a hushed voice, "Are you trying?"

"We are."

He grinned bigger. "That would be awesome to have all the little dudes grow up together."

"Yeah. Your kids, Thad's little one, and God willing, one for me."

"Just one?" Thano asked.

My hand pushed through my hair. "I'm not greedy."

Hitting me on the back, he peeked back over to Gabi. "It's a blessing, bro. And I have no doubt you'll be experiencing it soon."

forty-five

CHRISTMAS EVE

Gabi

To SAY THE DRIVAS HOUSEHOLD was chaos is putting it mildly. There were people everywhere. A Maria in nearly every single room.

Kids running in and out of the house screaming and yelling. It was insane.

But it was a beautiful insanity.

This was my new family. And no matter how much they were in our business, I knew it was because they loved us. And no matter how many times Katerina cracked a shot at my cooking, I knew it was because she knew I could handle it and would dish it right back.

I loved this crazy Greek family and so did my parents. My father and Dimitris were currently in a debate about a Greek god and the Roman Empire.

My parents, Antonio, and his girlfriend Kate, had flown in to spend the holidays with us about a week ago. I had somehow managed to talk both my mother and Katerina out of throwing us a reception. The idea of my mother and Nic's mom going head to head was not one I wanted to deal with. Especially since I hadn't been feeling all that great most of November. I'd kept it to myself, but Nic had noticed. When he didn't say anything, I knew he was trying not to get his hopes up.

"For the love all things good, Yiayia. Stop saying that!"

I glanced over to Charity who was sitting next to Yiayia as they both knitted. Covering my mouth, I held in my laugh. For someone who hated knitting club, Charity had really fallen in love with it.

"I'm just saying, child, you're having twins."

Charity sighed. "Yiayia, I know you're old as dirt, but there is this thing called a sonogram. They actually look at the baby. Hear the heartbeat. Here, look."

She shoved her phone in Yiayia's face. "That is a 3-D image of my child. There is only one! If there were two, we'd know."

Yiayia simply smiled then shrugged. "You're having twins."

Charity sighed. "Go back to knitting me a blanket, old lady."

Cole and Nic were outside playing football with some of the cousins' kids. Kate sat so close to me I thought she was going to crawl onto my lap.

"Kate, they won't bite."

She nodded. "I know, but Yiayia over there." Kate looked at me as fear laced her face. "She told me I had a good birthing vessel! What does that mean? I thought Antonio was going to fall to the floor with a heart attack."

I couldn't help but laugh. "Ah. Yiayia keeps you on your toes."

Kate agreed. "How old is she?"

Tilting my head, I realized I had never asked Nic. "You know, I'm not sure."

"My guess is a hundred. She started to speak to me in Greek earlier. I think I threw her off when I answered."

My head turned to look at her. "You speak Greek?"

Kate smiled. "Yep. I speak four other languages. Greek, Italian, Spanish, and Russian."

"Holy crap'ole! Do you work for the FBI too?"

When she didn't answer, I cleared my throat and looked away. "So, anyway."

She chuckled and glanced around the room. "How do you keep up with everyone?"

"It's kind of easy. Most of the women are named Maria. Or somehow they have that in their name somewhere."

Kilyn walked up and sat down on the other side of Kate.

"How's it going, ladies? Hiding from the family?"

Kate let out a nervous chuckle.

"Kind of. More like staying out of the way," I said with a wink. "Where's the baby?"

Kilyn rolled her eyes. "Katerina has him. I swear the woman has taken my son's penis out six times to show everyone he's a boy."

Kate choked on her drink. "W-what?"

I leaned over. "Don't ask."

She nodded then whispered, "I'm starting to see why you didn't want a reception, Gabi."

Nic walked in with Antonio and declared to my mother we were leaving. Katerina handed Alec back to Kilyn who promptly took off like a bolt of lightning. I'm sure to hide somewhere.

"What? Why are you leaving?" Katerina asked.

My mother walked up and said, "We need to still do the Feast of Seven Fishes."

Katerina frowned. "Oh right, the Italian Christmas Eve thing."

Nic kissed his mother on the cheek. "Bye, Mama." Turning to his father, he shook his hand and hugged him. "Bye, Dad. Enjoy the rest of Christmas Eve."

Dimitris smiled. "We will, son." He then shook my father and Antonio's hand before giving my mother, me, and Kate all a kiss on the cheek.

Katerina hugged me good-bye and held onto me a little tighter than normal. When she pulled back, she had tears in her eyes.

"Katerina, are you okay?" Her hand came to my face and I couldn't help but lean into the gentle touch. I smiled and she smiled back. I placed my hand over hers and silently let her know she was right. Covering her mouth, she turned and walked back into the kitchen.

"What was that all about?" Nic asked.

Shrugging, I replied, "Beats me. Maybe her way of silently thanking me for not kicking her ass at desserts tonight?"

Nic laughed as he placed his hand on the small of my back. About ten family members walked us out, each one having to kiss someone good-bye at least three times. By the time we got to my car, my parents were whipping out their antibacterial wipes and passing them around to us.

The rest of Christmas Eve was spent with my small family in our cozy little blue house that I gave up and Nic bought. After spending so many years apart, it felt amazing to be with my family again, especially with Nic by my side.

"How is the wine bar addition going?" Antonio asked with a smile.

Grinning, my father replied, "They're thinking by this spring it will be ready to open."

The look of pure happiness on my father's face was like a dream come true. When I told him about the wine bar, he immediately took over with the plans. I was happy to let him take on the project.

"That's awesome. I'm glad to see you have something to do you're enjoying, Papá."

My mother laughed. "So am I."

Antonio stood. "I'm exhausted, sis. I think Kate and I are calling it a night."

Standing, I kissed him on the cheek.

"It's all set up. You're lucky it's warm here right now," he whispered.

I squeezed his arm and smiled. "I know! Thank you."

"Mom, Dad? Are you bugging out as well?"

They both stood. "Yes. I think so, darling. It's been such an amazing Christmas. All those years I wished I could see your beautiful face and now . . . well now . . ."

She started to cry. Wrapping her in my arms, I held her tight. "I know, Mama. I know."

Once everyone was gone, I turned to Nic. "Are you tired?"

He laughed. "A little, but I'm thinking we should probably not be doing the nasty with your family in the house."

Hitting him on the chest, I shook my head. "No. I have a gift for you. But we have to go outside."

Nic pinched his eyebrows together. "Okay."

As we headed outside, I walked backward to face him. "Do you remember back in September when I got stuck on the roof?"

He laughed. "Yeah."

"Well, the whole reason I went up there was because Charity said it would be a romantic place to tell you that I no longer had to testify against Dante. But things kind of got ruined, and I ended up telling you that night before we left for Reno."

"Why tell me on the roof?" Nic asked.

I took his hand in mine and lead him over to the ladder Antonio had put out.

"If I go first, you'll make sure I don't fall, right?"

Nic laughed. "Gabi, what in the hell is going on? You want to go on the roof and what? Wait for Santa Clause?"

My teeth sunk down into my lip. "Maybe," I softly said. The excitement was building more and more as the seconds ticked by.

His eyes intensified. "All right. Let's go up on the roof."

Taking in a deep breath, I gradually made my way up. When I got up on the roof, I quickly walked to the middle of the roof. Looking up, I gasped as the endless stars in the sky.

Nic walked up to me and wrapped his arms around me. "Why is there a blanket up here, Gabi?"

Glancing down, I grinned when I saw the blanket and small basket sitting to the side of it. There were only two people who knew I was pregnant. Charity and my brother. It was her idea to try the roof thing again and my brother thought it would be a pretty cool way to tell Nic, so I decided to give it another try.

I looked up at the stars again. "Antonio put it there."

Cupping my face in his hands, he asked, "Why?"

The hope in his eyes had my heart beating so loud I was sure he could hear it.

Slowly starting to sit, Nic followed me. We sat on the blanket and I tried like hell to steady my shaking hands.

"I wanted to give my gift to you up here. Under the stars."

He smiled that brilliant smile that made my body ache for his.

"Lay back," I said with authority.

"Yes ma'am. I like it when you're bossy."

I opened up the basket and saw the two bottles of grape juice and the small box.

Charity. She thinks of everything.

"What do you see?" I asked as I reached in for the box.

"Stars. Endless stars."

"They go on for eternity."

"They're beautiful," he said so softly I barely heard him.

"When I was little, I used to lay out in our backyard and look up at the stars," I said as I laid back and looked up with him. "I would pretend they were wishes."

He chuckled. "Oh yeah? How did that work out for you?"

Taking his hand in mine, our fingers curled together. "I'd say it worked out pretty damn nicely. I wished for my own bakery."

"You got that wish," Nic softly said.

"Yes, I did."

"What else did you wish for?"

"A man to love me like my daddy loved my mommy."

Nic's head turned to face me. I could feel the heat from his stare. "I hope that wish has come true."

Meeting his stare, I nodded. "It has."

He smiled and my heart melted.

"Any other wishes?"

Tears formed in my eyes as I looked away and back up at the stars. "I wished I would be a mom someday."

Nic was still staring at me.

"Look up at the stars, Nic. Do you see it?"

He did as I asked. "Do I see what?"

With my free hand, I reached around and held the pregnancy stick out in front of us. "My wish coming true."

Nic stared at the test for the longest time before he sat up. My heart started to race. Maybe he wasn't really wanting a baby as much as he thought.

When I sat up, I was about to ask him when he looked up at the sky and said, "Thank you."

His head dropped back down and he wiped his tears away. Turning to face me, I could see the starlight reflecting in his hazel eyes. Cupping my face within his hands, he shook his head then pressed his lips to mine. Our kiss was filled with so much love it left me feeling breathless.

"Gabi, I've been wishing since that night before our wedding for this."

Warmth radiated through my body.

"You're happy?"

He kissed me again. This time he filled it with his answer.

"Don't you get it, Gabi Drivas? My love for you flows from the bluest of blue sky's to the deepest of deep oceans. I can't breathe without you and what you have given me has made me the happiest man in the world."

A sob slipped from my lips. "It's always been you, Nic. The moment I met you I knew I could only live this life with you in it."

He smiled. "Only with me, huh?"

Nodding, I clutched his shirt in my hands and pulled him closer to me as I whispered, "Only with you. My love for you will never stop, no matter what."

Nic's eyes searched my face. "The day you married me, I thought it was the most amazing moment of my life." He chuckled. "Now I see that was just a stepping stone to so many more amazing moments."

Dropping my head to his chest, Nic wrapped me in his arms.

"We're having a baby," he softly spoke.

I looked back up at him and our gaze locked. "Yes we are."

He furrowed his brows. "I wonder how long we can keep it from my mother?"

With a smile so big and bright, I brushed my lips against his as I replied, "She already knows."

Nic closed his eyes and said, "God help us."

epilogue

ONE YEAR LATER

Gabi

KATERINA AND MY MOTHER STOOD in the kitchen, both of them with their hands on their hips facing each other off.

"She likes the rice cereal," my mother said.

Katerina shook her head. "She doesn't. Look at her. She wants the Greek yogurt."

My mother sighed. "Katerina, you're only saying that because it has the word Greek in it. If I were to tell you this is Greek cereal, you'd be all over it."

I attempted to hide my smile. My mother and Katerina had become the best of friends. Competitive as hell in the kitchen, but best friends none the less.

"So glad your parents decided to move here," Charity said as she handed her son, Mick, a cracker then watched him wander back over to the pile of toys on the floor.

When my parents found out I was pregnant, they decided they had missed enough in my life. Three months later they sold their place in

New Jersey and moved to Colorado Springs. They loved it here and my brother Antonio and his wife Kate weren't too far behind. They lived in Denver though, since the FBI office was there.

"Me too," I said with a chuckle.

"Why don't you mix the yogurt into the cereal?" I said with a smile.

Both of them looked at me like I had lost my damn mind.

"I know the idea of compromise is something neither of you know, but my daughter is hungry."

Morgan was opening and closing her mouth each time the spoon came within reach of her.

"Oh, my sweet baby girl. Let Nonna feed you your yummy cereal."

Katerina reached over and dumped the Greek yogurt into the cereal, causing Morgan to laugh. She then leaned over and said, "Morgan, your Yiayia will not let you starve."

I couldn't help but laugh as they both took turns spooning food into Morgan's mouth.

Nic and Cole walked in and both stopped to look at the sight before them.

"Since when does she need two people feeding her at one time?" Nic asked with a chuckle.

"Hush," Katerina said.

Cole leaned down and gave Charity a kiss. "Hey," he softly said as she gave him a warm smile.

I couldn't help but smile every time I looked at how happy the two of them were. They'd gotten married this past summer in a beautiful wedding up in the mountains. Phoebe had been itching to get back into cake decorating and had done Charity and Cole's cakes. I loved the Italian cream cake so much I offered her a position at the bakery as our cake decorator. For years I'd had people asking me if I did cakes for weddings and showers. I never had the time. But with how well the bakery was doing, and Phoebe's desire to get back to work, she jumped on it. She could bring Michael to work with her anytime since we had turned half of the office into a playroom slash nursery.

Nic walked up to Morgan and bent down. Her smile grew so big my heart nearly leapt from my chest.

"Hey, agapiméni." Morgan kicked her feet and reached for Nic.

"No! She is eating!" Katerina said as Nic lifted Morgan out of her highchair.

"Well, right now she wants her daddy."

Morgan pressed her face against Nic's, covering him in yogurt cereal.

"Well, at least I won't have to worry about you being a good kisser with the boys."

I watched as Nic walked out of the room with Morgan. Softly talking to her, he held her attention like he always did. It was as if she was as mesmerized by him. Just like I was.

"You know what she is thinking, don't you?" Charity asked.

Shaking my head, I said, "No, what?"

"Damn, my daddy is one good looking Greek bastard."

Turning, I hit Charity on the arm.

"So, when are we going to introduce her to Liv?"

Groaning, I looked back over to where Nic was holding Morgan close to him as they danced. She leaned her head against his chest and smiled. Like everything she ever wanted in this world she had right there. My heart melted on the spot.

"Don't act like you don't have mad love for Olivia. Spread it to your daughter."

"The only thing I want to do right now is soak in this moment."

Charity stood and bent down to pick up Mick.

"Fine, but this conversation is not over. I will have my niece loving ONJ by her first birthday."

I ignored Charity as I got up and made my way into the living room where I leaned against the wall and watched my husband and daughter get totally lost in each other.

When his eyes met mine, he smiled and my stomach dropped. He then motioned for me to join them. As I walked up to them, I froze the memory in my brain. My stomach fluttered, and I never felt so happy in my entire life.

Nic pulled me to him as Morgan lifted her hand and put it on me. It was as if she knew how special this moment was.

Nic brushed his lips over my forehead and whispered, "Se agapó,

Gabi."

"I love you too, Nic."

Morgan pulled her head back and looked up at Nic. He laughed. "Se agapó, baby girl."

When she rested her head back against his chest, our eyes met.

Placing my hand on my stomach, I took in a slow deep breath.

"So, what are you doing later?" I asked.

He kept his eyes on mine when he answered. "Whatever you're doing."

My teeth caught my lip as I fought to hold back my emotions.

"I'll be on the roof. Looking at stars and finding more wishes."

Nic's eyes lit up as he said, "Just when I didn't think we could top this moment."

The End

acknowledgments

THANK YOU TO EVERYONE WHO helps me do what it takes to make a book happen! Your hard work is never unnoticed and much appreciated.

Thank you to my readers. I couldn't do this without y'all. Love you to the moon and back.

about the author

KELLY ELLIOTT IS A NEW York Times and USA Today best-selling contemporary romance author. Since finishing her bestselling Wanted series, Kelly continues to spread her wings while remaining true to her roots and giving readers stories rich with hot protective men, strong women and beautiful surroundings.

Kelly lives in central Texas with her husband, daughter, and two pups. When she's not writing, Kelly enjoys reading and spending time with her family.

To find out more about Kelly and her books, you can find her through her website.

www.kellyelliottauthor.com

other books

Book 5 Prequel—A Forever Love
Book 6—The Wanted Short Stories
Book 7—All They Wanted
Entire series available on audio book except Believe,
The Wanted Short Stories and All They Wanted

LOVE WANTED IN TEXAS SERIES
Spin-off series to the WANTED Series
Book 1—Without You
Book 2—Saving You
Book 3—Holding You
Book 4—Finding You
Book 5—Chasing You
Book 6—Loving You⋆⋆
Entire series available on audio book
⋆⋆Please note Loving You combines the last book of the Broken and
Love Wanted in Texas series.

BROKEN SERIES
Book 1—Broken
Book 2—Broken Dreams
Book 3—Broken Promises
Book 4—Broken Love
Book 1–3 available on audio book

THE JOURNEY OF LOVE SERIES
Book 1—Unconditional Love
Book 2—Undeniable Love
Book 3—Unforgettable Love
Entire series available on audio book

SPEED SERIES
Book 1—Ignite
Book 2—Adrenaline

BOSTON LOVE SERIES
Searching for Harmony (Available on audio book)
Fighting for Love (Available on audio book)

YA NOVELS WRITTEN UNDER THE PEN NAME
ELLA BORDEAUX
Beautiful
Forever Beautiful

HISTORICAL
Guarded Hearts (Coming December 2017)

playlist

(CONTAINS SPOILERS)

Tied Up—Olivia Newton-John
Gabi cooking for Nic

Magic—Olivia Newton-John
Nic kisses Gabi for the first time

Body Say—Demi Lovato
Nic and Gabi's first date

Landslide—Olivia Newton-John
Gabi getting ready for hiking

Never Got Away—Colbie Cailat
Nic and Gabi hiking

Queen of Swords—Idina Menzel
Gabi meeting Nic's mom

There's a Girl—Trent Harmon
The girls stuck on the roof

When a Heart Breaks—Ben Rector
Nic following Gabi in Italy

Cry A River—Amy Grant
Nic breaks up with Gabi

I Won't Let Go—Rascal Flatts
Gabi and Charity when she gets home from Italy

The Fighter—Keith Urban
Nic stopping Gabi from leaving

Yours—Russell Dickerson
Nic and Gabi getting married

God Gave Me You—Blake Shelton
Christmas Eve Gabi and Nic on the roof

Made in the USA
San Bernardino, CA
21 June 2017